IT'S THAT TIME AGAIN 2!

More New Stories of Old-Time Radio

Edited by Jim Harmon

IT'S THAT TIME AGAIN 2!

More New Stories of Old-Time Radio

Edited by Jim Harmon

BearManor Media
2004

It's That Time Again! Vol. 2
More New Stories of Old-Time Radio
All Rights Reserved © 2004 BearManor Media

Thanks go to the authors for their permission to use the following stories in this collection: "The Impossible Dream" © 2004 *Jim Harmon;* "The Stembottom Situation" © 2004 *William F. Nolan;* "The Adventure of the Duplicate Deceiver" © 2004 *Jim Harmon;* "The Maker of Werewolves" © 2004 Jim Harmon; "Out With Mommy" © 2004 Ben Ohmart; "Bad Business" © 2004 Mel Gilden; "The Adventures of Jimmie Allen in World War II" © 2004 Jon D. Swartz; "The Ghastly Dream" © 2004 Tony Albarella; "Fall From Grace" © 2004 Joseph Cromarty; "Jane's Side" © 2004 Barbara Gratz; "A Drink For the Damned" © 2004 Martin Grams, Jr.; "The Adventure of the Lady Prospector" © 2004 Jack A. French; "Little Beaver's Schooling" © 2004 Frank Bresee; "Crisis in Cairo" © 2004 Charles A. Beckett; "A Dancer, a Soldier, a Villain" © 2004 Bryan Powell; "The Fred Allen Murder Case" © 2004 Laura Wagner; "Murder in Pine Ridge" © 2004 Donnie Pitchford; "The Maltese Omelette" © 2004 Michael Kurland; "Last of the Legares" © 2002 T. Wayne Clay; "The Peltonville Horror" © 2004 Richard A. Lupoff; "Later Than You Think" © 2004 Christopher Conlon; "Saturday Morning Paper" © 2004 Justin Felix

Published in the USA by

BearManor Media
P. O. Box 750
Boalsburg, PA 16827

bearmanormedia.com

Cover design by John Teehan

Cover illustration by Bobb Lynes

Typesetting and layout by John Teehan

ISBN—1-59393-006-2

TABLE OF CONTENTS

FOREWORD
"The Impossible Dream" *by Jim Harmon* i

VIC AND SADE
"The Stembottom Situation" *by William F. Nolan* 1

SHERLOCK HOLMES
"The Adventure of the Duplicate Deceiver" *by Jim Harmon* 7

THE AVENGER
"The Maker of Werewolves" *by Jim Harmon* 15

BABY SNOOKS
"Out With Mommy" *by Ben Ohmart* 21

THE WHISTLER
"Bad Business" *by Mel Gilden* 29

THE AIR ADVENTURES OF JIMMIE ALLEN
"The Adventures of Jimmie Allen in World War II" *by Jon D. Swartz*... 39

HOUSE OF MYSTERY
"The Ghastly Dream" *by Tony Albarella* 49

RICHARD DIAMOND, PRIVATE DETECTIVE
"Fall From Grace" by *Joseph Cromarty* 59

MY FRIEND IRMA
"Jane's Side" *by Barbara Gratz* 69

THE COLUMBIA WORKSHOP
"A Drink For the Damned" *by Martin Grams, Jr.* 73

BOBBY BENSON AND THE B-BAR-B RIDERS
"The Adventure of the Lady Prospector" *by Jack A. French* 83

RED RYDER
"Little Beaver's Schooling" *by Frank Bresee* 97

THE MAN CALLED X
    "Crisis in Cairo" *by Charles A. Beckett* 99

NIGHTBEAT
    "A Dancer, a Soldier, a Villain" *by Bryan Powell* 109

THE JACK BENNY PROGRAM
    "The Fred Allen Murder Case" *by Laura Wagner* 119

LUM & ABNER
    "Murder in Pine Ridge" *by Donnie Pitchford* 129

HAROLD LLOYD COMEDY THEATRE
    "The Maltese Omelette" *by Michael Kurland* 139

HERMIT'S CAVE
    "Last of the Legares" *by T. Wayne Clay* 153

A WITCH'S TALE
    "The Peltonville Horror" *by Richard A. Lupoff* 167

LIGHTS OUT
    "Later Than You Think" *by Christopher Conlon* 183

THE GREAT GILDERSLEEVE
    "Saturday Morning Paper" *by Justin Felix* 189

BIOGRAPHICAL NOTES 203

FOREWORD

The Impossible Dream
by Jim Harmon

This book is a substitute for an impossible dream, and a good one for it.

The dream for all of us of a certain age, or even those younger but who share a certain love, is to turn on the radio and hear the ringing cry of "Hi Yo Silver!" and to know we are about to hear an adventure of the Masked Man we have never heard before, could never hear before, because it is brand new. We want to hear the haunting wail of a train whistle in the night and know that Jack, Doc and Reggie are encountering an exotically beautiful woman and a scientist, mad beyond doubt, but just perhaps on the side of right in an entirely original mystery we will love.

It is impossible.

There is virtually no economic incentive in producing new radio drama in the United States. The ranks of original participants in the Golden Age of Radio have thinned alarmingly.

Yes, there are re-creations. I like to think I have done some good ones on commercial recordings—*Tom Mix* with Curley Bradley and Jack Lester, and *I Love a Mystery* with Les Tremayne and Frank Bresee, original cast members. Anthony Tollin has done some excellent ones at old time radio conventions for *SPERDVAC* and other clubs. They can be good—very good—but never quite the same.

Our impossible dream is hearing not only great old program formats but unique performers like Jack Benny and Fred Allen youthful and vibrant again. A radio dial would be tuning us into the endless panorama of adventure, comedy, mystery, variety we once knew. Impossible, impossible, but…

If you have the power of imagination radio once gave you, you can return to a new feast of classic favorites.

The writing of William Nolan brings back *Vic and Sade* so deftly we can hear those voices speaking from the grand stage of illusion.

Similarly, we hear the voices of Snooks and Daddy from the writing of Ben Ohmart, and Jane and her friend Irma speak from the pages by Barbara Gratz.

Dr. Jon Swartz takes us beyond the skies flown by Jimmie Allen in his air adventures, to his inevitable entry into World War II.

I hope in one of my two stories, I have taken the Sherlock Holmes radio show beyond the place it was.

Award-winning mystery writer Richard Lupoff has developed *Witch's Tale* to literary heights beyond the original series. Mel Gilden offers a more subtle mystery than *The Whistler* was used to telling. I think Tony Albarella goes *House of Mystery* one better than sometimes went on behind its doors. T. Wayne Clay finds a new one from 'way back in *The Hermit's Cave*. Martin Grams, Jr., who seemingly can produce a whole book as fast as many can do a short story, settles for just a story from the *Columbia Workshop*.

A man who was really there, Frank Bresee (who along with Tommy Cook alternated in playing Little Beaver on *Red Ryder)* offers a new glimpse at the young Native American. Jack French is such an informed expert he portrays *Bobby Benson and his B-Bar-B Riders* as if he were in the studio for every broadcast. Bobby's mentor was a stalwart cowboy called Tex Mason, who was a prototype of screen idol Tom Mix. I believe the initials were no accident. The program with Bobby Benson and Tex Mason oddly anticipated the Tom Mix program where, of course, Tom was the star and the young boy, called Jimmie now, plus a young girl, Jane, were the sidekicks. Both programs featured a number of amusing characters on a big ranch.

Laura Wagner is the one who brings back a vibrant Benny and Allen.

Michael Kurland, best-selling writer and anthologist, Joe Cromarty, Charles Beckett, Bryan Powell, Christopher Conlon, Donnie Pitchford, and Justin Felix contribute to the impossible dream.

So read and dream on. I hope you think we have all done well by you.

Jim Harmon
Burbank, CA.
September 6, 2003

VIC AND SADE

The Stembottom Situation
by William F. Nolan
(Dedicated to the memory of Paul Rhymer)

Well, sir, it's three o'clock on a mighty hot summer afternoon in the small house half-way up in the next block. We find Mr. Victor Gook seated in his favorite easy chair, absorbed in the local paper, while Mrs. Sadie Gook converses on the telephone with her best friend, Ruthie Stembottom. Stretched on the rug next to the couch is Mr. Rush Gook, deeply intent on a volume titled *Third Lieutenant Stanley's Incredible African Adventure*…

"I just don't plain to goodness understand it," Sade is saying. "Doesn't make any fool sense atall to me. Isn't that I'm not just happy as a hog over your first place ribbon an' all, but them County Fair fellas must suffer a sunstroke ever time out. Heat must addle their brains. Last year they gave first prize to Olive Flankers, makin' a monstrous big elaborate lah-de-dah over her Prime Vanilla Custard Delight which certainly did not surpass my own Double Frosted Chocolate Triumph. An' this year it's clear as a horse that my Deluxe Strawberry Upside-down Cake should have won over your Sour-Lemon Surprise." She pauses, listening to Ruthie. "Uh-huh. Uh-huh. Well, *sure* I did. Had me a big bite of your Sour-Lemon Surprise and I can't deny that it was indeed tasty, but the plain honest fact remains that my Deluxe Strawberry Upside-down Cake was—"

Rush raises his head from his book, cutting into the flow of his mother's conversation. "Precisely how long are you gonna remain talkin' on the phone if I may so inquire? Promised I'd call Blue-tooth Johnson on a matter of dire urgency."

Sade puts her hand over the mouthpiece. "An' what's so monstrous urgent regardin' Mr. Blue-tooth Johnson that you gotta curtail my cake discussion with Mis' Ruthie Stembottom?"

"Me and Blue-tooth, we're both doin' reports at school on the same

1

book, an' I gotta pass along my personal impressions of said volume."

"Hold on, Ruthie," says Sadie. Her voice is tinged with scorn as she addresses her son. "An' pray tell, Willie, just what *volume* might you be referrin' to?"

"I refer to a classic tale of derring-do set amid primitive surroundings," says Rush. "The title is *Third Lieutenant Stanley's Incredible African Adventure.*"

"Oh, my," declares Sade. "I think we've had quite enough in this house of your Third Lieutenant Stanley."

"That may well be so," Rush replies, "but my discussion regarding Third Lieutenant Stanley will not require family participation or attention given thereto. My remarks will be directed entirely to my friend Bluetooth Johnson who, at this precise moment, sits eagerly by his telephone awaiting my comments on *Third Lieutenant Stanley's Incredible African Adventure.*"

"Well, he'll just hafta stay sittin' eager till your mother is through her talkin' to Ruthie Stembottom." Sade removes her hand from the mouthpiece. "You still there, lady?"

Now Vic cuts in. "Thunder! Seems that a fella can't read his paper of an afternoon without a clashin' of wills an' heated verbiage from those assembled in his near vicinty."

Sade ignores this, complaining to Ruthie: "Year before last they gave the doggone first prize to Dottie Brainfeeble for her Plum Passion Pie which, in all honestly, didn't *compare* to my Sweet-Apple Jumpcake."

"Uh-oh," says Vic, peering out the front window. "We got us some company comin' up the walk in the particular person of your Uncle Fletcher."

The doorbell rings.

"I'll get it, gov," says Rush, moving to the front door. He opens it. "Greetings, Uncle Fletcher."

"Howdy, Rush...Vic...Sadie," says the eccentric old man.

"Hi-de-hi, ho-de-ho," says Vic. "Sade's on the phone to Ruthie Stembottom."

She smiles and waves to Uncle Fletcher.

"Knew a man who spent most of his adult life on the telephone," says Fletcher. "Name of Y.I.I.Y. Skeeber. Had a son name of Slobert Skeeber who weighed one hundred ought nine pounds. Stood exactly five foot two inch. Married a four-hundred pound woman with a harelip. Opened a Five 'n' Dime in Upper Fishigan, Michigan. Sold gumballs six for a nickel. Didn't do well. Got into ladies underwear. Peddled these intimate garments door-to-door in Doregon, Oregon. Invented a singing tooth-brush that startled his neighbors. Later died."

"What did it sing?" Vic asks, looking over the edge of his newspaper.

"How's that?"

"The toothbrush. What did it sing?"

"Numbskull thing had just one song in its repertoire. 'In the Sweet Bye and Bye.' Song about drove Skeeber's dimwit neighbors crazy."

"If you folks won't mind cuttin' all the fancy chatter," says Sade, "I'll be able to continue to converse with Ruthie Stembottom on a subject of some great importance."

"Fine," says Uncle Fletcher.

"Just how much more conversin' do you plan on?" asks Rush. "My friend Blue-tooth Johnson is, at this very moment, eager to hear my—"

"Oh, ish!" declares Sade. Then, into the phone: "You still here, lady? Uh-huh. Uh-huh. Well, lands, I got me no hard feelin' towards your Sour-Lemon Surprise, but it just seems to me..."

Her voice drones on in the background as Uncle Fletcher sits down on the couch. "Hot," he says. "You could fry an egg on the lamebrain sidewalk."

"Take off your wide-brim hat," says Vic.

"What hat?"

"The one on your head."

Uncle Fletcher chuckles. "Didn't know I was wearin' the numbskull thing," he declares.

"Well, ya are," says Vic.

The old man removes his wide-brim hat and carefully places it on the couch next to him. "Got this wide-brim hat from over to the Y.Y. Flirch Mercantile establishment. Saw one just like it as worn by Godfrey Dimlock and a similar wide-brim on the head of Ike Kneesuffer."

"That so," murmurs Vic, deep into his paper.

"Yes, sir, I told myself I should be wearin' a wide-brim hat on my own head and subsequently made the purchase."

"Ummm," murmurs Vic.

"I am here due to a severe financial problem," says the old man.

"What's the problem, Uncle Fletcher?" asks Rush.

"It concerns Mr. Gumpox, the garbage man, who resides over to the

Bright Kentucky Hotel where them trains go roarin' pass lickety-split."

"What about him?" Vic asks.

"Owes me a dollar ought six. Loaned in good faith last October with a firm promise of full re-payment this summer."

Vic snorts. "Hasn't paid ya, huh?"

"No, sir, he has not—an' the problem at hand is that Gumpox, the garbage man, was slumberin' sound as a baby last month when a fright train came thunderin' past the Bright Kentucky."

"That would be a *freight* train," says Rush.

"Same numbskull thing," declares Uncle Fletcher. He continues: "Well, sir, that halfwit train jittered the entire building, the way they do passin' so close, and Gumpox, the garbage man, was flung from his bed *bang* into the wall. Ever since then he can't recognize anybody met prior to 1934."

"That's terrible!" says Rush.

"We met in '33," declares the old man, "so he don't know me from Adam. Says to me when I told him it was time to repay my loan of one dollar ought six that he never laid eyes on me in his sworn life and that he don't hand money out to total strangers."

"So I guess you'll never get paid back," says Rush. "That's a darn shame, Uncle Fletcher."

"Can't call in the numbskull police to a de-ranged individual," says Fletcher. "So I am bereft of my one dollar ought six."

"Sure looks like it," nods Vic.

"How can we help?" asks Rush.

"I am in present need of the aforementioned amount owed to me by the now de-ranged Gumpox," says Uncle Fletcher. "I am here for a loan of said amount."

Vic raises an eyebrow. "You want to borrow a dollar an' six cents?"

"Precisely."

"Well, I'm flat outa cash," says Vic.

"Me, too," nods Rush. "My last dollar went for the purchase of *Third Lieutenant Stanley's Incredible African Adventure*, the very tome I hold in my hand."

Sade has naturally overheard the conversation. "Ruthie, I hafta go help Uncle Fletcher. Call you right back." And she hangs up the phone. "I'll loan you the money," she tells Uncle Fletcher. "Just wait a sec. Be back soon as I fetch my purse from the attic."

Vic chuckles. "Hey, kiddo, what's yer purse doin' in the attic?"

"Just sittin' there I imagine, where I left it," she says, leaving the room.

"Your mother has quite a wit about her," Vic says to Rush, who is moving quickly toward the phone.

"Dimwit place to leave a purse," mutters Uncle Fletcher.

Holding the telephone, Rush dials, makes the connection, and says: "Blue-tooth? It's I, Rush. Uh-huh. Uh-huh. I *know*—but Mom was engaged in a heated conversation with her friend, Mis' Ruthie Stembottom regardin' the recent pastry contest at the County Fair and there was no possible way for me to—Uh-huh. I've got it right here." He flips open the book. "I procured my copy from the Tiny Tender Book Shoppe in the Glen, from Mis' Cora Bucksaddle, the owner. Uh-huh. *Third Lieutenant Stanley's Incredible African Adventure*. Concerns giant snakes, by George, an' includes a wide variety of enraged rhinos, elephants, baboons, leopards, gorillas, hippos, lions, alligators, an' striped tigers."

Vic cuts in. "Don't figure they have all them enraged animals together in *one* place. For example, take the striped tiger—"

"Uh-huh," says Rush to Blue-tooth, ignoring his father. "It's quite an amazing saga—in particular this dramatic scene from Chapter Six when the bloodthirsty tribe of flesh-eating pygmies have captures Lady Margaret."

"He's gonna read from the lamebrain book," says Uncle Fletcher.

"Ummm," murmurs Vic, lost in baseball statistics from the sports page.

Rush begins reading in a high, excited voice: "Third Lieutenant Stanley knew he had only moments in which to rescue Lady Margaret from her helpless captivity in the giant pot above the flames that threatened to boil the lovely flesh from her delicate pink body. 'Fear not!' he cried, drawing his service revolver, 'I shall deal with these fiendish little people!' And he fired point-blank into the fearsome horde of dancing pygmies. They fell back, shrieking in terror, as Third Lieutenant Stanley helped Lady Margaret from the boiling pot. 'Oh, how can I reward you for so brave an act?' she asked him, blushing furiously at her unclad state. 'You may reward me with a kiss from your fair lips,' cried Third Lieutenant Stanley and he—"

"Heavens to Betsy, what's going on?" demands Sade, having returned from the attic with her purse.

Vic chuckles. "Our redoubtable young offspring here is readin' aloud to his eager friend, Blue-tooth Johnson. When you left to fetch down your purse, he requisitioned the house phone and—"

Sade cuts in, red-faced with anger. "Willie, you get off this line this instant!"

"Hold it, Blue-tooth," says Rush. Then, to his mother: "I am simply fulfilling an obligation to my friend Blue-tooth Johnson who has been eagerly awaiting my impressions of—"

"Oh, ish! You put down that phone. I have to finish talkin' to Ruthie Stembottom."

"What about my one dollar ought six?" asks Uncle Fletcher.

Sade ignores this, glaring at her son. "Willie! Do as I say!"

"Okey-dokey," says Rush, expelling a heavy sigh. Then, into the mouthpiece: "I'll hafta call you later, Blue-tooth old scout. My mother urgently requires use of this instrument. Uh-huh. All right."

And he hands the phone to Sade.

Vic looks up from the entertainment page. "Think I'll mosey over to the Bijou this very evenin' to view the latest screen vehicle featurin' the talent of Four-Fisted Frank Fuddleman and Gloria Golden who are holdin' forth in *You're the Fireman of My Dreams, Ralph Razorscum*. Looks to be a dandy offering."

"Don't waste your time, gov," says Rush. "Me an' Smelly Clark we witnessed the latest Bijou attraction, *You're the Fireman of My Dreams, Ralph Razorscum*—an' it stinks."

"Don't recall that I asked for your personalized opinion, sonny," says Vic. "If and when it behooves me to base my picture goin' on the say-so of yourself and Mr. Smelly Clark then I shall retire from public life an' devote myself to the raisin' of muskrats."

"I'll just bet that Ruthie Stembottom is mad as a hornet," declares Sade, dialing her friend's number. "Ruthie *hates* waiting for telephone calls. Claims it's one of the things she detests most about modern life."

"We all have our cross to bear," mutters Vic.

"What about my dollar ought six?" asked Uncle Fletcher.

And the afternoon sun continues to shimmer down on the small house half-way up in the next block. ♦

SHERLOCK HOLMES

The Adventure of the Duplicate Deceiver
by Jim Harmon

My name is Grover Petrie. I was one of the announcers on the Sherlock Holmes radio series heard over several American radio networks during the thirties and forties. It was my job to go to the retirement cottage Dr. Watson had in California at this particular date and interview him about his adventures with the world-famous detective, Sherlock Holmes. The program was one of the earliest to employ remote equipment to broadcast directly from the retired doctor's home.

By this time, Watson was getting quite along in years. I always had a lurking fear he would lose his place and somehow ruin the broadcast, but it never happened.

I want to tell you about one particular show and certain events that occurred after the end of the broadcast of which the general public was not aware. This program was sometime in the late forties. My personal records were lost in a house fire, and I must admit my own memory is not as exact as Watson's was as I approach the age he was then. But I remember that evening well enough to relate it now, although I do not guarantee the dialogue is word for word as Watson told it and as I witnessed it.

The old doctor's cozy house was just off the sea coast of Santa —— —— and although Watson was a California resident for the health of his aging body, the house reflected much of his life in Britain and particularly London. A dart game hung on one wall, a game I found the elderly medico could beat me at handily, and somehow he had acquired the Persian slipper for his pipe tobacco from his old digs at Baker Street. There was a mantle clock whose chimes reminded one of Big Ben.

The man himself was very trim for an old gentleman of his years, one reason he had reached that age, no doubt, dressed in dark trousers, white shirt, vest and tie, but no jacket, his gesture towards West Coast informality.

I came into the house as the technicians were making their final checks of the equipment in the corner of the necessarily large living room.

Watson asked me if I would like some coffee or a beer.

"Just the usual glass of water to keep the old pipes open, Doctor," I told him.

I took my seat in one of the two chairs facing each other in front of the fireplace, after the fashion of the old doctor's rooms so long before.

We both had our scripts which we had marked for emphasis and pauses on the rehearsal from the previous day. We had more the rehearsal pattern of the *Lux Radio Theatre* than, say, *The Shadow*.

The sound man knocked on the two-foot-tall model of a door and opened its doorknob.

"Come in, come in, Mr. Petrie. Ready to hear another of my tales of the great detective, Sherlock Holmes?"

"Indeed I am, Doctor Watson. What better way to spend a brisk California evening than sitting in front of your fireplace and hearing you relate another of the cases of the Master Sleuth!"

"I appreciate you listening to the reminiscences of an elderly physician, Mr. Petrie. But before we start, I believe you have something to say about what our listeners should do these chilly days."

"Why yes, doctor, there's nothing better to prevent colds and other illnesses than fortifying yourself with Simmons' Colon Health Tonic. Simmons' Tonic has been around for eighty-one years, and it is still helping people build up their health with a refreshing draft of sparkling taste."

Unseen to the radio audience, Watson made a face. He hated the taste of the stuff although he had assured himself it did contain some vitamins and minerals and couldn't harm anybody.

"Yes, Simmons' Colon Health Tonic – good yesterday, good today, and good for your tomorrow! Now what is our story tonight, Doctor Watson?"

"Tonight, Mr. Grover, I think I shall tell you another encounter Sherlock Holmes had with that Napoleon of crime, Professor James Moriarty…"

It was a year near the end of the last century (Watson continued). Holmes and I were in our rooms at Mrs. Hudson's, 221B Baker Street. We were both in our favorite chairs, reading and smoking. Finally, Holmes folded his newspaper.

"So Watson, you found that when you purchased your copy of *The Woman in White* at the Tower Book Shop you were shortchanged a shilling by the clerk in the worn brown sweater who had the slight limp in his left leg?"

"You continue to amaze me, Holmes. How on earth did you deduce that?"

Holmes shrugged. "I read the letter to your old classmate, Billings, you left on the secretary."

"I say, Holmes, you are becoming a bit of a snoop."

"I am a snoop—a pry, a detective. I see and observe. It is my life. Do not leave the secrets of your life around and not expect me to find them out," Holmes said.

"Hardly a great secret, I suppose. Although, I would not care for you to read all of my private correspondence."

"And those letters you do not leave lying about," Holmes said. "We have learned to accommodate each other's ways."

Below in Baker Street we heard the sound of a horse and wheels pulling to a stop.

"Were you expecting a client, Holmes?"

"Yes," he said. "You may remember that I do sometimes keep secrets large and small."

"Should I excuse myself?"

Holmes gave one of his quick, nervous smiles, lasting no more than the blink of an eye. "How many times have you asked that question? You are forever my Boswell, Watson."

Mrs. Hudson climbed the stairs with another lady, from the sound of her footfall. The door opened and our landlady introduced "The Honorable Mrs. Harry Grimesby."

We stood and Holmes assured the lady she could say anything before me she could before him, and that I was also bound by my medical oath. He gestured her to my old chair, and I took a hard-backed seat from the breakfast table.

The woman was past thirty but still retained the ashes of her youthful beauty. Her garments were those of a woman on the edge of wealth. "Mr. Holmes, I shall come right to the point."

"Always the best procedure," he assured her.

"My husband is being sucked dry of his life's blood," she said.

"A blackmailer, madam?"

"I mean he is being drained of life's very essence. A vampire, Mr. Holmes!"

Holmes was silent for an instant. "Madam, I have upon one or two other times come across what was considered to be a supernatural demon of the night, but in the end, there was a mundane explanation."

"Pray that you find one here! I can only tell you what I observe to be the fact of the matter."

I could not help interjecting. "Madam, you have actually seen this creature drawing blood from your husband?"

"Not that, Doctor. But I have seen the results. After a midnight meeting with this cloaked caller, my husband showed himself in the morning with hollow eye and sunken cheek, pale and wan, his life's energy sucked from him."

Holmes arose from his chair to his full impressive height. "When you speak of a 'midnight meeting' are you merely making a poetical reference to the nether part of the night, or do you mean this caller always comes on the very stroke of twelve?"

"Near it, Mr. Holmes," she said. "There may be a difference of a few minutes either way."

"Is this a call of business, Mrs. Grimesby?"

"My husband is a building contractor. He does not do business from his residence in the middle of the night."

"Yet do you expect another call this very evening, Madam?"

"Yes, I do, Mr. Holmes. Each call is proceeded by the delivery of a simple miniature wooden box. One of these arrived by carrier this day."

"Have you seen what these boxes contain?"

"I have found the opportunity to examine two of them. They contained nothing."

"May I inquire as to where you reside, Mrs. Grimesby?"

"In the ——— Gardens quarter, Mr. Holmes."

"I think it best my associate, Dr. Watson, and myself go with you to your home and prepare for the arrival of this visitor. You say the visitor is cloaked? You have not yet seen a face?"

"Never. Harry greets him at the door and quickly escorts him into the study, and the door is bolted. In the morning, Harry emerges in the condition I have described."

"When and how does the visitor emerge?"

"God only knows, Mr. Holmes. I have never seen the creature again after he disappears behind the door with Harry."

"Have you spoken to your husband about this seeming apparition?"

"It would not be a good wife's place to do so."

"Of course. Come, Watson. We will join you downstairs in a moment, Madam."

After Mrs. Grimseby had left our quarters, Holmes turned to me. "Bring your revolver, Watson."

"I have no silver bullets, Holmes."

"Oh, I should think lead will do as well in this instance, old fellow."

We two interlopers made ourselves secure in the clothes closet of the Grimsby Manor, which was nigh on to being fit for a gentleman. The cabinet was large and smelled of cedar, designed to hold the greatcoat of guests in starker weather.

A crack of the cabinet door revealed the main door. We were getting hot and nigh smothering as the midnight hour drew on. At last came the chime. The servants had been dismissed, and Grimesby himself went to the door. He was a man of not yet middle years, growing a bit thick in the middle from the good life.

He threw back the door, and we saw the figure Mrs. Grimesby had described, not tall, face hidden in the collar of a rather theatrical cloak.

I heard a sharp intake of breath from Holmes beside me. "No disguise could hide that identity from me! Watson, may I relieve you of your revolver?"

I gave the weapon over to him. My first thought was that only one person could make Holmes wish to be armed so quickly—Professor Moriarty himself.

Grimesby escorted his guest towards the study door, but before the portal could close them off, Holmes sprang from the cabinet like a tiger.

"Hold, there! I would have words with you!"

Grimesby's face did not have to wait until the dawn to take on an ashen look. "What are you doing in my house? Who are you?"

"I am Sherlock Holmes, and I know everything!"

The visitor laughed in a high, almost effeminate way. "Another of your egotist claims, Mr. Sherlock Holmes. And are you accompanied by your Watson who knows nothing?"

I left the cabinet. "I am here to support Holmes, should he need any assistance."

"I can handle this matter, I should think, Watson. Did you think your disguise would fool me a second time? This is not the first time you have worn men's clothes, Irene Adler."

The cloak was thrown back, revealing the beauteous face and high-piled hair of the one-time opera diva who had engaged in a battle of wits with Holmes on a previous occasion. "You do not care to address me by my married name, Mr. Holmes?"

Holmes laughed sharply. "There was no marriage. Weddings were not a subject that I had studied because I felt such knowledge would be of no use to me in my work. But I reconsidered and investigated. You had me murmuring responses as a witness to your supposed wedding. I now know witnesses are called upon to make no responses at an English wedding."

"There was no wedding then," Irene said. "But perhaps there could be with a man near my equal, one to whom I could give a son to carry on his work."

Holmes gave another laugh that resembled a pistol shot. "I may have called you 'the woman' but you are not a normal woman. There is a reason why you can only fake a wedding and why you enjoy male dress. You can use your charms to entice men, but only to destroy them."

"Normal? What do know of 'normal,' you besotted drug addict, closeted in your unkempt rooms? You will live to see the day my kind earns equal respect to your nineteenth century views of normality in a world fast approaching the twentieth century."

"Yet you can ape the worst of your apparent sex as you destroy this fool for some purpose of your own."

Irene smiled, if that would be what her facial expression could be called. "Only to lure you here, Sherlock, to your own destruction."

In frustration, I could only ask, "What is all this about, Holmes?"

"Since I have sent Mrs. Grimesby away, I can tell you Grimesby himself was drained of his energy on many a night by Miss Adler in an excess of passion. The skills of Miss Adler have left more than one lover spent almost to death."

Grimesby tried to speak, but could not.

From the study which the pair had not entered there emerged a new figure on the scene. The great cranium rotated from side to side in a reptilian manner. It was Professor James Moriarty.

"Yes," Moriarty hissed. "I thought this puzzle would lure you to me, Mr. Holmes. I had hoped to play the hand out a bit more by Miss Adler developing the theme of giving you an heir to carry on your work when you are done. I wanted you to see that image as a possibility … before I told you that I have achieved that goal, and I will have a successor to carry on my great plan in the twentieth century."

Holmes snorted in ridicule. "You have mated with this vixen to produce a child? That would indeed be a demon to tempt the retribution of the heavens."

"I have no need of a woman, even the formidable Miss Adler. My successor will be another version of myself. My great mind can conceive of things other than criminal plans. I have developed a method by which an offspring can be cloven from the very atoms of my body. You might say it will be a 'Clove' of myself."

"A hideous prospect," Holmes admitted. "And you have drawn me here only to inform me of this?"

"No," the professor said. "I wanted you to know that in a new form I will carry on into the next century, but you, even in your ever aging body, will not be there to interfere in my plans. Adler has done more than to arrange a stage setting to appeal to you. She had been transforming Grimesby, more or less selected at random, through her wiles, drugs, my mesmerism. He has been transformed into an execution machine. He only awaits the signal from me to kill you. A bullet in the heart or head will not stop him from wringing the life from you, Holmes, in a body strengthened by early years of great labor."

Holmes turned to Professor Moriarty. "I will not waste a bullet on that poor soul. A number of times in my career, I have made my own laws, to let go free those guilty by the unbending laws of the empire. But it can work the other way, Professor. For the good of and on behalf of all mankind, I sentence you to death."

There was time for a look of surprise to cross Moriarty's face before Holmes fired a bullet from my revolver into the plotter's heart.

I sat in my chair across from Watson at the radio broadcast in a state of shock. Surely the continuity department of the network had not approved this script. It was not the one we had rehearsed. The old doctor had substituted this script for the approved one at the last moment.

"Yes, Mr. Petrie, the method of demise was not as picturesque as, say, Holmes carrying off Professor Moriarty over Switzerland's Reichenbach Falls, but just as final. Miss Adler escaped in the confusion, and poor Grimesby was delivered to a mad house."

"But Scotland Yard, Doctor—how did they react?"

"Oh, the professor was about to kill Holmes with a hidden weapon when the great sleuth fired. It was ruled justifiable homicide."

I somehow made my final pitch for Simmons' Tonic, and I was hardly aware of the story Watson promised for the following week.

We said goodnight to Basil and Bruce and the other Hollywood actors who had played the parts of Holmes, Watson and the others in the body of the show.

I was left alone with the aged Watson himself and at a loss for words when a tall figure emerged from the bedroom as the technicians were striking their equipment.

The man had a white goatee and rather resembled the cartoons of Uncle Sam. Watson glanced up at him and gasped. "*Holmes!*"

"Yes, dear old Watson, I thought it time I visited America and you at one of these wireless sessions." The man—Sherlock Holmes—sighed. "You must forever be creating melodrama, Watson. You know I only fired a warning shot as Moriarity made his escape. His dupe, Grimesby, was far too spent to be any danger."

"Yes, I know, Holmes," Watson said. "But I did not want to worry the public that fiend was still out there plotting his evil."

Holmes produced a pipe, tamped it, and lit it. "I think we have no need to worry about that. You and I are getting to be quite ancient fellows, and the professor was far older than we. He could not be alive."

"What of his talk of making an exact duplicate of himself, a 'clove'?"

"Watson, do you think there was any concept Moriarity could conceive that I could not at least equal him in? If you suppose a new Moriarty, you may as well suppose a new Holmes to combat him. And one conceived without the cooperation of Irene Adler."

"You did have a weakness for her, Holmes."

"I had an attraction to her, as I am attracted by crime. You know, my brother Mycroft and I had much the same genes. But Mycroft was driven to overeat, perhaps, I fear, by frustration over all the notoriety his younger brother achieved. Perhaps a new Holmes might more resemble the more ample Mycroft due to the pressures of this modern age. But enough. Perhaps you and your young associate can join me for a nightcap on this first evening of my all-too-short visit."

That was half a century ago. Holmes and Watson have disappeared into the shadows of time. But I know if there is a new Sherlock Holmes I wish I could announce one of his new adventures just one more time. If there were radio like that once again. ♦

THE AVENGER

The Maker of Werewolves
by Jim Harmon

Jim Brandon handed a cup of coffee to his lovely assistant, Fern Collier. They sat back on the lab stools and took a few minutes out from their work in the laboratory. Yet somehow Brandon never seemed relaxed. His lean, athletic body belied the studious nature of his work.

"Jim, can you tell me once again why you don't share your secrets with the official police?" Fern asked, after a sip of the hot beverage.

Brandon shook his head. "They wouldn't believe me about what the telepathic indicator would do. They couldn't accept the fact that a small portable device could register brain waves from the mind of a person about to commit a crime, a work of evil. Years of testing and investigating would go by, preventing me from doing what I could to prevent or avenge such crimes. As for the diffusion capsule and the power of invisibility…"

"Yes, Jim?"

Brandon turned away. "Who can be trusted with such a power? Even some member of the police might give way to the temptations it offers. Sometimes I wish I had not uncovered the secret. It is a terrible duty to uphold.

I have to bear it, but I won't trust it to anyone else. Perhaps the world will change in time, but until then, only I shall be The Avenger."

Suddenly, both noticed the signal light on the device they were discussing, the telepathic indicator.

"Jim, the light is red. That means someone is plotting a crime."

"Yes, Fern, and from the intensity of the light it is a monstrous crime. The new locator dial I've installed indicates it about to happen somewhere in the city's major park. The light…stronger, faster. Fern, this monumental evil is happening right at this moment!"

Moonlight gleamed off the fangs of the wolf.

A lean hand stroked the fur of the Northern gray wolf. "Quiet, Bela, quiet. You must be taught to kill, but we must be careful. The part of your

15

master, Professor Krueger, must not be known. My plan will change the world, and I must not be interfered with by the simpletons of the police force."

The wolf licked the hand of the tall, white-haired man, and then turned his narrowed yellow eyes back to the shadowed footpath of the trail.

The professor's own eyes were glazed and dancing in anticipation. "Yes, soon you will know the glorious pleasure of inflicting death. I have done it many times, and it is always a wonderful experience. You must be taught to kill, to enjoy killing, to make it a part of your very blood. And then—then that blood will be transfused into the body of one of my super-beings, those the ignorant might call werewolves but who in time will rule the world!"

The wolf whimpered as if in appreciation of the professor's plan.

The scientist could not restrain a giggle that burst into full-fledged laughter. "And to think—they called me mad—the fools, the simpletons!"

The neck bristles of the wolf rose, and with them, a low growl.

"Someone is coming down the foot path. Ah, I have seen him on previous visits in preparation. Officer O'Malley."

The heavyset man in police blue came down the trail on his usual nightly rounds, swinging his nightstick casually, and softly whistling "When Irish Eyes are Smiling".

Krueger stifled the laughter in his throat, and wiped a fleck of foaming spittle from his lips. "Now, Bela, now—*kill!*"

The policeman's round face registered surprise, fear, horror.

"Saints preserve us—what in the name of all that's holy—?"

The wolf launched its furry length at the blue uniform and the throat above it. Both tore.

Professor Krueger could no longer hold in his laughter. "The first step! The first step in my plan to create a super-race of werewolves!"

Only a few pathways further on, Jim Brandon and Fern Collier were walking a different trail, carefully watching the greenery at the sides of the path.

"Fern, you should have stayed behind. The telepathic indicator registers some terrible vibrations from around this area."

"I couldn't let you go alone," Fern said. "I only wish we could have brought some police with us."

"It is the same old story," Jim said. "They would not have believed the evidence of my indicator. We have to investigate this alone."

The high wailing cry of a wolf pulsated through the night.

"Jim, that terrible sound!"

Jim gave a chuckle. "We are near the zoo, Fern. I believe they have a few timber wolves on display. I might be wrong, but I expect what we have to worry about are human wolves."

The beautiful girl hugged Brandon's arm tightly. "Jim, are you armed?"

He looked grim in the moonlight. "Only with the powers of…The Avenger!"

The wolf cry sounded again.

"We must be getting closer to the zoo," Fern said.

"No. We are going away from the zoo, but the wolf howl is closer to us. I was wrong! That wild animal must have something to do with the crime that is happening tonight!"

"What shall we do?" Fern asked.

"I've got to investigate this. But I don't know what about you… Wait, someone is coming."

Down the path walked a tall, white-haired man in a leisurely stroll.

"Fern, I recognize that man. He's an old professor I know." Brandon raised his voice. "Professor! Professor Krueger!"

The older man looked up sharply. "What? Why, James Brandon. I haven't seen you since that science conference in Rome two years ago."

"Great to see you, Professor. Especially under these circumstances."

"There is an urgent matter I have to attend to. Could I ask you to take care of Miss Collier for me?"

The white-haired man smiled. "Why, yes, I shall be happy to take care of Miss Collier."

"Just see her home," Brandon said.

"I'll see that she gets to the right place."

"Fern, you know I have to go."

"Take care, Jim," she said, watching the young scientist go off into the night.

The old professor patted Fern's arm. "And now, my dear, as James suggested, I will take care of you."

"So this is your home, Professor Krueger?" Fern asked. "It is very European."

"Yes," the professor said. "Some have even said it resembles a damp old castle. We will be here for just a moment. I must get my glasses for night driving, and then I can take you home in my car."

"Yes, then perhaps Jim will call me at home, and I can find out what happened."

The white-hair man gave a soft chuckle. "I think I can tell you what happened, Miss Collier. My wolf, Bela, killed young Mr. Brandon as I have trained him to do, as Bela has already killed once before this night."

Fern felt as if cold lightning had struck her.

"Wait—I think I hear Bela scratching at his special door even now."

The old scientist threw a switch and in a moment a huge wolf came padding into the room.

"Ah, is that fresh blood on your snout, Bela—the blood of Mr. Brandon, I presume."

Fern looked around desperately for a way out.

Krueger smiled. "Oh, you can get out of this room. You can go to my laboratory where you will be strapped down to receive a transfusion of killer blood from my wolf, Bela, where you will become the first of my race of slaves to myself, the first of my super-werewolves!"

Fern found herself strapped down on an operating table, a white sheet covering her body. Her breasts heaved up and down as a white mound as she struggled useless to free herself.

Krueger had anesthetized the wolf and had the long grey length of fur that was the creature fastened down to another table, standing side-by-side with the one that held Fern.

"Ordinarily the blood of an animal transfused into the body of a human being would kill that person. But I believe I have solved that problem by my invention of a universal transfuse solution. If I am wrong—well, science learns from mistakes and I will just have to try again."

"Dr. Kruger, try to think rationally," Fern demanded. "You are raving like a madman."

"They said Di Vinci was mad. They said Edison was mad. They said Hitler was mad. What will they say about Kruger? That was not even always my name. In another life, I was known by an Irish name—Moriarty. But I changed it to a German name in honor of my associate, Dr. Swartz. A brilliant man—although he sometimes did object to murder."

There was a *pop* as a cork from a bottle, and then the hiss as of escaping gas.

Krueger looked startled. "What was that? One of my experiments going wrong?"

A deep, echoing voice filled the laboratory. *"No, Professor, it is I, The*

Avenger, to make things right!"

The old professor's face contorted in fury. "Where are you hiding, you so-called Avenger?"

"I am cloaked in the power of invisibility, a power created by the science you defile!"

"You can't interfere with me. You are just a voice. I will proceed with the transfusion by inserting this needle into Miss Collier's arm..."

Fern gave a short scream. "Oh, Avenger, I'm so glad you are here. But don't let him—"

For the first time a look of concern, of fear, crossed the white-haired scientist's face. "Something is holding my hand with the needle, something I can't see."

"You can't see me, but you can feel the power of The Avenger! Drop that needle!"

The needle clattered to the floor. The strapped-down wolf roused slightly at the sound and looked up.

"You have delayed me, Avenger, until my wolf has come to. But it is just as well. He has killed twice this night, and he can kill again once I unstrap him. A wolf doesn't have to see you, Avenger. He can smell you out."

"Do not release that beast, Professor. The Avenger is cloaked in many ways. The wolf will not find me."

The deranged scientist paid no heed. He unbuckled the giant wolf.

"Kill, Bela, kill as I have taught you...Wait, Bela...do not look at me. No!"

The wolf sprang. The creature sank his fangs into the soft throat of the doctor, and the two beings fought in a bath of crimson blood. Then came a gun flash from empty air, and the beast fell dead beside his slain master. The marksmanship of the Avenger was true as ever.

"Oh, how terrible, Jim," Fern said.

"Yes, Fern, the wolf could only see one person to kill. Professor Krueger has learned that crime ends in a trap that justice sets!"

Jim Brandon and Fern Collier were back in Brandon's laboratory.

"That poor animal didn't know what it was doing," Fern said.

"Yes, Fern," Brandon said. "It was an innocent creature taught to kill by my old associate. Krueger was wrong about him being able to sense me. The diffusion capsule offers a complete sensory screen – sight, sound, movement, and even smell. Only when I exercise the force of my will-power as I have trained myself to do, can I be heard or felt. Hidden from him, I was able to follow him home to Krueger's house. Then when he was ordered to kill, the wolf was aware of only one target for its violence – Kruger."

A haunting laughter filled the room. "**You have done well, Jim Brandon, but I watch closely those who use the power of invisibility. Use it wisely, use it justly, or I will know.**"

Fern paled. "Jim, someone has discovered your power!"

"No, Fern, not my power. I heard no sound of the decanting of the diffusion capsule. This being must have some other secret for his invisibility."

"But he knows your identity, Jim," Fern said. "What do you think we have to fear from him?"

"Perhaps nothing, Fern. He only advised me to stick to the path of justice, and that is always the path taken by The Avenger!" ◆

Baby Snooks

Out With Mommy
by Ben Ohmart

Her dainty, ill-washed feet crept soundlessly into the bedroom. On the tray in her young hands: burnt toast, pared figs right off the backyard tree, half-scrambled eggs with plenty of crunchy shell, twelve strips of mostly-cooked bacon and wax paper, and a side cup of coffee/sugar. Between the tray and the greasy plate rested the poor Friday paper, minus the best part.

Snooks had already been through the gist of the funnies when she had a sudden inkling to fix Daddy breakfast in bed after his ordeal the previous night.

"DA-ddy!" she exlaimed when plenty close.

Lancelot Higgins awoke with a pained start, hitting his head on the solid-oak bedboard. He groaned, still clutching the perpetual headache he always seemed to keep on hand.

"Oooooh…Snooks! What is it?"

Scooping up one long breath, she began hurriedly. "Eggs n bacon n coffee with sweet jus' like you like 'n' some fruit cuz it's good for you in the mornin' n toast with bean dip—"

"Please!" the poor father shouted. He had the one eye open and was working on the other.

"If you wanna pancake, they're downstairs."

"Couldn't you fit everything on the plate?"

"Oh yeah! It all fit on the plate good. But now it's downstairs."

By now, Daddy read her like a banned book. Her response was code-word for Pancakes on the Floor. Still, being a father meant looking on the bright side of the nimbostratus cloud.

"Well!" he began, sitting up in his hideous Oxford Don pj's. "This looks fulfilling. Eggs and shell, bacon and paper. Mmmm-*mmm*! Did you fix all this by yourself, Snooks?"

The child nodded vigorously. "Yeah. But Mommy spoiled it. She got to do the fun part and got to whoosh the gas stove!"

"A smart woman, your mother," Daddy said with grave respect. "I knew there was a reason I'd married her originally. It's a little warm right now, Snooks, if you don't mind I'll just have a look at the paper."

"It's in there, Da-ddy. I left it in 'cuz there's where all the juice 'n' goodness is."

"Yes. Of course."

Thoroughly engrossed in the Platt's scientific column, Daddy was the last to notice the hanging plant come down on his head with gravitational force.

"Ooooooooooooo…!"

He clutched his lumpy nut as the demon they called Snooks frowned and fell off the bed, broomstick still in hand. She'd always wondered what kept that potted green thing suspended from the ceiling. And here it turned out to be boring ol' piano wire or somethin'.

"Snooks!!"

It was too early in the morning for understanding. He was too groggy for parental self-editing. But it was just the *right* time for a spanking worth of de Sade himself.

Even before his face made the leer and the inevitable right sleeve began to roll up his arm, Snooks knew that look. She backed up as the parent advanced. Only a miracle would save her now-

"Lancelot!"

In came a cheery miracle by the name of Mommy. She was full of good Friday smiles when she breezed into the bedroom, already dolled up in a cute but functional blue suit. But now, faced with the familiar old sight, her tone turned automatically harsh.

"Lancelot! What are you doing to the child? And why are you covered in dirt this time of morning?"

"I always wash my face in dirt before I eat pared figs. It's the only way to live!"

Snooks bit her tiny pinky and quietly asked, "Is it?"

A low groan escaped the man of the house, as he rolled down his unhappy arm and trundled back to bed.

"I'm going out for a bit, Lancelot, I shan't be long…"

She was halfway out the bedroom door when she heard the anguished cry. "WAIT! Take Snooks!"

It was the first time she'd heard that kind of language coming out of her husband's mouth.

"Are you feeling all right?"

"NOOO! Take Snooks!"

It was all he managed to say for the three minutes she remained. The man was raving. Snooks chuckled and grabbed her mother's hand.

"Just like Uncle Louie when he was petting that red zebra!"

Mommy jerked the child away with such force, the hand almost came off.

The car ride was usual: Snooks jumping up and down, pushing all the dials she could and couldn't find, singing EE-I-EE-I-OOH to herself and out the half-down window at every opportunity. For some reason she found it incredibly easy to ignore. But not today.

"Okay now, Snooks, settle down. We have to be dignified when we go to the bank."

"Whyyy?"

"Because we must show respect. And there's still a lot left on that mortgage…" She begin thinking dollar thoughts.

"What's respect?"

"It's a wonderful gift you give people so you can get the same thing in return."

"Then why don't you just keep what ya got?"

She smiled at the little darling. "Respect means observing a person's rights. Letting them be who they are."

"Who are they?"

"Who are who?"

"Who?"

"Just sit still, Snooks. Here, play with this."

It was a plastic puzzle that slid one square at a time until the drawing came out correctly in place. To Snooks' mind, it was also a first class stinker as a toy. She let it drop.

"Where we goin'?"

"To the bank, I said. Didn't you hear me?"

"What was that?"

The questions began again, but unlike Daddy, Mommy knew how not to answer. Eventually, they would stop. Mommy prayed for a good car accident or a spotty dog to follow the car – something to stop them sooner.

The bank was crowded that day. End of the week traffic, no parking places. Mommy drove around in circles four times waiting for a space.

"Why are we drivin' crazy?"

"It's not crazy, Snooks, it's—oooh!"

An old man was pulling out and the Higginsmobile made a mad dash for it. In her zeal, the feminine adult in the car pulled too close to the brown Ford on Snooks' side. Unfortunately, Mommy's cries of "Wait! Snooks!" were as useless as the doormats in their house. The little girl quickly opened her door, banging it into the side of the Ford. Not once, not four times, not eight times but –

Mommy could stand it no longer. "Snooks!"

Nor could the 55-year-old banker coming out of the smart side door of the First Union Bank.

"What's going on here? Look at my car!"

Mommy began groveling early. "I'm sorry, Mr. Preston, really I am. I have my little girl with me today, and she's so anxious when we go on these little trips—"

He wasn't interested. The car was a showpiece in a different way for him now. "Look at the side of this! This is special paint—I have to send away to New Zealand to get this stuff!"

At this, a joyful Snooks began bounding up and down, sometimes on the poor executive's corned foot. "I wanna go! Haha, I wanna go!"

"Go where?" her mother asked with fixed exasperation.

"I wanna go see the funnies! I wanna go get the paint!"

"The funnies?" the man asked, despite his wounded ego. "What are you talking about?"

"I wanna go to Newsland! I wanna go to Newsland!"

Snooks did her little dance around the adults, laughing and giggling and grabbing their hands to take her to Newsland. It broke the ice holding Mr. Preston in place. Now he knew what this young mother was up against.

"Let's speak inside, Mrs. Higgins."

The interior of the First Union was cool with the smell of rich men's air conditioning. Mommy instantly sat Snooks in the corner with the chair and potted ficus, and shook her finger right up against the girl's nose.

"Respect, Snooks."

"Respect, Mommy…"

Mommy strode away after the hurried Mr. Preston. Had Snooks any concept of body language, she would know who controlled the situation. Mommy just hoped they wouldn't take her house away for this.

Snooks sat. For fifteen seconds. There was too much activity. Too many new faces. Too much flashy cash moving past.

Innocently, the young little thing with the pink ribbon in her hair strode up to a homely 55-year-old male in a green suit well past its expiration date.

"Is this where you give out the money?"

He smiled a few teeth. "That's right, little girl. Do you have an account?"

"What's account?"

"Well, you have to put money in before you can get it out again."

"Sounds screwy to me."

The man reacted as if struck by a wet wife. "It's the way we do business, I'm afraid."

"I'll just keep my three cents, then."

"Ah!" The teller was feeling fruity and talkative today. "But if you do that, you'll never get interest."

"Interest..." Snooks thought to herself. "Ain't that when you pass the peep show and you have a look in at the dame with the —"

"No!" His voice was so loud, three women looked up, and had to start counting their fifties again from scratch.

"No," he continued quietly, stooping down until his glasses touched the counter. "Interest means that you give us, say, one dollar, and we give you back one dollar and a dime in a little while. We give you *interest* for loaning us the money. You see?"

"Yeah." Her nose wriggled. "It's like a pawn shop." Before the man could summon up enough dignity to protest, Snooks asked, "How much will you give me on this three cents?"

The cash came out of the child's dainty dress pocket—along with a dead frog, two glazed rocks, some remnants of lemony-orange candy and a piece of knotted string: all pretty much in one fistful.

The cringing man, now intensely glad of his bachelorhood, tried to summon a smile from the deep revulsion of his inner being. He did it.

"I'm afraid there's a twenty-five dollar minimum required for opening and keeping a savings account here, little lady."

Snooks looked at the money as if it had just been sneezed on, and cast her full brown eyes back at the man. "No good, huh?"

He shook his head, and tried to hide by stamping already stamped checks.

Still, she stood. "How long would it take for what I got to grow up into twenty-five bucks?"

"I'd be an old man by then."

Cheerfully, energetically Snooks re-took the pennies from her pocket and standing on tippy toes, shoved them over the counter. "Gimme the money!"

It took the clerk a full five seconds to realize he'd been subtly but greatly insulted by this—this—

Out went his hands, ready to strangle that kid!

"Marvin!"

Mr. Preston ran over just in time to restrain the enraged clerk from clutching his pink hands around that scrawny little neck! Mommy followed the executive out into the lobby, and knew her cue when she saw it. She grabbed her child like a rag doll and flew from the business.

"Bye!" Snook yelled, smiling respectfully as the door closed.

She promised she'd never hit the child—no, that was wrong—but it took her the entire seven blocks to eek all the fume out of her system. When Mommy put the squeaking breaks down in front of Phil's Garage, she had 70% of her sanity restored.

"Hey there, Mrs. H," Mike called, coming to the window. He always had a greasy grin and a bag of conversation for the lovely ladies.

"Nice to see you out and about with the kid. She's growing, isn't she? I heard if you put a brick on their head, it'll stop 'em doing that. Ha ha! What's the problem today?"

"I know I should've called first, Mike, but just yesterday the breaks seem to squeak a little. But more importantly—there's just the tiniest ding in the rear left. Looks like someone hit it while I was at the drug store. I swear I didn't hit anyone! But Lancelot would never believe me if I told him—"

She stopped when the smiling man held out a greasy hand.

"I believe you completely, Mrs. H. Happens all too frequently, guy just backs up too far and either doesn't know he's hit so lightly or else just doesn't have *time* to be a good guy, I remember last week when I..."

His voice faded as he went in the "grease pit" to grab a blank form.

"He talks a lot, don't he?"

"He's just being friendly, Snooks."

"Sure hope he ain't too friendly with Daddy..."

Mommy's face went a granite color. "What do you mean?"

"Oh...nuttin'..."

"Now Snooks—I didn't hit that car, if that's what you're referring to. It's just a little ol' ding anyway."

In her smallest voice, her child replied, "Just a li'l one?"

Mike came back after a quick but professional appraisal of the rear. He set his muddy grin on standby, and squatted to keep his head in the open window frame.

"Well, Mrs. H, we're looking at around two twenty-five for the alignment of—"

"Two hundred and twenty-five? Dollars??"

His voice tried to remain compassionate. "It's quite a banged up piece of work back there, missus. I can labor alone running you almost a hundred and—"

Her face went white. "Mike? Are you kidding me? Is it April first?"

Instantly, she gently bumped the mechanic out of the way with an opening door and trotted her pink high heels around to the back of the vehicle. Mike began his knees lifting up to join her. But Snooks was too quick.

"Can I see yer mask?"

The grease monkey smiled with indulgence. "What mask is that, honey?"

"The one you use when you're out on the highway."

"Highway?"

"Ain't you a robber?"

Slow as Mike's thought reaction might have been, the man had had a full two months of high school. He shifted his face to Hard Mode, because he got the little tyke's wretched drift.

"Who told you that?"

"Can I see it?" she barked excitedly.

"I ain't got it with me. Who said that, your mommy?"

"Are you twins?"

He was simple man, and blinking helped his mental processes. "Huh?"

"Are you twins? You got a brother or sister that looks jus' like you?"

"What are you talkin' about, kid?"

"Well, when Daddy gets a piece of paper from you in the mail, he clutches on his head and asks how can you live with yourself at the prices you—"

That was enough. Snooks went on, and Mike went to join the perplexed Mommy who still couldn't figure out what was wrong. Snooks stood up in the car seat to watch the argument in the rear view mirror. Perhaps Mike was usually reasonable with his estimates, but now, all sorts of new costs were coming out of the little ding which barely had scratched a millimeter's worth of paint off the light-blue automobile.

It was fun! The more and more they talked, waved their arms about and shouted to the wind, the more Snooks jumped up and down, up and down, giggling to herself like a giddy lion cub.

In less than a minute, the right back tire blew. ◆

THE WHISTLER

Bad Business
by Mel Gilden

I am the Whistler, and I know many things for I walk by night. I know many strange tales, many secrets hidden in the hearts of men and women who have stepped into the shadows. Yes, I know the nameless terrors of which they dare not speak...!

A twin-engine plane lands on the field outside Bascolm City and taxies to a stop before the shed that serves as its terminal. One of the passengers is Fred Barton, a big man with big appetites. He is returning in triumph from Detroit where he was installed as a member of the exclusive businessman's organization, the Great Caribou.

Waiting for him at the gate is his wife of many years, Gladys. Fred smiles as he walks toward her across the tarmac, but his smile hides his real feelings. He is noticing once again how old Gladys looks. He is thinking once again that she is not an appropriate companion for a member of the Great Caribou. He is thinking about Sylvia LaTour, who is so much younger and more beautiful.

Gladys waved enthusiastically. "Hey, Fred! Hello," she cried.

Fred waved back. He walked through the gate and touched her cheek with his own without bothering to drop his bags.

"How was your trip?" Gladys asked.

Fred said nothing but only puffed out his chest, showing off the Great Caribou pin on the lapel of his gray pinstriped suit. It was a cloisonné pin of a butterscotch-colored caribou with enormous antlers.

"Oh, Fred," Gladys said, "I'm so proud."

Fred beamed at her.

Gladys put her arm through his, and together they walked toward the parking lot. "Arthur is at home preparing the perfect dinner for the conquering hero," she said. "Steak, mashed potatoes, and green peas. And for dessert, apple pie and ice cream."

"My dear," Fred said, "that sounds wonderful. I've missed Arthur's cooking. What have you been doing with yourself while I was gone?"

You barely listen as she goes nattering on about the bridge club and the garden. Is she really the most boring woman in the world, or does it only seem that way to you? Though you try to take an interest, it's difficult, nearly impossible, isn't it, Fred? But a successful businessman such as yourself possesses many skills, among them is the ability to act.

At last you arrive at your home, a large gray mansion which you can barely see because of the all the trees and flowers Gladys has planted. But you give her only compliments because if it wasn't for her garden, she would be under foot all the time.

You are surprised to see Sam Dirkin's car parked out in front, and sure enough when Arthur opens the door the Sheriff is standing just behind him. You and Sam have been friends for many years, but his presence will make what you have in mind more difficult. Still, you cannot see spending this evening alone with Gladys, or even with Gladys and Sam—not when Sylvia LaTour is waiting for you at Blaster, a club on the edge of town.

Sam seems impressed with your Great Caribou pin, as well he should be. Many years ago each of you made a decision. And it wasn't your fault, was it, Fred, that Sam went into law enforcement instead of sales?

Arthur hovers over you, making sure that your needs and the needs of the others are met instantly. He is more like a member of the family than like a servant, isn't he, Fred? And though the dinner he's prepared is good, it is nothing like the spectacular meals you were treated to in Detroit.

The three of you eat on the balcony 30 feet above Gladys' carefully planted garden. The view of the gray-green mountains in the distance is spectacular. Then, as Arthur clears the dirty dishes, the moment you have been waiting for all evening arrives.

"Wonderful dinner, Gladys," Fred said.

"Yes," Sam agreed. "Very good."

"Thank you, both. Though you must know that Arthur did all the work."

"You inspire him," Sam said.

Fred nodded. "If we ate like this every evening I would have to buy some new pants." He chuckled. "Now what did I do with my cigars?"

"Right here, dear."

"Have one, Sam?" Fred asked.

"Don't mind if I do."

"Let's step up to the railing."

"It's a beautiful view," Sam said as he puffed.

"Yes," Fred said as he cut the tip off his cigar and lit up, "Gladys has done a handsome job with the garden." A cloud of gray wool from two cigars rose to mix with the thin evening fog.

"Let's have another look at that pin of yours," Sam said.

Fred leaned forward.

"Can you pass it over here?" Sam asked.

"I'm afraid not, Sam," Fred said. "I never take it off."

"He's going to shower wearing it," Gladys said. They all laughed.

After a short silence, Fred spoke again. "I'll have to go out tonight," he said.

"Oh, Fred," Gladys said, sounding distraught. "I was hoping that on your first night back I might be able to spend some time with the new Great Caribou."

"Sorry, dear. Business. That's one of the reasons I was made a Great Caribou—because I'm always ready to do business."

"I know, dear, but—"

"But nothing, Gladys. It's settled. I'll be home late. Don't wait up."

"Yes, dear."

"Welcome home, Fred," Sam said.

"Thanks, Sam."

You don't like them laughing about your wearing the Great Caribou pin, do you, Fred? But it was either go along with the gag or you would have to explain once again to Gladys and Sam what an honor it is to be chosen. You know that no matter how many times you explain, they will never understand. A housewife and a policeman—how could they?

You're not a bad person, are you, Fred? You don't really enjoy hurting Gladys, but without coming right out and saying it there is no way to tell her you will not be home this evening. Thank goodness she grew used to your need to go out at odd hours all the times you were really going out to wheel and deal. She doesn't have to know that now, something other than business is on your mind. You smile when you think about Sylvia, and you feel strong emotions you have not felt for Gladys in many years.

You go to your bedroom where Arthur is already laying out your clothes for the evening. It's almost as if he can read your mind. That bothers you a little, doesn't it, Fred? You laugh at your own foolishness.

"Something funny, sir?" Arthur asked as he hung up the suit Fred had been wearing on the plane.

"No, Arthur. Just glad to be home."

"We're glad to have you, sir. Here's your Caribou pin. I took the liberty of removing it from the lapel of your gray pinstripe suit."

Fred looked at him with suspicion. "How did you know I would want it?

"Why, sir," Arthur said with surprised, "I overheard you and Mrs. Barton and Sheriff Dirkin talking about it. I assumed that if you were going to a business meeting you would want to wear it. I hope I did not overstep my bounds."

"No, of course not, Arthur. You never do. Thank you for your thoughtfulness. And I meant to tell you that dinner was superb."

"I do my best, sir. It is my pleasure to please you."

Yes, Arthur is a wonderful servant: punctual, accurate, talented, and caring. You are lucky to have him, aren't you, Fred? And he is certainly a lot less work to be around than Gladys.

As you drive along the familiar streets of Bascolm City you think about how perfect your life would be if Gladys wasn't in the way. You imagine what life would be like with just the three of you—you, the beautiful and sensual Sylvia, and the useful and discreet Arthur. But Gladys is a fact of life—like, like gravity. You're not quite ready to dump her, are you, Fred? But soon. Very soon.

At the edge of town Blaster pours a splash of light onto the gravel parking lot. From inside comes laughter and rock music. Gladys would certainly be surprised to see you in a place like this. But you feel young here.

Humming to yourself, you park your car and go inside. The place is crowded. Couples are dancing up a storm on the small dance floor. At last you find Sylvia sitting alone at a table in one corner. She looks good, doesn't she Fred, in her crop top and jeans, her blonde hair cascading to her shoulders? She smiles as she rises. You kiss her hard on the lips and she responds. Home was never like this. You smile as you both sit down.

"Welcome home, Fred," Sylvia said.

"Thanks. You look wonderful tonight, Sylvia."

"How could I not? My man is with me."

"Look at what your man is wearing. Can you see it in this dim light?"

Sylvia peered at him. "You were accepted into the Great Caribou," she said with delight, and leaned across the table to kiss him again.

Fred took a deep breath. "Well," he said.

"How is Gladys?" Sylvia asked.

"Fine. Do we have to talk about her?"

"As long as she's your wife, we do."

"She's my wife in name only," Fred said. "I love you."

"I know you do, Fred. That's why this situation is so awkward."

"I don't think she would give me a divorce," Fred said.

"Then perhaps we need to work out something else."

"Must you be so melodramatic?" he asked suddenly.

"Your life is a melodrama," Sylvia said. "What I am if not the 'other woman'?"

"If she won't divorce me what do you want me to do?"

"There is always murder," Sylvia said.

Fred said nothing while the music played. "You talk of murder very calmly."

"If Gladys won't give you a divorce, what else are you to do?"

"Why do anything?" Fred asked. "What we have right now isn't so bad."

"I don't enjoy being the 'other woman', Fred."

"You're not the 'other woman' to me, darling," Fred said.

You and Sylvia talk far into the night. The club gradually empties. Instead of hot rock, the band plays cool jazz as if for themselves alone, and still the two of you sit at the back table discussing what to do about Gladys. It's been a long day. You're tired, and the three beers you've had make you a little buzzy. Murder sounds better and better all the time, doesn't it, Fred? After a while it seems as if killing Gladys was your idea all the time. It seems so easy, especially the way Sylvia blocks out the moves.

You drive home carefully, aware that you're a little tight, and sigh when you arrive at home in one piece. Quietly, you enter the house. You walk to Gladys' room and stand in the darkness staring down at her. She breathes noisily as she sleeps, sounding like a truck in need of a tune-up. Putting a pillow over her face would be a pleasure, wouldn't it, Fred? The "other woman" would become the "only woman." But then the pillow would be a murder weapon, and somehow it might lead back to you. Besides, Arthur might hear the two of you struggling. No. Bide your time. Follow the plan that you and Sylvia worked out together. That's best.

The next day at breakfast Gladys seems distant, inattentive, not nearly so glad to see you at home as she had been the night before. Each of you spends a lot of time looking at the distant mountains. Like a ghost, Arthur moves silently between you and the kitchen and Gladys. You stand up and invite her to join you at the balcony railing. You put an arm around her and she stiffens.

Gladys took a step away from Fred.

"What's the matter?" he asked.

"You think that hunk of tin on your collar makes you smarter than everybody else."

"What?"

"You're not the only one with secrets, Fred," Gladys said, her voice shaking with anger. "You're not the only one who knows how to deceive."

"Are you cheating on me with Arthur?" Fred asked, and smiled at the ridiculousness of it.

"It would serve you right if I did," Gladys stated.

"Gladys, what are you talking about?"

"Were you convinced last night, Fred? Did you believe I was glad to see you?"

"I did. I had no reason not to."

Gladys laughed. "I thought I was pretty convincing, myself," she said. "But you still insisted upon going out. You still insisted upon seeing that woman."

"Woman? What woman?"

"I don't know her name. But she is pretty and blonde and much younger than I."

"I don't know where you get your information, Gladys, but— "

"I hired a man to watch you, Fred," Gladys said, interrupting. "He's been watching the two of you, you and that tramp. You were together last night."

"You're imagining things, Gladys," Fred said, and dismissed her with a wave of his hand.

"I don't think so," Gladys said. "I saw the pictures he took."

"Pictures? What pictures?"

"Very handsome head shots. Would you like a few for your wallet?"

"Where are they? Let me see them."

"They are in a safe place."

Neither of them said anything for a long time.

Arthur came out onto the balcony. "May I do anything else for you, Mr. and Mrs. Barton?" he asked.

"No, thank you, Arthur," Fred said. "That will be all."

"Very well, sir." He went away.

In the distance a bird shrieked and dived at something in the garden below. After that the silence was complete.

"You don't want to give me a divorce," Fred said sounding weary. "What do you want? Money I suppose?"

"Of course, money would be very useful. But what I want most, Fred, is nothing so simple as money, or even freedom. I want revenge."

"Go on."

"I want you to stop seeing that woman."

"Why? Seemingly, you won't give me a divorce no matter what I do. What's in it for me if I stop seeing her?"

"Oh, Fred. You have absolutely no imagination at all, do you, poor boy? You will stop seeing her or I will ruin your reputation. I'll send my little album of photos to the Great Caribou board, complete with an explanatory paragraph on the back of each."

"You wouldn't."

"I would and I will."

You're heard enough, haven't you, Fred? Arthur has gone back to the kitchen, where he will be washing up. It is time to put Sylvia's plan into effect. You grab Gladys and the two of you struggle for a moment. Then suddenly she is flying through the air. Her cry as she falls is very much like the shriek of that hunting bird. There is a solid thump as she hits the ground. Her broken body lies like a discarded marionette in the garden among flowers whose names you could never remember.

You stagger back from the railing a little short of breath. She was stronger than she looked.

"What happened, sir?" Arthur asked as he ran out onto the balcony. "I heard someone cry out."

"Mrs. Barton," Fred said, still trying to catch his breath. "She jumped."

Arthur rushed to the railing and almost doubled himself leaning over it. "Oh," he said. It was less a word than an excited exhalation of breath. "Oh, sir," he said. "We must call a doctor immediately. She may still be alive."

"Yes, yes. By all means. And the police, too."

Arthur hurried away.

You must get a grip on yourself, mustn't you, Fred? Nothing about Gladys' death indicates it is anything other than an accident. Arthur seems convinced, and so will the police. Though you settle on the living room sofa, the picture of the anguished husband, in reality your main concern is not Gladys' untimely death but the honor of the Great Caribou.

Arthur joins you and reports that both an ambulance and Sheriff Dirkin will be there soon. You thank him, and Arthur waits for a moment before he leaves the room, as if he wants to say something but can't find the words.

When Arthur is gone you look down at your collar, hoping to take strength from the Great Caribou pin's reassuring glimmer. But the pin is not there! Where could it be? Could Gladys have clutched at it as the two of you struggled, grabbed it, carried it with her when she fell? It will look mighty suspicious if the pin is found near her body in the garden. You must go down to where she fell and retrieve it immediately. Hurry to the garden, Fred. Hurry as if your life depends on it.

The trip down the wooden stairs and along the gravel path seems to take forever, doesn't it, Fred? But you arrive in the garden at last. You don't like touching Gladys' body—so twisted, so still, so dead—but you force yourself. You open her right hand and find nothing. The same again in her left. But she could have dropped it during her fall, couldn't she, Fred?

You get down onto your hands and knees and desperately move the dirt around. Nothing! Nothing! Time is growing short, isn't it, Fred? Sam Dirkin will arrive soon!

Fred was surprised to find a shinny black shoe. He looked up at Sam Dirkin.

"Searching for something, Fred?" Sam asked.

"Thank goodness you've come at last," Fred said as he clambered to his feet.

"It must be important if you're looking for it at a time like this," Sam said as he gazed down at Gladys' body.

"Yes," Fred said. "Poor Gladys. She was already dead when I reached her."

"What are you looking for?" Sam asked again.

"Well, as a matter of fact," Fred said in a reasonable voice, "I'm looking for my Great Caribou pin. Gladys had it with her when she fell. She was taking it to a jeweler to have the clasp repaired."

"Seems odd that the pin should matter at a time like this," Sam said.

"You're right, of course. It doesn't matter at all." Fred glanced about him. "Still, I know it's down here someplace. She must have pulled it off me when she fell."

"Did she put up much of a fight?" Sam asked innocently.

"Not much," Fred said. "She—" he went on, and then stopped instantly.

Neither Fred nor Sam said anything for a long time.

"I think you'd better come along to the station with me," Sam said as he gripped Fred tightly by the arm.

"What?" Fred asked as if he were in a trance. "Yes. Yes, of course."

Together they left the garden and walked up the driveway to Sam's official car. Sam was about to thrust Fred into the back seat when Arthur ran up to them. "There you are, sir," Arthur said. "I found your Great Caribou pin behind a sofa cushion. I know it means a lot to you, so I brought it right out." ◆

THE AIR ADVENTURES OF
JIMMIE ALLEN

"The Adventures of Jimmie Allen in World War II"
by Jon D. Swartz

Capt. James Allen of the USAAF started firing as the single engine, low-winged Focke Wulf 190 was completing its turn in his direction. The 50s found their mark, a hail of shells directly on the target. The enemy plane straightened out and flew directly toward Jimmie's Mustang. Jimmie held the trigger down and his sight on the enemy's engine as the planes approached head-on. The Mustang's tracers and his 50s spattered on the enemy plane. The two planes were close—hurtling at each other at hundreds of miles per hour. Jimmie eased back on his controls. He flew his *Blue Bird Special II* not with his hands but with the tips of his fingers. His body was the body of the Mustang, and there was little difference between them. The Focke Wulf suddenly zoomed upward with extraordinary sharpness, and the enemy plane—before as small as a toy in Jimmie's sight—now loomed huge in size. Seconds passed. Jimmie could see the round nose and the outstretched wings of the Focke Wulf and the enemy pilot in his shallow cockpit. The pilot was smiling, but it was an ironic smile. There was a jolt of air as the enemy plane shot past. Jimmie's keen blue eyes swept the sky in all directions. Only other Mustang P-51s and the Axis plane he had just shot down could be seen. The air battle had lasted only seconds, but it had seemed like hours to Jimmie and his fellow pilots. The Allied pilots thought the Axis planes they had encountered recently—whether Focke Wulfs, Messerschmitts, or Stukas—were more aggressive than any they had met before in any action of the war.

It was early January in 1943, and it was bitterly cold. In addition to being cold, Captain Allen was tired, bone-tired, as he taxied his Mustang to where his groundcrew could service it easily and quickly. He never knew just how long it would be before he was in the air again. Allen loved his

Mustang, felt it was by far the most "honest" airplane in service, and had no bad flying habits. The P-51D answered all a fighter pilot's dreams. It was a wonderful flying machine, with a view of the world around, a fantastic gun platform, and designed to combat all enemies at any distance from base. Moreover, its relatively small cockpit made it possible to have all instruments within easy reach. With its top speed of 437 mph, six .50 caliber machine guns, and 2,000-bomb load, Jimmie thought that—with a good pilot aboard—the Mustang was a match for all comers. Before his *Blue Bird Special II*, he had flown other fighters, including a Lightning P-38. He had liked his Lightning a lot, and flown it with great success, but for some reason had never named it. No, his Mustang, which he had almost immediately nicknamed the *Blue Bird Special II*, was the fighting ship for him. And he felt lucky to have it. Just the year before 25 Mustangs had been lost at sea in transit from the United States. The Atlantic crossing was very hazardous, with German submarines taking a heavy toll of Allied shipping.

Allen got out of his cockpit, stood briefly on the starboard wing as he examined the outer skin for any damage. Then he saw the groundcrews approaching, and jumped to the ground. He stood for a few seconds, looking at his plane. Tall and fair, in his twenties, Jimmie still had the appearance of a teenager. He was almost six feet tall, with ice-blue eyes and wavy light-brown hair. Although lean, he carried himself with an air of strength and competence. There was an aura of authority about him, especially when he spoke to you. His fellow pilots thought Jimmie was a great pilot. Great because, in an emergency, whenever the moment came, his coolness was great, his courage was great, and his flying instincts were great. He didn't really fly a plane, he merely followed his instincts—and they had never failed him.

The wind was biting cold, but he tried not to think of the weather, or his tiredness. He had flown back-to-back missions as the Allies attempted to halt the advance of the Germans in France. Instead, he tried to concentrate on the Headquarters mess room, with its comforting fire, as he walked the mile or so to Headquarters.

"Hi Allen," called Lt. Milton Clark. "How did it go?"

"All right, Milt," said Jimmie, "although it was really cold up there. I just wish a Mustang's windshield heating were a bit better. It really isn't sufficient at higher altitudes."

"I agree. It's the only complaint I have about the Mustang. But, Jimmie, I was told to meet you and tell you the old man wants to see you. He's been asking if you had landed yet every ten minutes or so. He's waiting for you in his office right now. The scuttlebutt is he has something important to tell you. If it's what I think it is, you and I may be going on a mission together…and soon."

Two members of the ground crew walked together as they approached Allen's plane.

"Do you see what I see on this Mustang, Sergeant Lewis?

"I don't know, son. What do you mean?"

"The victory symbols on it. Look for yourself. There's a ton of symbols, and for all the Axis powers, meaning the pilot is an ace several times over. But look right there, next to the last German swastika. Unless I'm mistaken, that's a *Stars & Stripes*!"

"Oh yeah, I forgot you were just assigned to my crew. So many of you are new around here. That's Capt. Allen's *Blue Bird*, or to be more precise, the *Blue Bird Special II*. It's famous around here. Capt. Jimmie Allen was our squadron's first ace."

"Jimmie Allen? He was my hero. I listened to his radio show, belonged to his flying club, had all the premiums from the program. I wanted to be a flyer just like him, and would have if my eyes had been better. And now I'm part of his crew! But a *Stars & Stripes* symbol on his plane. How can that be?"

Sergeant Lewis answered slowly, as if he were talking to a child: "What it means, private Evans, is that Capt. Allen, in addition to a bunch of Axis planes, also shot down one of ours. A Douglas C-47 transport, I think. What's more, his girlfriend was on board!"

"You're kidding. He shot down one of our planes, and it was carrying his girlfriend at the time?

"Yeah, a nurse named Barbara Croft. She's a looker too. Raven-haired, good figure. She and her family helped raise Capt. Allen when he was orphaned as a kid. His father was Scotty Allen, killed trying to cross the Atlantic in 1927."

"I think I read about him in the papers. He was quite a daredevil, wasn't he? And got killed trying to set the record before Lindbergh. But what about the C-47? Why in the world did Capt. Allen shoot it down? And did he know his girlfriend was on board?"

"Let's finish our work, and then I'll tell you all about it inside. It's too cold out here for story telling. It's a long story…but a doozy. I may be the only person who knows the whole story."

Later, Master Sergeant Aloysius "Flash" Lewis and Private Charles Evans, the young groundcrew member, completed their work and vanished into the warmth of the mess hall.

Capt. James Allen stood at attention in front of his commanding officer. The CO, Colonel John Boynton, did a church-and-steeple with his fingers, and gazed over them at Jimmie.

"At ease, Capt. Allen. I have a request to make of you."

"Yes, sir."

"I need two volunteers for a dangerous mission. I have one already, and Army intelligence has recommended that you be the second."

"What's the mission, sir?"

"Special Operations has reported that German scientists have developed a kind of unmanned rocket that they plan to use on our cities. The scientist in charge is a Professor Proteus."

"Professor Proteus!" exclaimed Jimmie. "I knew a Professor Partenon Proteus back in the States, but I thought he was dead. He was a madman. Nearly wiped out an American city with a poison gas he invented."

"That's the man," said the CO. "He's very much alive, and been working for the Germans since the war broke out. And now he's about to unleash unmaned rockets on civilians. We have to stop him!"

"I agree, sir. What can I do?" asked Jimmie.

"Intelligence has had men working behind enemy lines, gathering information. One of them, a colonel, has managed to find out Proteus' plans. But he and some of his men are trapped behind enemy lines. Someone has to rescue them before Proteus can act. It's a two-man job, and Lt. Clark has already volunteered. But he's inexperienced. This mission requires a hot pilot, someone who's accomplished the near impossible before. We think you're that man."

"I'm your man, sir. A madman like Proteus can't be allowed to remain at large. My *Blue Bird* and I will get the job done."

"That's another thing, Allen. You won't be flying your Mustang. Instead you'll be flying a German reconnaissance aircraft we just captured, one they won't even try to shoot down. It's a Blohm and Voss 141, a most unusual plane indeed. Here, read this report."

Jimmie read the following:

I & R Confidential Report No. 406/TW
    The Blohm and Voss 141 is a radical departure in asymmetric design. This odd-looking craft is used by the Germans for reconnaissance and strafing. It is powered by one Bramo Fafnir radial air-cooled engine of 1000 hp. The wings are low, with the left shorter than the right. A nacelle on the starboard wing houses the personnel. The engine is set in the fuselage and of equal diameter with the forward end of the fuselage which is long and circular in section, carrying the engine in front and the tail behind, with no provision for personnel. The tail is set high on the fin with only port half present. An extremely tall single fin and rudder is curved forward to accommodate tailplane. Specifications: Span 66 ft.; length 49 ft; gross weight 9700 lb. No further data available at this time.

Jimmie looked up from the report.
    "I don't guess an observer could mistake such a plane, so I can see why we'll have an advantage flying over enemy territory. But will it hold all of us? According to this report, there's no provision for personnel in the fuselage, and the nacelle won't hold all of us, once we pick up the intelligence officer and his men."
    "Come with me, Capt. Allen. I want to show you our captured Bv. 141. It's in the south hanger. Now that our people have had a chance to study it, we'll to able to add to that I & R report. I think you'll be surprised at what Sergeant Lewis and his men have been able to accomplish in a very short time."

    The crossing had been uneventful, and Jimmie was becoming accustomed to the foreign controls. He didn't especially like flying the German plane, not after his *Blue Bird*, but he was getting used to it. He and Milt Clark had maintained radio silence as they crossed the Channel, following the map given to them by Major Cardwell, an intelligence officer, just before they took off. As they approached the coordinates indicated on their map, Jimmie saw flares outlining a small, makeshift airstrip. Approaching the site, however, they saw a series of explosions. Then, something resembling a giant flying cross shot past their plane, heading for the airstrip.

"What in the world is that?" asked Clark. "I've never seen anything like it!"

"That must be one of Proteus' unmaned rockets, the ones we were briefed about before we took off," answered Jimmie. "Weren't we told it looked like a flying cross?"

The young aviators listened to the rocket's buzzing sound as it flew over the small airstrip. Abruptly, the buzzing stopped and the rocket fell to earth. A few seconds later they heard a loud explosion. As they came in for a landing, they saw that the device had hit the airstrip and almost demolished a small building next to it. Purposely flying over the strip, now almost completely destroyed, Jimmie decided they had to clear a stream and land in a small clearing beyond. Coming in, the plane's tail dragged on the frozen stream. The German ship lost speed; and the wheels, held up for an instant by the drawn-back stick, touched the ice. The ice held—but the wind, whistling along the surface, lifted the tail dangerously. The enemy plane finally came to a stop. Jimmie had brought the Bv. 141 in safely.

"Wow, Jimmie. How did you do that?" asked Clark. "I don't think I could have set down a plane in such a small area, especially one I'd never landed before."

"I remembered the last words my father said to me," replied a grim-faced Jimmie. "Keep your tail up. And remember, whatever happens, fly into the wind."

He looked over at Milt.

"Besides, no plane ever got the best of me yet."

Jimmie smiled.

Leaving Lt. Clark to guard the plane, Jimmie hurried to the small building next to the airstrip, now a tangled mass of smoking wreckage. Picking his way through the rubble, and pushing the larger pieces of debris out of the way, he finally reached the men lying there. Jimmie carefully checked each one for signs of life. Only two were still breathing, one he was able to identify as a colonel.

"Sir, what happened?" asked Jimmie, as he bent over the wounded man who lay almost exactly in the middle of the blast area.

"A German reconnaissance plane flew over about an hour ago. It must have reported the position of our airstrip . . . then, a few minutes ago, the rockets started coming in. It seems like all the Axis powers have been after us since they learned of our intelligence activities."

"Are you all right, sir?"

The colonel looked up through slitted eyes in a face black with soot and dirt.

"Yes, captain, I'm all right," he said. "How are my men."

"I'm afraid only one is alive, sir. The rest didn't make it."

The colonel struggled to stand up. "Please help me to my feet. I want to check on my men myself."

Jimmie helped the colonel to his feet, bracing him against a partial wall that still stood. Moving slowly and with difficulty, the colonel managed to examine each of his men. Only one, a lieutenant named Ferguson, was still alive. While he was examining his men, the moon shown through the smoke and the colonel's face was revealed. Jimmie looked closely at him and let out a gasp!

"Speed!" cried Jimmie. "Is that you under all that dirt?"

"Yes, Jim, it's your old flying buddy all right. I was wondering how long it would take you to recognize me. I see they picked the right man for this job."

Colonel Robertson put his hand on Jimmie's shoulder and looked intently into his eyes.

"I've been out of touch. How are things back home? Are Barbara and the Colbys okay? He paused to catch his breath. And have you run into Flash anywhere?"

"Everyone back home is fine, but Barbara is in England right now. She's been there for almost a year, serving as a nurse." Jimmie paused for five full seconds. "I'm afraid I first heard she was over here when I shot down the plane in which she was flying."

"You shot down Barbara? How in the world did that happen?"

"It's a long story, and I don't like to talk about it. I made a mistake. If you insist, I'll tell you about it on our way back to England. But right now we need to get in the air quickly and fly with a wide-open throttle. Lt. Ferguson should be in a hospital."

"You're right, of course. And I must tell our people what we've learned about these new unmaned rockets, and all the other enemy plans we were able to uncover. Did they tell you that Professor Proteus is behind the rockets?"

"Yes. Lt. Clark and I were briefed on Proteus and his activities before we left England."

"I find it hard to believe that the Germans would order rockets to bomb this part of France. The Germans have so many of their troops deployed around here. Someone must have been desperate to stop us. Those devices aren't all that accurate yet, and they could have killed some of their own men. As far as we know, the only other time the Germans used one of these new rocket-bombs was a couple of months ago. That one was launched from a site near Calais and intended for London. Special Ops reported that Proteus himself was responsible for that order. I wouldn't be surprised if he gave the order to bomb our position here."

"Speed, we were told that Proteus is the scientist who's been coming up with most of the recent Axis nastiness. He's a madman."

"You have that right," said Speed. "He has to be one of the most dangerous men in this war. Human life means little to him. You remember what he did in the States."

Later, flying over the English Channel, Jimmie looked over at his old friend. "Are you all right, Speed?"

Robertson nodded, and asked: "I'm okay. Don't worry about me. My injuries are minor...but how's Lt. Ferguson?"

"Lt. Clark is looking after him in the renovated fuselage. We have a first aid kit and some other medical supplies there. So you're in Special Ops, are you? I guess I shouldn't be surprised."

"I was in Special Operations, but now I'm with OSS." Speed replied.

"OSS, what's that?" asked Jimmie.

"Office of Strategic Services, created about six months ago. We're charted to carry out clandestine operations against the Axis powers on a worldwide scale. OSS wants me to put together an undercover team to go after Proteus. Jim, I'd like you to be a part of that team. We were able to stop him before, and I think that together we can do it again. What do you say? I can get you transferred to my unit as soon as we get back."

"You bet, Speed. I want to help any way I can. Madmen like Proteus and Hitler must be stopped. Don't you think we could use a master mechanic like Flash on our team too?"

"That's certainly something to think about. Tell me about Flash...and Barbara. What have they been up to since we got into this shooting war."

"Flash is a master sergeant, head of the groundcrew that takes care of my plane. He can still get any plane in the air and keep it there."

"I'll bet he still always has the right tool on his person, no matter what the problem," Speed laughed.

"You bet he does. And the fact that he does never ceases to amaze everyone around him. He was in charge of getting this Bv into flying shape...and of redoing the fuselage so it would carry personnel."

"Old Flash. What a guy! Some things just never change, do they? It sounds like we *could* use him in the OSS. But, Jim, tell me about Barbara. Did you really shoot her down?"

"Well, Speed, that's a long story. Barbara may never forgive me for what I did. And, with all the missions I've been flying lately, I haven't really had a chance to talk with her about it." Jimmie gazed out the bulletproof windshield of the Bv for a full minute before he spoke again.

"Say, Speed, don't you think we could use a nurse on our undercover team?"

Men from several aircrews and groundcrews sat around a large table in the warmth of the mess hall, drinking coffee. Sgt. Lewis was sitting at the head of the table and had been holding forth for nearly an hour.

"Well, I guess that's the whole story, and I believe I'm the only one who knows it. Capt. Allen doesn't like to talk about it. I was against his putting that *Stars & Stripes* on his plane, but I think he felt it was the honorable thing to do. He said that if you shoot down *any* plane, you have to acknowledge it. Personally, I think he keeps it there as a reminder that he isn't perfect...and maybe, that he should be more careful in the future. One thing is certain, it really makes his *Blue Bird Special II* special." Flash laughed, leaned back in his chair, and sipped his coffee. Another sergeant walked in.

"I heard Flash was telling the *Stars & Stripes* story again," he said. "And probably making an epic out of it. I can tell all you new men what happened in less than a minute."

"Oh, you can, can you? asked Flash.

"Yeah. That American transport was where it wasn't supposed to be. Capt. Allen was on a mission, and happened to see it while he was waiting for help for one of our downed planes, another ship in his squadron. He tried to communicate with the transport, and when it didn't respond, he reasoned that—despite its marking—the transport might be enemy-operated. You see, no friendly transport was supposed to be in that hostile area. So he carefully shot up each engine, and the transport was forced to ditch. All 12 occupants escaped unharmed. It was later discovered that the C-47 was ours, but hopelessly lost. The pilot didn't know what to do. I guess he had his mind made up for him. Capt. Allen didn't find out until later that his girlfriend and some other nurses were on board. No one was hurt, and the pilot of the transport later said he was actually grateful. Not only was he lost, but he was running out of fuel…and just didn't know what to do. "

"But what did Capt. Allen's girlfriend say when she found out it was her boyfriend who had shot them down?"

Flash leaned back in his chair. "Now, that's an even better story," he laughed. ♦

HOUSE OF MYSTERY

The Ghastly Dream
by Tony Albarella

This is Roger Elliot, otherwise known as The Mystery Man, inviting you to join us for another storytelling session here at The House of Mystery. And now I see it's time for today's story…so if you're ready, I'll begin "The Case of the Ghostly Dream."

I had just settled down to a freshly brewed coffee and a bowl of Corn Toasties when the phone jarred me into wakefulness.

"Good morning, Elliot residence," I answered, stifling a yawn. There was a brief moment of silence on the other end of the line, as if the caller could not decide on a response.

"Roger? Roger Elliot?"

The voice immediately struck me as familiar, but remained tucked away in some far corner of my mind, a memory that I could not yet recognize, covered with dust.

"Yes, this is Roger Elliot. To whom am I speaking?"

"Roger, it's Phil. Phillip Donaldson. 'End Zone' Donaldson?"

The moniker caused a recollection to flare and bloom in my head. "Phil! Why, I haven't heard from you since we graduated!"

"I'm glad that you remember me, Roger."

"Remember you?" I replied with a smile in my voice. "Why, I'm the one who threw many of those rather perfect passes that earned you your nickname!"

I sipped my coffee as we spent the next several minutes catching up, reminiscing about our school days, and familiarizing each other with our current lives. Before long Phil came to the point of the phone call.

"Thing of it is, Roger, I'm aware of your reputation for—shall we say—making sense of unsettling situations. And I'm afraid I could use your help."

"Of course," I replied, eager to help and guessing that the man would rather give details to me in person. "Are you in town?"

"I can be, in a matter of an hour or so," he replied, and I sensed in his voice a measure of relief. "I don't live awfully far off."

"Then how about this," I offered. "Meet me at noon at the Crescent Diner on the corner of Central and Third. We can talk it over there and then."

"Wonderful, Roger. I really appreciate it. See you then."

I returned to my Corn Toasties, still crisp in the bowl, and looked at the clock. The call had roused my interest and I now eagerly anticipated our meeting.

Tucked away in a quiet rear nook of the smoke-filled diner, we had a light lunch and talked more of school and the life that followed. I gave Phil plenty of time to settle in and finally, over coffee and cake, he reluctantly ventured forth with his tale.

"It's like this, Roger. The last few years have been pretty rough; both of my parents are gone. My dad was out fishing when his rowboat capsized, and he drowned. My mom lost all desire for life after that, and her health failed. She followed Dad last year."

"I'm so sorry to hear that," I said, imagining the hardship endured by Phil and his family. "They were good people."

"Yes," he nodded, tracing a circle on the Formica table and avoiding my gaze. "They were good people indeed, and thank you for that. They're greatly missed. However, the reason I looked you up, and the thing that has wholly disrupted my life of late, is something beyond mere grief."

He paused, still not looking up at me, waging some internal battle with himself.

"I think I'm being haunted," he confessed, his voice a self-conscious whisper. "Or 'visited,' I guess one would say. By my mother's ghost."

Phil cautiously raised his eyes to gauge my reaction. He must have expected a look of incredulity or amused skepticism, and was happy to see none. "I suppose you hear a lot of this sort of thing," he added.

"You bet," I reassured him. "You'd be amazed at the sheer number of irrational things that happen to rational people. Now go on, please."

"Well," Phil said with a newfound confidence, "since my mom's death, I've had a reoccurring dream. It's hit almost every night for the last eight months and I'm at my wit's end. I haven't been able to make heads or tails of it." I absorbed the information without comment, and he continued.

"It's nearly the exact same thing each time. In the dream, I'm seated at the old baby grand piano in the living room of my parent's house. Suddenly I turn and my mother is beside me on the bench. She mumbles something unintelligible about my father, becoming more and more distraught as I struggle to make out her words.

"In time, I become aware of the peal of a clock. It grows progressively louder, a deep bass sound, over and over, a resonant din. Just when I think my eardrums are going to explode, I wake up.

"And here's the kicker: when I awaken, it's three-seventeen in the morning. It's *always* three-seventeen. That same exact moment, every single time."

I nodded, contemplating the story and carefully weighing my response. "You know," I said cautiously, "it's not uncommon for the subconscious to play tricks on one's mind following such a tragic double loss, and…"

Phil reached for my hand to cut me off. "I know that, Roger. At first I tried to convince myself of that very fact. But I know this is real and it's happening, I can *feel* it. My mother is coming back to me with some message and I have to figure out what it is."

I looked Phil in the eye and could see the resolve within him. "So," I said at last, "you think that I might be able to help you piece together the clues of this message?"

"Not exactly," he countered. "I've already sought out professional help, the only kind that can be of any use to me at this point. I've scheduled a meeting with Madam Helena, a medium. Tomorrow evening we're going to hold a séance at her house, and we're going to try to contact my mother."

I was a bit shaken by this, and felt trepidation at his reliance on a psychic. Genuine mediums may well exist, but I have seen far too many that rely more on shadow than substance. I feared that Phil, in his grief-stricken and frustrated state, would blindly put his trust in some stranger who may likely harbor an ulterior motive.

"So where do I come in?" I inquired.

"Well," Phil shrugged, "everyone I've told thinks that I'm going crazy and need some sort of medical help. My solution of a séance would surely confirm their suspicions…but it's something I have to do. This is right up your alley and I knew you'd believe me. It's tough to do it on my own; I was hoping you'd be willing to accompany me when I visit Madam Helena."

I paused for only a brief moment. I was relieved that he'd asked me along; in his fragile state he would surely need looking after. Yet I hoped that

I wouldn't shatter Phil's optimism and trust in the supernatural. "My friend," I said as I signaled the waitress for the check, "I'd be honored to join you."

Madam Helena greeted us at the door and led the way through a marble foyer that opened to a foreboding, gloomy drawing room. All four walls were lined with heavy scarlet drapery, and the room reeked of sharp incense and stale air. The mahogany furnishings were so weathered and dark that they seemed to sink into the shadows. We were asked to sit at the circular wooden table that squatted in the middle of the room. It was small and close, with a large crystal ball mounted in the center. Over this hung a tired, dusty chandelier that cast off an insufficient glow.

The medium herself formed a haggard figure; the bent, withered body covered with a shawl, the face drawn and wrinkled with skin like crushed parchment paper. Her wiry hair, pulled into a tight bun, held a color reserved for storm clouds just prior to the release of their heavy, wet burdens. She shuffled about the room lighting candles with her bony fingers and muttering ritualistic prayers in some ancient tongue. At last she dropped into the chair next to Phil and cast a wary gaze at me. The only trait that belied her careworn visage was a pair of steely blue eyes.

"So," the furtive woman said to me in a coarse tone of voice, "you are a friend of Mister Donaldson here, is that right, Mister Smith?"

"I am indeed," I replied, glad that I had convinced Phil to introduce me with a false name. I didn't want my reputation to affect the proceedings in any way.

"That is good," she remarked, patting Phil on the hand. "He will have need of a friend in this time of peril. You may bear witness as we cross over tonight."

I nodded, looking to Phil. He seemed uncomfortable, lost.

"Well," she announced, "shall we begin? Please take each other's hand and my own, that we may complete the circle."

We did as instructed. Madam Helena then released my hand and, with a murmured chant, slowly passed her gnarled fingers over the crystal ball. The chandelier dimmed and the room fell away to darkness before I could read the expression on Phil's face. In the gloom I sensed the medium again reach for me. When she closed her cold fingers around my hand, I felt as if a skeleton had seized me.

"Spirits of the netherworld," she began, "we call upon you this eve that we may speak with Eleanor Donaldson, dearly departed mother of

Phillip Donaldson. Come to us, Eleanor, join us and lay to rest the doubt in your son's heart."

I felt Madam Helena sway side to side as she tightly clutched my hand. A soft mantra fell from her mouth, the pitch of her voice undulating, until at last a slight tremor rose from the table. The vibration in the wood grew more pronounced in rapid increments, until the table began to violently shudder. I felt Phil's grip harden with fear and anticipation.

"Yes, Eleanor," the conjurer continued, "we are here, closing this circle and completing the circuit in order to bridge the gap between worlds. We beckon, come to us, now."

A high-pitched wail chilled the dark, and I was positive it hadn't come from Madam Helena. It emanated from the far corner of the room. After several extended, blood-curdling seconds, the shriek congealed into a shaky feminine voice.

"P-Phillip," the voice called out, "Phillip, is that you, my son?"

A beat, then I heard Phil enthusiastically call out. "Yes, mother! I'm here."

In the darkness I leaned toward my friend. "Is that your mother's voice?" I asked.

"I'm not sure," he answered. "I-I can't really tell. I think so."

"Silence!" hissed Madam Helena. "Keep silent lest you break the connection established with the beyond. Speak only when spoken to, and allow me to question the spirit. I am the conduit between the living and the dead."

The old woman turned from us and once again addressed the air in as loud a voice as she could muster. "Oh spirit of Eleanor Donaldson, answer my inquiries so that peace may befall your troubled son."

"I am here," the voice offered, "and I hear you, Madam Helena. Your power is great, and I thank you for arranging this meeting. I have come willingly, anxious to share with Phillip the secret I have carried with me through the mists."

"Excellent," exclaimed the medium. "Then answer my plea. Your son's sleep is plagued with dreams of you and your message. Explain to us now the meaning of the clock sound, the piano, the garbled talk of Phillip's father."

The voice shrilled a woeful sound, and then began. "Phillip, I am in pain. I am lost in the fog, trapped between worlds. I long to move beyond and be with your father, but there is only one who can help me find my way to the light."

I felt a tremble pass through Phil's hand. "What is it, Mom?" he begged. "Tell me; I will do anything it takes to free you!"

"My dearest son," the voice answered, "I fear that the only release for me will come at the hands of Madam Helena. It is her skill that beckoned to me tonight and drew me from the crowd of lost souls; it is she that holds the power to complete my journey. I sent to you the dream clues to indicate my need for the other side. I apologize for this vague game of charades, but without the aid of a master medium, the dream remained my only form of communication.

"The grand piano," the voice continued, "represents the sweet music that awaits us when we pass over. Your father waits also; we cannot be whole until we are together. The sounding of the clock symbolizes the countless hours we will enjoy as one, waiting for you join us in Heaven, where time will become a glorious perpetuity for us all. And three-seventeen, the hour that haunts you, is my scheduled time to cross over. That is, of course, if you employ the services of Madam Helena. Grant her whatever price she asks, for material goods will be of no use to us in our blissful infinity."

"I will indeed help you," cried Madam Helena. "When the stars are right and your son returns. Tomorrow night I will send you on your way."

"Bless you, most powerful oracle," warbled the voice. "Bless you and thank you for freeing me from my prison. Remember, my son, return to Madam Helena at dusk tomorrow and pay her fee. Until you do I shall remain trapped, and you shall suffer the ghostly dream in all its restless monotony. The grand piano, your father, and the clock."

As the voice lulled in the distance, a glowing timepiece appeared and floated over our heads. It crossed to the far side of the room and returned, sweeping back and forth over the table.

"Over and over," droned the voice, "until we are both put to rest. The dream, the grand piano, your father, and the clock." The floating timepiece slid back and forth in a hypnotic dance.

"Dream…Grand…Piano…Father…Clock…"

As the shimmering clock swooped low over my head, I rocketed from my chair to seize it in my hands. "Now!" I yelled, and the lights flared into existence.

The three of us shielded our eyes from the sudden brilliance, and Madam Helena leapt to her feet. "What is the meaning of this?" demanded the medium.

"I'll tell you," I said to her. "But first let me introduce you to Police Chief Robert Collins."

I gestured toward the door where a portly uniformed man stood with one hand on the light switch and the other on his gun. He released the switch, tipped his hat and silently smiled.

"Chief Collins was kind enough to join us tonight, to my knowledge alone, though he of course lagged behind and stole into the foyer after we had been seated. You see, when Phil informed me of this appointment I did some checking with my buddies at the Bunko Squad, and found a number of complaints listed against a certain 'Madam Helena.' The police haven't had enough evidence to charge you as of yet, but the events of tonight will change all of that."

"Rubbish!" exclaimed the medium. "Lies! I demand you leave at once."

"I don't understand," Phil confessed. "You mean the whole thing was a trick?"

"Every bit, I'm afraid," I told him. "A most impressive swindle. See here, the floating clock that I hold in my hands. It's nothing but an ordinary table clock coated with luminous paint, strung across a piano wire, and pulled back and forth with an invisible thread."

"Pulled by whom?" Phil asked, trying to absorb it all. "And what of my mother's voice?"

I walked over to the corner of the room, tracing the clock wire to a spot behind the drapery. "Allow me," I said as I pulled away the drape, "to make a second introduction." Behind the curtain stood a startled, fuming woman. She glared at Madam Helena and muttered curses under her breath.

"This is Madam Helena's assistant," I continued. "Without her, the show could not go on. I suspect that this woman was responsible for dimming the lights with a hidden switch, shaking the table in the dark, operating the hovering clock and supplying the 'voice from beyond.'"

"I told you!" screamed the assistant at Madam Helena. "I told you we shouldn't have allowed an unscreened mark!"

"Shut up, you fool!" retorted the exposed medium.

Phil slumped in his chair, stunned. "I can't believe it. I almost fell for it hook, line and sinker. So much of what they knew and said seemed believable."

"They knew only what you explained to Madam Helena when you set up the appointment," I reminded him. "She took the elements of your dream and worked them into a story that would placate you. Tomorrow, after you'd paid her a most princely sum, this charlatan would proceed to 'free' what she called your mother's spirit and you would leave, most contented. Perhaps the dream would stop, now that the problem was resolved in your mind. But even if not, and you returned for a refund and an explanation, you'd find this an empty house, just as it was before these two rented it several days ago."

Phil sighed. "How could I have been so gullible?"

I put a hand on his shoulder. "Don't feel bad, my friend. They do this for a living and have become quite good at it. You were right to call Madam Helena a professional; she's a professional cheat. And the worst kind…she takes advantage of people at their most vulnerable, in a time of bereavement, when they are desperate to say goodbye to a lost loved one. It's a vile, cowardly way to make a quick buck."

"Sadly," added Chief Collins, "they are not the first nor will they be the last to pull this cruel charade." He handcuffed Madam Helena and her assistant. "But rest assured that these two, at least, won't be fleecing any more mourners. See you down at the station, Roger, and thanks for the tip." He led the disgraced women out of the house and to a waiting patrol car.

Phil slumped in the front seat, silent for most of the trip home. I pitied him and had no words of condolence. Suddenly he bolted upright as if struck by lightning. "Roger! Don't take me home just yet. Drive me to my parents' house on Main Street, please!"

I was shocked. "What is it, Phil?"

He shook his head. "Something just hit me, something the spirit— I mean, Madam Helena's assistant—said tonight. I've been going over it in my head. I'll explain when we get there."

Several minutes later we arrived at the vacant house that belonged to Phil's parents. It was on the market but as yet remained unsold, and Phil kept the key to the front door on his key ring. No furnishings had been removed; the entire house stood as it had on the day his mother died.

As we rushed up the walk, I begged Phil for an explanation, and he relented.

"It was the way that assistant lady repeated the elements of my dream. Grand piano, my father, the clock. 'Grand…Piano…Father…Clock.' Then it hit me, as they blended together: grandfather clock! And I remembered the old grandfather clock that used to be in the living room. My mom loved to hide jewelry and small valuables in it, in case the house was robbed. She figured it would be the last place anyone would look. When the clock got to the point where it kept breaking down, my folks didn't have the heart to throw it away. They just put it up in the attic and forgot about it."

"So it's still up there," I added as we entered the house.

"Yes," Phil confirmed as he removed a flashlight from the hall closet. "And that grandfather clock must hold the key to unlock my dream."

We climbed the stairs to the top floor of the house and rushed past the bedrooms. At the end of the hall hung a chain connected to the attic steps. Phil pulled it down, unfolded the creaking hinged stairs, and we climbed into the musty darkness. He panned his flashlight over the wooden beams until he located a hanging bulb, then pulled the attached string. In the lighted gloom I could make out the remnants of his family's life—toys, clothes, luggage, furniture—piled high all around. A walkway was fashioned down the center of the stacked belongings.

At the end of this path, wedged upright under the eaves of the roof, was a grandfather clock covered in dust and mold. Wordlessly, Phil rushed to it and tore open the small wooden door beneath the murky faceplate. Inside was the key and winding mechanism; below that a small scalloped drawer that might have once been intended to hold replaceable parts or maintenance materials. Phil opened the drawer, reached into it, and withdrew a small bundle of faded cloth. He let out a gasp as he unwrapped it, and I caught a glimpse of something shiny.

"What is it?" I asked.

"I-I don't believe it," he responded, holding up an opulent pocket watch, suspended on a gold chain and lavishly set with several large diamonds.

"This," he said, regarding the treasure in his hands, "is a very old, very valuable family heirloom. My mom always told me that it came from my great-grandfather; it belonged to my dad and would eventually come to me, that I should someday pass it to my children. It was very special to her, a link to the family's past. She often argued that my father should put it safely away, but he loved it and wore it often.

"I had forgotten all about this until after mom passed away, and when I didn't find it about the house, I assumed my dad had been wearing it when he drowned. I thought this was forever lost at the bottom of Chesterfield Lake. Yet here it is, safe and sound, and found at last."

I noticed something about the face on the grandfather clock and pointed to it. I watched as realization dawned over Phil's expression, and his mouth fell agape. We exchanged glances and together smiled.

The hands of the broken clock were forever frozen at three-seventeen.

I called on Phil a week later and he answered the telephone with a cheery voice.

"I still can't get over it, Roger. It's been seven nights since we found the watch, and I haven't had the dream once."

"I doubt you'll have it again," I explained. "Perhaps a memory of the pocket watch, and its importance to your mother, festered in your subconscious mind. The matter eventually manifested itself as a reoccurring dream until you satisfied the need for it."

"Well," chuckled Phil, "how analytical of you. I, however, have my own theory. I think my mother really did visit me to offer the location of the pocket watch, because she alone knew the location and she couldn't rest until it was passed to me. The clues she placed in my dream led me to it. Remember, I thought the heirloom was forever lost, so I had no reason to go in search of it. However you slice it, my parents can now rest in peace, and I can dream of happier things."

"And to think," I added, "this would not have happened without the intervention of Madam Helena. It's wonderful to know that some good came from her evil deeds."

"How true," Phil agreed. "Who knows? Maybe that old woman had some hidden power after all, a gift that allowed my mother to act through her without Madam Helena's knowledge. I'd like to think so. At least one thing is crystal clear."

"What's that?" I asked.

"None of this would have happened without the aid of my good friend, Roger Elliot, The Mystery Man."

I laughed. "Well, I had a good deal of help on this one. Together we solved...The Case of the Ghostly Dream."

And that was the mystery I call "The Case of the Ghostly Dream." Join me next week as I unravel another tale of supernatural suspense. I know you won't want to miss it so be sure to be with us next week at this same time and this same station. I'll be waiting for you at...The House of Mystery. ♦

RICHARD DIAMOND, PRIVATE DETECTIVE

Fall From Grace
by Joseph Cromarty

"What kind of day is it, Rick?"

"Why, it's a good day for singing a song, and it's *a*—" I sang before being cut off.

"Nooo. I mean business!"

"Do you, Helen?"

"No monkey business, business business." She sighed. "Honestly."

"Honest to a fault."

The lovely young thing on the other end of the phone was Helen Asher, an extremely wealthy woman I was madly in love with and who felt the same way about me. It was only her extreme wealth that kept us from that chapel in the moonlight.

"At the moment slow, but you never know when things are going to pick up."

And that was the exact moment things picked up. The door opened and in walked a *very* good-looking lady. Good-looking despite the bad look on her face.

"Mr. Diamond, I need your help."

I held my hand over the receiver and said, "Have a seat. I'll be with you in a sec." Into the phone I said, "I'm sorry, Director Hoover, but right now would be a bad time. I'm always happy to help the Feds. Unfortunately, right now I'm up to my ears in work. But feel free to try me next month."

I hung up the phone before Helen's reaction came through and turned my smile on the woman I hoped would be my next client.

"What can I do for you, Miss…?"

"*Mrs.* Mrs. Grace Thompson." She fooled around with the clasp on her handbag for thirty seconds or so while I waited her out. "It's my husband."

It usually was. "What seems to be the trouble with him?" I was

59

hoping it was something I could send her down the hall for Dr. Kildare to treat but suspected it wouldn't be.

"He's been moody of late. He——" She got up. "I'm sorry, Mr. Diamond, I shouldn't have come here."

I let those lovely legs of hers get her as far as the door. "I have to disagree with you, Mrs. Thompson. You need help and you came to the best helper in the business. Sit down and tell me all about it, won't you? Worst that can happen is I can't help you. If that turns out to be true, I'm sure I know someone I can send you to who can help you, Philip Marlowe, Richard Rogue or one of those fellows. How about it?"

A small tentative smile and she sat. "Maybe you're right." She rearranged herself and began.

"I thought——*think*——we've had a good marriage. But lately Hart's been so uptight, so quiet. I'm afraid he's contemplating suicide." She stopped.

I don't know whether she was waiting for me to jump in and say something or was surprised I hadn't. She took a deep breath and went on. "He's been saying things to himself when he thinks I'm not around. Just this morning I caught him arguing with himself about stocks and bonds. When I asked him what he meant, he told me I shouldn't be listening in on private conversations."

She forced a smile, then fumbled in her bag, bringing out a dainty handkerchief and dabbed at the corners of her pretty eyes.

I'm not much with weeping women, but I try. "What would you like me to do?"

"I don't know exactly. Could- could you follow him, you know, shadow him, whatever it is detectives do? And if he *is* going to- to- to kill himself, stop him?"

Then came the flood.

"Tell me about your husband, Mrs. Thompson."

She wiped away the downfall. "What is it you want to know?"

"Oh, the usual things: how does he earn his daily bread, do you suspect him of seeing another woman, things like that."

"Hart with another woman?" She actually sounded as though the thought was unthinkable.

"Uh-hmm."

"No. No, there's no other woman in his life. Not even a secretary. He doesn't have one. I'm not even sure *I'm* in his life. Hart spends more time at his office than any man I know."

"I see. Tell me about his work. What is there about it that keeps him there? Are you sure he doesn't have a pretty secretary?"

"No, he *doesn't*. I *told* you—" She slumped a little. "He runs a sort of mail drop."

I raised my eyebrows.

"Not what you're thinking. Some people don't want other people to know where their business is located, so he handles their mail for them. He has post office boxes for clients that don't want to get their mail at home. You know, to keep their business mail separate from the family mail."

She coughed. Her voice was a bit rusty. I got her a glass of water from the little sink stuck in the corner.

I tried to look as though I believed Hart's business was legit, but wasn't sure she believed my innocent look.

"Okay, I'll give it a look-see," I said, and gave her a warm, comforting smile.

I got her address, phone number, and a retainer. Also a photo of Hart Thompson and his business card. She got my home phone number and, something I rarely gave out, Helen's. Just in case.

The hubby was a peculiar-looking geek, if his photo was a true reflection of the man. He was rail thin, with red hair as wild as the west once was. His horn-rims were thick enough to be the floor of a glass-bottomed boat.

Hart Thompson's business was located opposite the elevator on the fourteenth floor (which was really the thirteenth) of the Blake Building. By the look of the space between office doors, they couldn't have been much bigger than large closets. Ah, the price of real estate in metropolis. The office next door was open and had no name on its door, so I suspected there was no tenant. The incisive brain of a trained detective at work.

I rode back to ground level, found the real estate agent's name and phone number, and gave her a call.

"Miss Del Valle? Hi, I'm looking for a small office to get my widget business underway. I was in the Blake Building the other day and think it would be perfect for starters. Got something I can afford?"

"As a matter of fact, I have a vacant office on the fourth floor." She started extolling the virtues of it, including the price, which was hardly virtuous, but I cut in on her.

"*Brother, can you spare a dime?*" I sang. "I was looking for something a little higher in the building and a little lower in the price range."

She laughed. "Nice voice. Have you considered singing as a career?"

"What, become another Dick Powell? No, thanks."

I was beginning to like her laugh. "I do have a smaller office, but it's on the fourteenth floor."

"No problem; I don't have acrophobia."

"How about claustrophobia?"

"Nope. Not even triskaidekaphobia."

"Ah, you noticed."

"Hard not to, walking up all those flights."

Her laugh was a hearty one. "Want to see it?"

I didn't need to; I was going to rent it no matter how bad it looked. How else could I keep a private eye on Mr. Thompson?

It turned out to be awful, but she didn't. The room was like a railroad car with a window where the observation platform would have been. She turned out to be luscious.

By noon I was ensconced in the place, my equipment waiting to be put into Thompson's office when and if he ever left.

It wasn't until mid-afternoon that he did. He got on the elevator whistling, badly, *Jimmy Crack Corn*.

In less than two minutes, I'd jimmy-crack-corned my way into his office. I took care of the important detail first, putting a mike in the desk's kneehole. Then I cruised through his files, but found nothing out of whack.

I was closing the door to my cubbyhole when Thompson returned via the elevator. I hummed *Time Waits For No One* as I closed the door.

For the rest of the day, I watched and listened. Nothing was going on, so I called Helen and serenaded her, just for the fun of it.

At six p.m. he locked up and left. I made it to the elevator before the doors shut. We rode down in silence.

I kept a half-block back and followed him home to wife and slippers, where I felt aforesaid wife would keep watch over him.

Breakfast had been donuts, and lunch air, so I headed for my favorite diner. The sign had once read 'Good Food,' but the first 'd' and the 'ood' in 'Food' was out of commission. It read 'Goo_F___,' so it became known as 'Goof's.'

I put the blue plate special and the exorbitant tip on Mrs. Thompson's expense account, tarried awhile and headed for Helen's.

Francis, the beautiful Helen Asher's butler, opened the door and welcomed me with a grim smile and a drink.

"Rick!" Helen rushed to the foyer. "You cut me off this morning. I sulked by going to the movies."

"Nice to see you, too, baby. By the by, did you know that some day in the far distant future the movies will come to you?"

"I don't believe it."

"Trust me, as the lawyers say."

"I don't care what the lawyers say, tell me why you cut me off after saying that silly thing about the FBI's top man."

"Work, love, work. I had to toil in the salt mines of the detecting business."

"Is she pretty?"

"No."

"No?"

"No. Beautiful. But she has a mate."

"And she hired you because…"

"Ah, no can tell. Detective/client thing. You understand."

"Do I?"

Francis came in with the telephone in his paw. "For you, Mr. Diamond." In hopes of embarrassing me, he added, "A woman."

"Francis, you dog, you." I took the phone from him and said "Hi" into it.

"Mr. Diamond?" It was Grace Thompson and there was a tremble in her voice. "My husband just called to say goodbye to me. He's— he's going to kill himself."

"He *called*? He's *there*. I followed him home earlier this evening."

"You…he—he went back. He said he'd forgotten something. I think it must have been an excuse, because he just called."

"He called to tell you he was going to kill himself?" Something was screwy here. "Why would he do that? What did he say? Exactly."

"He said, 'I'm sorry, Grace, I just can't go on. I'm going to jump. It's easier this way.'"

"Then he must have taken the high dive already. Call the cops."

"No!" Her 'no' was so loud I almost lost my hearing. "I—I—that is, he hasn't jumped yet. I asked him to wait, I told him I wanted to say goodbye in person. Meet me there, Mr. Diamond. Hurry!"

Before I could answer, she'd hung up.

"Helen, call Lt. Levinson and tell him to meet me *here*." I gave her Hart Thompson's business card, retrieved my hat from Francis, and hurried out.

When I got to the Blake Building, Grace was waiting for me at the front door. I unlocked it with my tenant's key. We raced to the elevator and rode up in silence, the same sort of silence her husband and I had ridden down in, except that she stood at the front of the elevator staring at the little numbers that kept changing.

When the doors opened, she rushed out ahead of me.

Thompson's office door was open and he stood framed in the window. There was just a desk lamp on and it was aimed at the door.

She yelled, "Hart!" and stopped in front of me.

"Goodbye, my love," he called and, throwing her a kiss, stepped off.

Grace fainted, falling back and grabbing me as she slipped to the floor.

I disentangled myself with some effort and stepped to the window. Thompson lay in the center of the alley, as flat as a bug on a windshield.

I picked Grace up off the floor and plunked her in her dead husband's chair.

As soon as we'd gotten off the elevator, the doors had closed. Now they opened again and out of it strode Lt. Walter Levinson and his faithful idiot companion, Sgt. Otis. Walt was a longtime friend and Sgt. Otis was, well, Sgt. Otis.

"What's going on, Rick?" Walt asked.

"The usual, a dead body."

He was looking at Grace and I swear I saw a question mark over his head.

"No. This is Grace Thompson, *wife* of the dead body. You'll find him in the alley."

I pointed to the window and he stepped over to it.

Otis asked, "How come we never see you except when somebody's been murdered, Diamond?"

"'Cause I keep hoping the next one I come across is going to be you."

Walt turned from the window. "What happened, Rick?"

"Mrs. Thompson and I walked in. The dead body—who wasn't dead at the time—was standing in the window. He said, 'Goodbye, my love,' threw his wife a kiss, and stepped off into the Big Nowhere."

Grace was coming back to life.

"Otis, take Diamond outside. I want to talk to Mrs. Thompson."

I preceded the sergeant and waited for him to squeeze his bulk through the doorway.

As soon as he'd closed the office door, Otis said, "Geez, they got a bathroom around here? I really gotta go."

I indicated where it was. He trotted off around the corner and I slipped into my newly-rented room next door.

I rewound the voice-actuated tape. It began, "What are you doing here? Stay back!" This was followed by vague sounds, some whispering, and silence. After a minute, the phone was dialed and a voice, presumably Thompson's, said, "Call that (something) of yours."

I couldn't make out whatever the "something" was because of the whisper. He might have been saying "pizza," but that didn't make any sense.

There was no answer from the other end of the line.

I rewound the tape, slipped it into my pocket, and stepped out into the hall.

Otis, who'd returned from the little boys' room, stood in the hall looking as though he'd lost something. When he saw me, he asked the question that would have been burning a hole in his brain if he'd had one. "Hey, where you been?"

"I was thinking about moving my office to higher quarters, so I was checking this one out."

"Oh?"

"I don't think so."

"You don't think so *what?*"

"What do you mean, so what? You trying to pick a fight, Sergeant?"

"Who, me? I don't know what you're talking about."

"Do you ever? Say, the lieutenant's been in there a long time with Mrs. Thompson. You don't think…? No, of course you don't. You haven't the equipment."

Otis chortled. "Mrs. Thompson's gone. The lieutenant let her go while you was checking out that office."

I went back into Thompson's place. Walt was pacing, a difficult thing to do in that room.

He turned at the end of his pace. "Rick, something's wrong here, but I can't put my finger on it. Say, what were you doing here, anyway?"

"Me? I was working for the widow. She was worried about hubby, thought he might be contemplating doing away with himself."

"Looks as though she had reason for her contemplations."

"Yes, it does, doesn't it? Well, I'll leave you to your pondering, Walt. My job's over. Bye."

"Where you going?"

"Where do I always go when a case is over? Helen's."

I rode down one flight, knowing Otis wouldn't be watching the indicator, and got off to visit the room directly below Thompson's. After which, I thought it was time I had a little talk with the new widow.

Later, I dropped in on Helen. Francis, who looked as though he hoped he'd seen the last of me for the day, let me in and announced me.

"Rick, you rushed out of here without telling me anything. I've been on pins and needles ever since."

Helen looked as lovely as ever. "First you hang up on me and then, before I can finagle any information out of you, you're gone. It's been hours."

She lounged on the couch and patted the spot next to her. "Come. Tell Mama everything."

I lounged next to her and brought her up to date.

After I'd left Walt, I'd gone right to the Thompson apartment and knocked on the door.

Grace was wearing a filmy black thing that just about covered another filmy black thing, and was holding a black cat with a slash of white at its throat.

"Richard! What a surprise." The look on her puss— not the one she was holding—told me it really was a surprise.

"May I? As the fly said to the spider."

"Yes. Yes, of course." She stepped aside to let me enter.

"Who's the outfit for?"

She was setting the cat down and she stiffened. Pussy put a claw in her arm and Grace dropped the little beastie.

"Sorry about that. Didn't mean to startle you, but those aren't exactly widow's weeds you're wearing, though the color's right. Who's the lucky man?"

She had the audacity to hang her head, as though in shame. "You're right, of course. There is another man."

She lifted that beautiful head, defiantly. "And why not? I told you Hart spent all his time working. You should have inferred I'd need a man in my life, a *real* man."

She was good. Not as good as June Allyson, but good.

"Maybe so, angel, but that's no reason to murder your husband."

"Murder him? That—that's crazy! You saw him jump out the window. We both saw him."

"Uh-uh. We saw *somebody* go out a window. But I'm of the opinion that it wasn't Hart and that he didn't jump to his death."

"You saw him there, in the middle of the alley."

"Yeah. And that's what bothered me. That and a tape I listened to."

"Tape?"

"Oops. That must have slipped my mind. I put a tape player in your husband's office while he was out for lunch."

"You—"

"Yep, me. When I listened to them, while you were having a chat with Lt. Levenson, I thought it was your husband on the phone. But he said something that made no sense at first. Crazy, but it sounded as though he was asking you to order pizza. But he couldn't have been, since he'd had lunch less than two hours before. Skinny people don't usually eat that often.

"Anyway, it took me a while to figure—"

"What was it you figured, Diamond?"

He'd slipped into the apartment without my hearing him.

"Dr. Livingston, I presume?"

"Don't presume too much, Diamond." He was a thin, good-looking man, but all his charm seemed to be in his looks. "You were saying?"

"No, I was presuming. I presume you and the new widow were in the murder together."

"Murder? Why, Mr. Diamond, where would you get an idea like that? I understand Hart jumped."

"Did he jump or was he pushed? I'm of the opinion he was helped out the window. You the helper? Of course. You would be.

"You would also be the one who committed 'suicide' wearing that red wig. You'd rigged a net one floor below to drop into.

"There were a couple of things that bothered me. The first was that Grace didn't faint. People who faint relax completely. She didn't; she hung onto me, to keep me from getting to the window too soon. After all, you needed time to get inside the room below and drag the net in after you. The 'faint' kept me back long enough. By the time I got to the window, the only thing to see was Hart's body in the alley.

"That was the second thing. Hart's body was in the *middle* of the alley. It should have been right next to the building, since he, that is you, dropped, rather than jumped."

"You're a regular Sam Spade, Diamond. Well, that was our mistake. Yours was in coming here. Tomorrow, I'll go back and get rid of the net and no one will be the wiser."

"Tomorrow you're going to be in the hoosegow, friend."

He started a hand inside his jacket, and so did I. But I'd been to more Hopalong Cassidy movies than he had. I shot the gun out of his hand. I wouldn't tell him I'd been aiming for his heart. No harm in him thinking I was better than I am.

The door flew open and I turned, still holding the gun.

"Don't shoot, shamus! We're the good guys."

"Otis turned out to be a bit brighter than expected," I said to Helen. "He'd noticed the elevator had stopped for a while on the floor below and mentioned it to Walt on the way to headquarters. That made Walt have him turn the cruiser around and go back to the Blake Building, where they found the net, and Walt deduced what I'd deduced. That sent them on their way to the Thompson apartment, where they arrived in the proverbial nick.

"I also suggested to Walt that he look into the late Hart Thompson's business."

"But what was that business about the pizza?"

"Oh, that. As I started to tell the boyfriend, I thought he'd asked her to call for some pizza. What he'd really said was, 'Call that P.I. of yours,' meaning me, because everything was all set up for the 'suicide.'"

Francis came in with drinks, and I took a good look at him. "Francis, do you have a brother on the police force?"

"Why no, sir."

"Funny. I could have sworn…"

"No swearing, Rick." Helen smiled and sipped the excellent martini. "Singing, but no swearing."

I moved over to the piano and ran my fingers across the keyboard. *"Tonight we love,"* I sang and hoped it might be true. ♦

MY FRIEND IRMA

Jane's Side
by Barbara Gratz

Everyone will have many friends during a lifetime, and if one happens to be single and living in New York where the rents are high, at least one roommate. But of all the friends I will ever have and all the roommates, the last I will ever forget is my room mate, *My Friend Irma*.

Irma and I both work as secretaries. I hate to admit it, but I'm in love with my boss, Richard. Hopelessly in love with Richard. He's smart, successful, generous, not snobbish, likes and respects me, but somehow just doesn't get around to asking me to marry him.

I'm an attractive, comely brunette; Irma is a knockout. Most people like and respect me. This category doesn't exactly apply to Irma. With her blonde hair, blue eyes, and very classic figure, young men never get past their eyes. Everybody else responds to her genuineness and sweetness, and she brings out the best in everybody.

Like the other day, Irma was walking past a group of street beggars. One came up to her and said, "Lady, if you could just give me a fin, I could get my life back together, go home to Nebraska to my wife and six children, and hold my head high in the community."

Irma said, "Of course. Come with me."

Irma proceeded to lead him to the Fulton Fish Market.

The guy was getting more confused by the minute. "Where are you taking me?" he protested.

"I know where you can get several on each one," Irma said sweetly.

"Here, lady, take this." He handed her a twenty dollar bill, and ran off.

"See, he's getting more successful already," Irma remarked.

Irma works for Mr. Clyde. He's married, older, and is alternately exasperated and fatherly toward Irma. Did I mention that Irma has her own logic and filing systems? Mr. Clyde could never fire Irma, not even if he wanted to or as he is occasionally tempted to, because without Irma to interpret Irma's system, all previous data would be lost. It works for Irma and gets the job done for her boss.

Like, just the other day, Mr. Clyde called Irma at home because he needed to locate the Murphy-Bronson file, but couldn't find it under M or B.

Irma said, "It's easy: Murphy reminds me of a murphy bed, which reminds me I'm sleepy, and since July is the month with the longest days and the least amount of time available for sleeping, the file is in the last two-thirds of the J's." You see what I mean.

Our apartment is New York tiny, but it's clean and cozy. Sharing expenses makes if affordable. We have caring neighbors.

There's a knock at the door. I open to our landlady, Mrs. O'Reilly, a small pudgy ruddy lady, whose reddish hair and blue eyes proudly proclaim Ireland. "Hello, girls," she says. "I just did a bit of baking, and thought you might enjoy these."

She hands me a pan of biscuits. The aroma hits the room. Then we hear the sound of footsteps coming up the stairs in the hall.

"I'll be going," she says. "You know that old expression, absence makes the heart grow fonder. Well, I'm trying to avoid Professor Kropotkin. When he doesn't see me every day, he will grow to miss me, and that should spark his interest in me. I'll get him yet." She scurries out.

A minute later there's another knock on the door. Professor Kropotkin enters. He's tall and thin. He looks the sensitive artist he is. He plays violin at the Gypsy Theatre and also teaches. He will never catch up nutritionally from the deprivations he suffered in Russia and since as an immigrant.

"Hello, Janie, hello, Irma," he says. "I just finished giving my last lesson of the day, and thought I'd see how you girls were getting along. What's this I see on the table?" He points to the pan of biscuits.

"They're biscuits Mrs. O'Reilly baked," I say. "I'm sure she would want you to have some."

"No, girls, thank you just the same. I can't be sick during tonight's performance."

He hesitates, "You know, I haven't seen Mrs. O'Reilly for the longest time. I'm almost beginning to miss her. I keep expecting to hear her nagging. When I don't hear it, I feel like something's wrong. I feel like I left the house without my violin or umbrella." He leaves gracefully and elegantly.

I leave the house too. "Irma, since Richard hasn't called by now, I don't think he will. I'm going to the museum to see about life in Egypt. Want to come?"

"No, I like it here," Irma says.

After I left, the phone rang.

"Hello," Irma said sweetly.

"Hello," said Richard in his well-modulated voice. "Is Jane there?"

"No," Irma replied. "She went down to see about life in Egypt."

Richard seems a little puzzled.

"Yes," asserted Irma. "Jane says you can understand your own culture better if you also understand other cultures. She's on her way right now."

"Oh." Richard paused, waiting for comprehension to catch up with hearing. "I can't stand in the way of what she wants. I'd better start interviewing for a new secretary. But I'll never find a woman as intelligent and gracious as Jane. Thanks, Irma." He let the phone receiver slip out of his hand onto the cradle.

There was another knock on the door. Al, Irma's boyfriend, entered. He's a smallish man, with dark, oily hair. He looks like a weasely, devious runt, straight out of a Damon Runyan story. Except, he has one saving grace. He truly loves Irma, and that just might make him a good man some day, if only he'd give up his get-rich-quick and quasi-shady schemes.

"Oh, Al, I've ruined my best friend's life," Irma moaned. "I might have told Richard Jane was going to Egypt. Now he's looking for a new secretary."

"Okay, Chicken," reassured Al. "There's only one way to handle this. Give me the phone."

He dialed a number rapidly, one that obviously he had dialed many times before. "Hello, Joe."

Pause. "Al. Got a problem. This guy's going to replace his secretary because he thinks she's going to live in another country. But she's not, and doesn't want to be replaced."

Pause. "Ahunh."

Pause. "Ahunh."
Pause. "Ahunh."
Pause. "Unh-unh."
Pause. "Unh-unh."
Pause. "No."
Pause. "Well, thanks, Joe."
"Well?" inquired Irma hopefully.

"Joe suggests we get a copy of the Yellow Pages, look up employment agencies, call every employment agency in town, and tell them that Richard is facing indictment for tax fraud."

Irma started to cry.

I was never so hurt or shocked as when I heard Richard on the phone talking with various employment agencies about a new secretary.

"Oh, Irma," I moan. "What am I going to do? Now I won't even be Richard's secretary, let alone his wife. I can get another job, but it won't be the same without working with Richard every day."

"Oh, Jane," Irma whimpers, then starts crying.

"Oh, no," says Jane. "You didn't."

More crying.

"You did."

Irma bawls uncontrollably.

There's another knock on the door. I open it, and look adoringly up into the face of Richard Rhinelander. He's so strong, so handsome, so manly, so everything a man should be—so everything except mine.

"I don't know what to say," Richard does say. "You're perfect. You're everything any man could want. I can't sleep. I can't eat. I can't do without you. Whatever you'll be doing in Egypt, I'll offer you better. I'll match it. I'll double it. Just say you'll stay on as my secretary."

Well, I still see Richard every day. I still see him forty hours a week. I'm still his secretary. I'm still not Mrs. Richard Rhinelander, but then neither is anybody else. As Al would say, I have the inside track. And I do have a very nice raise, thanks to **"MY FRIEND IRMA."** ♦

THE COLUMBIA WORKSHOP

A Drink For the Damned
by Martin Grams, Jr.

The sound of the quarters rolled down the chute and clinked in the container. The jukebox began preparations. After a pause the lights dimmed and "It Don't Rain in Southern California" poured from the speakers. Walking back to his stool, Dalton danced his way to the counter. It wasn't much of a dance, really. More like a drunken attempt to walk straight and fly without wings. With tie loosened and jacket tossed flopped across a table, Dalton reached for the drink he ordered. He was alone—just him and the young waitress behind the bar. She wasn't even paying much attention to him. The waitress was blonde, mannequin-shaped perfection with a voice that could train a canary.

Dalton admired her shoulders, back and thighs as she bent over to clean the evidence. Peanut shells needed to be swept. Ashtrays to empty. Wet napkins sticking to the seats.

"This joint is pretty nice," Dalton commented. "How long has this place been here?"

"Two years. What another?"

Dalton finished the last of his drink and ordered another. "You're the only one left here tonight?"

"Everyone leaves when the crowd goes. I need the money. Some nights are busier than others."

"Think I can buy you one?" Dalton asked, sliding a five across the counter.

"A little bit of soul will come your way," she remarked…seriously. "Best to put it away and finish up so I can shut down." She turned and walked into the back room, stacking glasses and plates on a tray.

"I think she likes you," said a familiar voice. Dalton turned to discover he was not alone. A figure dressed in black hopped on the stool next to him.

73

"If you intend to join me, you're two drinks behind," Dalton joked.

"I had a couple down the road," remarked the stranger. "Hey sweet cheeks! I'll take one of what he's having!" And with that, the stranger took off his coat and hat and tossed it across the room. On the same table next to Dalton's. The blonde brought the stranger his drink, gave him a sly look, and slowly walked out of the room to continue her routine.

"You know, I think she has an eye for you."

"Think so?" Dalton asked.

"I know so. When the scenery shines bright, don't admire it. Pull at the roots."

"I might just do that," Dalton pondered. "I'll wait a little first."

"Why wait?"

"Because after this, she'll really be something worth looking at."

The stranger laughed. "Let the night never end." Dalton realized he was missing his watch. Glancing across the cigarette smoke-filled room, Dalton read the clock on the wall. Half past two. The dim red lights didn't offer an accurate reading, it could be half past three.

"Mind if I make an observation, pal? You look like a man who doesn't know what he wants."

"Why do you say that?" Dalton asked.

"A great wife, two kids to go home to. Successful on the financial side—I can see that by the way you dress, but you lack the human qualities so richly desired from deep within."

"How did you know I was married?"

"Ring on the finger. But that's not what's important. What is important is you are here, drinking faster than an alcoholic, for two reasons. Self-indulgence in a deadly ritual, or loneliness."

"You're wrong there, brother."

"Oh? Something bad happen today?"

"Third time's a charm."

"Nah...the day looks brighter when you look ahead, not behind. My laundry is never clean but I shine just the same." Dalton looked at the stranger. He was certainly in favor of black, right down to the Fu Manchu beard. "Wouldn't you know it? I come in here to escape the heat and I find it hotter in here than outside. The evenings are not what they used to be—it's like a night-life oven."

"So where are you from?" Dalton asked. "For reasons I can't place it, I swear I've seen you before."

"I have that kind of face."

"No—do you live around here?"

"I'll let you in on a little secret. Just between you and me." The stranger leaned over to whisper loud enough for only Dalton to hear. "I am the Lord of the Flies."

Giving the stranger a queer look, Dalton took a swallow of beer. Looking around to see if anyone else was in the room, he leaned back. "And I am Joan of Arc, sister of the Brotherhood."

The man in black leaned back and laughed again. "I like you. A sense of humor. I'll have to remember that when you come and visit."

"Just who are you really?" Dalton asked, feeling off the stool.

"I told you. I'm on vacation. Momentarily, that is. I know all about your little mistake today. With Corless Palmer."

"You her boyfriend?" Dalton asked nervously.

"Nah. I know Corless because of what she did. Let me point out that she lives in a world within the four walls of Corless Palmer. If the rules don't work her way, she'll bend or break them."

"And step on toes," Dalton defended. "I should be thankful her boyfriend didn't get involved."

"There are two ways to success in this world. The first is the slow rise up the ladder, one rung at a time. The second is overnight fame. But for every person's toes you step on, is another person you'll have to face going down."

"Don't forget I was the victim."

"'Course you could also rise in the world by killing the boss."

"She already did. I put the best four years of my life in that job and today she tells the boss what she thinks of me and I'm asked to leave the organization. She was against me from the first day I arrived there."

"And now she has your job. Happens to the best of us."

"And now I have read the classifieds."

"Oh, that sounds like murder," sarcastically spoken by the man in black, leaning behind the bar to fix himself a drink without assistance from the waitress. "Want to know what I have to go through every day? Lectures on the pedestal. Invitations to the criers. I admit it's fun, and I get my jollies, but even the most pleasurable job has its faults."

"What?"

"Stressful it's not." The stranger poured Dalton another glass. "But it never stops and on nights like these, I take a break and surface for a little conversation. Nothing short of a labor dispute. Maybe I shouldn't be so forgiving. Felt tips on whips. Snowcones on Sunday mornings."

"You're already drunk," Dalton theorized.

"Think so? Say, how would you like to come down for an hour and check it out? It's better than a roller coaster. You can see them grovel. A few blowhards were talking about forming a union against me, with God as their Shop Steward. I tell you it's as useless as rain on Lake Michigan."

"Labor disputes? In hell?" Dalton humored his new-found friend.

"Why not? They have good cause to gripe. Take this guy Sisyphus. I've been having him push this huge rock up a very steep hill every day. It takes the fellow about twenty minutes to reach the top, sweat it out a little, and then the rock moves. Rolls back to the bottom and he turns to find himself back at the bottom having to perform the task again. All he does is complain, complain, complain."

"Sounds like you're describing me. I'm back at the bottom," Dalton recalled. "I kept to myself and worked hard to get where I was. Maybe I should have griped. Maybe I would have gotten somewhere."

"Employees will form resistance. It starts with uncertainty and during policy changes, they don't know how to react. It's a little unsettling at first, but give them time to trust and understand . . ."

"Not Corless."

"You had something for her, didn't you?"

"No..." Dalton turned to admire his drink. He could feel the stranger's eyes upon him.

"Don't deny it. Lust can hold a man together."

"Makes me all the happier that I'm not on that route."

"There's still time to change."

"I'm still thinking about it." And with that, there was a moment of silence to think real hard about their positions. The music stopped and Dalton gathered his senses for a moment. Realizing it was all in the bubbles, queer things began to form. Notions too vivid. "Between you, me and the liquor here, I think Tennyson was wrong. Tis better to have never loved at all than to have loved and lost."

"So is this a personal agenda or are you just against everyone in the phone book?"

"I think I'm losing my faith in humanity, that's all."

"The world on your shoulders."

"Like Atlas."

"You are not as drunk as I thought – yet. So you've partaken of the ultimate desertion. You for yourself."

"And why not? That's all we have in life. Ourselves."

"Some women live on the thoughts that men drool over them."

"Or their pillow."

"Now you're talkin'. Your wife would think differently."

"You know what makes the world go round?" Dalton asked.

"Love?"

"Problems. And mine is apparently a three-drink problem."

"Seven. The evening is not really over yet. The night is young and so are the barmaids."

"Bar maid. Singular," Dalton corrected.

"You're pretty fast."

"You have to be, to get ahead of the game."

"A rat race…"

"Well, someone will just have to teach Corless that it's always the second rat that gets the cheese."

"If I wasn't as old as I looked, I could have her…"

Dalton turned his head to look at the stranger, with perplexed eyes. "You?"

"The pressure cooker is still steaming."

"Maybe I'll use some of that spunk myself and try for the girl when she returns," Dalton pondered.

"You'll get her if you make a try. You missed with Corless but try and try again…"

"And just how do you know? Do you have a crystal ball in one of your pockets?"

"As a matter of fact, I do. Call it a sixth sense. Like you, she just wants to feel like a real woman."

"I don't want to feel like a real woman."

"You know what I mean." The stranger finished his drink while the girl returned. She asked Dalton if he wanted another, and he nodded. Both glasses were replaced and the girl returned to the back room.

"Women are attracted to me like magnets," Dalton remarked. "Only with the opposite poles pushing each other away."

"You're allergic to blondes?"

Dalton chuckled. "Look—even if Corless wanted my job, a relationship wouldn't have worked out. My wife would have eventually found out."

"You can still have your job back."

"How? Sell my soul to you?"

"You already have. She has too. But maybe she can be taught a lesson."

"That's your job. Temptation. Urge people to move in on the actions of others."

"All in a game. Don't get heartbroken over this. You'll enjoy a little revenge now and then. How about Super Glue in her tire valves? Prank calls at three in the morning. That would make *you* sleep better at night."

Dalton disagreed. "And get a sock in the jaw for friendship."

"You plan it right, and no one would know…"

Dalton still disagreed. "Disgruntled women of the workplace—kill your oppressors. That's a switch."

"A wise Nigerian would say the same. It only takes a pull of the trigger, a simple phone call, a couple of harmless letters – scare her a bit. Make her think she was vulnerable. Sooner of later, a larger predator takes over."

"Maybe I will. If it's good enough for Bobby McGee, it's good enough for me."

One Hour Later…

"So tell me, what's it like in hell?"

"Fire and Brimstone is Hollywood. The real hell is Inner Man."

"Both sexes?"

"Sure thing," the devil acknowledged. "I have a job 365 days a year, 100 years a century. Pay isn't bad, but the benefits are superb."

"Can you make flames from your fingertips?"

"Better than that. Watch this." The stranger held out his hand and within seconds, every fly in the bar was in the palm of his hand.

"Nah—that's not impressive. Sugar water. I made my hands bleed when I was in high school using a thumb tack. Made people think I was Jesus Christ."

"I know. I saw that. Pretty creative. Watch this." As the man in black took a couple sips from his seventh glass, the entire tavern started to shake. Glasses and plates rattled. After a few seconds, the quake stopped. "Believe me now?"

"You're a prince of a fellow." Dalton, knowing he'd had enough, took another swallow. "So any regrets? What I mean is—don't you wish you could be doing something else?"

"What else is there? I take pleasure in the vile things others do. If Benjamin Franklin was still alive today, he would probably say, a blind man will not thank you for a looking glass."

"If Benjamin Franklin was still alive today, he would probably drop dead. I think I'm just losing my faith in humanity, that's all."

"And so you've partaken in the ultimate desertion. You for yourself."

"And why not? That's all we have in life. In a perfect world, we would all be living in clover."

"In a perfect world, we'd all be complaining about how the clover smells. Sometimes all you little people need is a little TLC."

"Well, all I get is TNT instead. I would like to crawl into the wood-work and not come back until the second coming."

"And that's supposed to solve all your problems? I'd still consider revenge. It will make you feel better."

"That's what these drinks are for."

"Want some good advice?" asked the devil.

"From you? What is good advice?"

"Unknown to those in need of it, and unheeded by those who know of it." Once again, the men paused to reflect on their drinks. "I'll give you another word of advice. Everyone has skeletons in their closets. You're not Saint Francis of Assisi yourself."

"Say, what are you trying to do? Brainwash me?"

"I'll leave that job to psychiatrists."

"So why don't you? Instead of sitting in here telling me what I should do. You know, if I want to keep myself unemployed, so be it. My father gave me the rare gift that I can become anybody and do anything, so long as I want to."

"And you believed him?"

"Why shouldn't I?"

"Life isn't a string of pearls. I would have thought you'd learn that by now. The older you humans get, the dumber you become."

"I believe in the American Dream. My mother believed in love at first sight."

"And I believe I'll help myself to another drink," said the man in black, leaning over the counter to grab a bottle of whiskey.

Three Hours and Three Drinks Later...

Round one was the same as round two, except that round one was less foggy. By now both men are drowning their sorrows and, making up like all decent people (those who qualify for having some decency in them), were having a contest to see who could retain their senses the longest. Mutual friendship with alcohol—the universal language.

"...so this guy says, 'Hey bartender, give me another drink before the trouble comes.' The bartender does, but this time he slams the bottle on the counter. The bartender by this time had had enough and says, 'Look bud, that's the third drink I've given you the past half-hour. So when's this trouble supposed to come?' The fella says, 'The trouble comes when you realize I haven't gotten any money'!" The men roared with laughter, pounding fists into the table.

Dalton wiped away his tears and stopped laughing for a second. "So I have to ask you. I just gotta know. What city in the United States has the most sinners? New York or Los Angeles?"

"Philadelphia."

"The City of Brotherly Love?"

"You got 'em."

"No," corrected Dalton, "You got 'em." The men roared with laughter again. "Why is it when we talk to God it's called praying, but when God talks to us, it's called schizophrenia?"

"On your time, not mine. I used to enjoy a good witch hunt. A burning at the stake. You need to get that tradition up and going again."

"Are we guilty of just bad thoughts?"

"You're all guilty of something. It's how much you are willing to admit to."

"Well, here's one you forgot. Commandment number eleven. Thou shalt not cheat and steal jobs and promotions that belong to other people."

"That still burning you?"

"Mistaking my words for thoughts. Whatever I meant to do, I forgot it now."

"Shame. Revenge is a sweet-smelling harmony."

"I guess deep down inside all of us we have a little Mr. Hyde."

"The next time you look at someone," the man in black remarked, "remember that people are like trees. Many stand tall and many bloom brightly. They protect and serve. But deep down inside, underneath our very noses, they all have crooked roots."

"For a man of pure bile, you sure have a bit of wisdom to you."

"If you want, I can take care of Corless and her boyfriend. Just say the word and thy wish will be granted."

Dalton took a swallow and wiped the sweat from his brow. Looking about him he noticed the waitress was nowhere to be seen. Where was help when he needed it? Where was his conscience? He thought deep and clear for a brief moment. "A wise answer," Dalton spoke out loud, "would be to turn the other cheek. But at the moment, I am not quite too sure about things. If I sign myself over to you, by agreeing to see her fry, then I would be just as guilty as she."

"And so like a righteous man, you throw the blame on your own shoulders?"

"The understatement of the century. I'll admit I'm no Romeo. My wife and I have problems but perhaps we can talk about them as married couples should. At least for the sake of the kids. I'll tell her about me and Corless. Tell her it was a fling and that it's over between us. I lost my job over it, but what the hell—I can get another. I still have myself, my pride and a suitcase of respect from all those who pay tribute to a 'preserved,' dressed-up body that one day will enter a mahogany box and be remembered for who he was—not what he accomplished. I believe that is what merits the value of good and evil. It tips the scales of immortality and damnation on a sole leverage."

"Now I know you're drunk."

"No—no I am not. How was it phrased in the Bible? Forgive us our debts, as we forgive our debtors? Do unto others? Am I really drunk? It's not alcohol that I'm intoxicated with."

"In some religions, you gain admittance to heaven by being buried with your ancestors."

"You can't confuse me now. I made a mistake, I'll label that under 'E' for experience. We all make mistakes."

"That's why they put erasers on pencils," the man in black chuckled.

"Charles Churchill. By different methods different men excel, but where is he who can do all things well?" Dalton got off the stool, walked over to the table and picked up his hat and coat. "My conscience is clear. I think I can go home now and sleep it off. Tomorrow morning I will explain it to my wife. You were right, the seventh drink would be the cure. Time heals all wounds. Or as a writer name Bloch put it, 'Time wounds all heels.'"

The devil turned to thank his host for the enlightening evening. "I've got the drinks covered."

"Thanks." Dalton looked around to clear his head for a second and regain his senses. The lights started turning off, one by one. The waitress walked out from the back room. Dalton watched as she walked over to the devil, wrapped her arms around his neck and hopped on his lap. She giggled with almost the same laughter he heard Corless give last week. Then the man in black wrapped his fingers across her waist. Dalton made for the exit.

"Hey kid!"

Dalton turned. "Yeah?"

"Keep your chin up."

That was the last thing Dalton ever saw or heard from the stranger as he stepped outside the bar. He breathed in the summer air, the evening moisture, the fresh air and for a short moment the dizziness cleared. The only sound he could hear was the crickets. The sky started to lighten up on the eastern side. The sun would probably rise in another hour. It's going to be a beautiful day, Dalton thought. Remembering what the stranger said, he lifted his chin a little high. Almost immediately a fist came across his face, knocking him to the ground. Trying to break through the blur of the evening skylight, Dalton saw a familiar figure lean over him. It was the face of the boyfriend. Another fist took out the view. ◆

BOBBY BENSON AND THE B-BAR-B RIDERS

The Adventure of the Lady Prospector
by Jack A. French

The midmorning sun was climbing high in the blue Texas sky over the B-Bar-B Ranch, slowly removing the spring chill from the air, as a lone rider on a buckskin mare rode through the main gate and up to the ranch house.

"Here comes Irish with the mail!" yelled Bobby Benson, the slender dark-haired youth who owned this sprawling ranch in the Big Bend Country of the Lone Star State. In response to his cry, three men came out on the porch. First was broad-shouldered

Tex Mason, the ranch foreman. Closely behind came a tall and handsome Apache Indian, Harka, dressed in soft, fringed leather clothing.

"Doggone it, Harka," complained Windy Wales, the third in line, "can't you let a feller through, if he's expecting an all-fired important package?"

"Wind-man be in plenty hurry," Harka observed, as the spry old-timer pushed by him and hurried over to grab the reins on Irish's panting horse.

"Now don't be getting too anxious, Windy," said Irish, as he dismounted from the saddle, his left arm crooked around a bundle of mail, "there should be mail for everybody." To Windy's consternation, Irish slowly passed out the various pieces of mail.

"Gee, Tex, it looks mostly like bills and circulars," Bobby said, sorting through the mail Irish handed him, "but what's that big package you have left?"

"Well now, Bobby, this large box came all the way from San Diego, California," Irish replied, "and it's from the Continental Correspondence School, addressed to Walter Wellington Wales."

Windy blushed at the sound of his full, proper name, but it did not deter him from quickly grabbing the package from the smiling Irish.

"Now you looka-here, Irish, a feller has to use his actual full name when ordering educational material; it's only right," Windy said as he clutched the package to his chest. "Inside this box are my first lessons on the road to fame and fortune."

He sat down on the top porch step and began to carefully cut the wrappings with his pocket Barlow knife, as Bobby, Tex, Harka, and Irish watched his progress. Soon the wrappings were discarded, the box was opened and it revealed a large gray bound notebook, upon which was written in capital letters, "THE ART OF BULLFIGHTING." A little below that were the words, " How to become a Matador in Twenty Easy Lessons." And at the very bottom of the cover of the notebook it read "Lessons One through Five." Windy removed the bound notebook and held it proudly for the others to see.

"This is it, fellers, soon you'll be shouting 'Ole," as I drive a raging bull to complete distraction," the old-timer predicted.

"Why, Windy, you don't expect to become a skilled matador just by reading that book, do you?" Tex asked.

"Of course not, Tex," Windy replied, "this here's just the first five lessons. After I master them, the rest will come to me in other packages. But now I've got what I need to get started on my new career."

"Bull-fighting can be very dangerous," Irish said. "You might be headed for a peck of pain."

"That right, Wind-man, mebbe you stop now or big trouble come," Harka added.

"Now doggone it, Harka, seems like you and Irish agree so much, sometimes I think I'm talking to the same person. What you fellers don't know is that the Continental Correspondence School guarantees every course, and that's a fact," Windy said.

"Gosh, Windy, it still sounds pretty risky to me, too," said the Cowboy Kid. "Whadda you think, Tex?"

"Well, son, I've got to agree with you. Windy, I want you to promise me you'll stick to just reading your lessons and not climbing in the corral with any bull until it's safe," Tex replied.

Before Windy could reply, Bobby spotted something else in the box. "What's that red cloth in the bottom of your box, Windy?"

"Why, shucks, Little Boss, I was afraid no one was going to ask me. That's my small cape; it's called a muleta. See here, you put this dowel through the one end, and now it hangs straight, kinda like a flag, only it's not a flag. It's what I use to get the bull to miss me when he charges. I'll show you fellers how it works after I get some practice in." Windy waved the scarlet cloth around as the others watched with a mixture of amusement and anxiety.

"That's enough for now, Windy, we've all got chores to do," Tex interrupted. "You'll just have to do your reading and practicing on your own time, after your work is done. Do you understand that?"

"Dag-nabbit, of course I do, Tex," the old-timer agreed, "but that means it'll take me a little longer to become a famous matador and put the B-Bar-B on the the map."

"That's fine with me, Windy, now all you fellers get to work; there's a lot to do before supper," Tex said.

The Riders of the B-Bar-B spent the rest of the day in their assigned chores. Bobby curried his palomino, Amigo, and the rest of the horses in the barn. Irish and Slim worked on fencing around the hay field. Windy and another cowhand, Waco, took the wheels off the buckboard and greased the axles. Harka was in the tack shop, making repairs to some harnesses. Tex Mason went into the ranch house and concentrated on the accounting books, paid bills, and ordered some summer supplies.

That night, after a steak and potatoes supper cooked and served by Tia Maria, Windy got out his correspondence course and was reading portions of it to the other Riders. "The noble sport of bullfighting dates back to the 12th Century in Spain and its success requires three basic elements: courage, skill, and grace," Windy read aloud and then paused for effect: "What do you fellers think about that?"

"Well, it looks like you've got your work cut out for you, Windy," Irish said. "You're a fine cowboy, but nobody ever called you graceful."

"Shore, Irish, but the grace comes with the costume. That'll be comin' later, with Lesson 15. You see, them fancy, pink pants are called 'Traje de luces' and they fit real tight so the bull can't hook you with his horns. And, of course, any feller looks graceful in tight pink pants. You'll see when I get in the corral with Lucifer. "

"Hold on, Windy," Tex said. "Lucifer is a very large and dangerous bull. That's why he has his own corral at the B-Bar-B. When you want to practice with an animal, use one of the older steers, so you won't get injured."

"Doggone it, Tex, how am I going to become the toast of Mexico City at the Plaza de Toros if I only get to practice with some dumb old critter?" Windy complained.

"We'll worry about your success in the bull ring later, Windy, but for right now, stay out of Lucifer's corral," Tex ordered.

Windy sadly put his small cape and his notebook in the box and walked out on the porch. He sprawled out under the porch light and began reading again. Irish and Bobby came out later and were watching the fireflies in the dusk when Windy interrupted their quiet observation of nature. "I'm gonna let you fellers help me when I start matadoring with Lucifer. I read where the matador has some assistants, and they are in the ring with him. They're called picadors and they ride these horses who are padded with thick blankets. Now I figger that Bobby, you could wrap Amigo up in some old quilts and then saddle up and be my picador."

"Golly, Windy, I don't think that I—" Bobby started to say but was interrupted by Irish.

"He'll do no such thing, Windy," said the angry cowboy. "None of us are going to be your horseback picadors."

"All right then, all of my assistants don't have to be on horseback. There's some other assistants who are called bandilleros and they just come in on foot, as smart as you please. You reckon you could do that for me, Irish?"

"Glory be! C'mon in the ranch house with me, Bobby, we're not going to listen to any more foolishness," Irish said and led Bobby back in the house.

The next morning the Riders of the B-Bar-B were just finishing their flapjacks, bacon, and fresh fruit, which was the breakfast specialty prepared by Tia Maria. Alerted by the barking of Hero, his dog, Bobby went to the window and saw a rider approaching the B-Bar-B. "Looks like we've got company," he said. "A man is riding this way on one horse and leading another."

Harka's sharp eyes took in the rider and he corrected the Cowboy Kid. "No, Bobby-boy, Harka see woman in saddle, not man, and her animals be mules. "

Bobby and Harka went out on the porch, followed by Irish, Tex and Windy. As the rider drew near, they could see that Harka's observations were correct. A tall, smiling lady of indeterminate age, wearing a broad western hat, a man's denim shirt, scruffy boots, and a long, dust-covered skirt. Her saddle was on a large, dark mule, and tied behind her, was another smaller, gray mule.

"Howdy, boys, are you the reception committee?" she said with a warm grin.

"I reckon we are," Tex replied. "Welcome to the B-Bar-B Ranch. I'm Tex Mason, the foreman on this spread. This is the owner, Bobby Benson, and these other three fellers are Windy, Irish, and Harka."

"Wal, I shore am pleased to make your acquaintance, boys," she replied, "My name is Claudia Johnston, but everybody calls me 'Pokey.' This here's my riding mule, Gertrude, and this other one is her colt, Sunny Jim, who does his best to carry our supplies and keep up with us. I've worked with mules so long, some people think I can read their minds."

She let herself down from the saddle and joined the others on the porch steps. "What brings you to our ranch, Miss Johnston?" Bobby asked.

"Well, I'm a prospector, sonny, and I travel the wide West looking for whatever I can find that has value. Just me and my mules. And please, call me 'Pokey'. You might scare my mules if they hear you using my given name."

"What are you prospecting for now, Miss John—I mean, Pokey?" Irish inquired.

"Ma'am, if you're prospecting for gold or silver, I can give you some tips" Windy said, "I've spent many years in the Rocky Mountains, looking for gold, silver, and such. Why shucks, I never will forget the time I—'"

"Thank ye kindly," Pokey interrupted Windy, "but I'm prospecting for uranium. I got me a Geiger Counter and everything else I need."

"Glory be, uranium!" Irish said. "Is there any around here?"

"That's what I'm fixin' to find out," Pokey replied. "There's several hundred acres of government property just north of Cougar Mountain and I've gonna go over every inch. The Atomic Energy Commission pays a hefty finders-fee to any prospector who can locate uranium and I reckon to do just that."

"Mighty interesting, Miss Pokey." Tex said. "Now, you're welcome to water your mules at our trough by the barn. And mebbe you'd like a glass of buttermilk and a sandwich. Where do you plan on staying while you're doing your prospecting in this region?"

"Me and the mules just camp out where we find ourselves. 'Course, it's a mite chilly this time of year, but we do all right. I'm not such a good cook, but the mules never complain," she laughed.

"Why don't you be our guest here at the B-Bar-B?" said tex, "You can bunk with Tia Maria in her place out back. I'm sure she'd like some female company, and it would be a durn-side more comfortable than sleeping out in those stoney foothills."

"Well, that is mighty kind of you, Mason, I'll take you up on that.

But I expect to pay you for my room and grub; Pokey Johnson don't take charity from nobody. But now I've still got about nine hours of sunlight left, so if me and the mules can get some refreshments, then we'll be on our way."

"That'll be swell, MIss Pokey," Bobby said. "Be back here by six or you'll miss supper."

After the lady prospector departed on her mules, the B-Bar-B Riders went at their ranch chores with a will. They worked all day and then were joined, as planned, by Pokey for their evening meal. She told the Riders that while she had not discovered any uranium today, there were some encouraging signs of underground radioactive materials in the region.

When supper was finished, Tex announced that Tia Maria had baked a lemon-and-marshmallow dessert in honor of their lady guest, and it would be served around a campfire that Waco had made behind the bunkhouse. All the cowhands, and Pokey, went outside, sat around the campfire, and enjoyed dessert. As they finished, Windy spoke, "Darned if this ain't right nice. This-here campfire reminds me of the time I was a-sitting around a fire with fellers from the 7th Cavalry. They had been searching for gunrunners along the Rio Grande River and were pert-near worn out when I showed up. Of course, when I heard about their troubles, I throwed in with them so's I could give 'em the benefit of my tracking experience, yessiree. Well, it twarn't but a day later when I found the the trail of those varmints. They'd been sloshing through some creek beds to hide their tracks, but they couldn't put nothin' past ol' Windy Wales. Well, sir, I tracked them to a tiny canyon. There were at least three escape routes out of that canyon so I told the Officer in Charge to hold his troopers back whilst I snuck up on the gun-runners with just my lariat. And, doggone it, even I was surprised when my first throw roped all nine of them owlhoots together. Later, the 7th Cavalry wanted to make a big fuss over me, with an engraved plaque, but of course, I refused cuz I was just doing my duty."

"Golly, Windy, did that really happen that way?" asked the Cowboy Kid.

"Why, Little Boss, darned if every word ain't the truth," Windy replied. "And that's a fact."

Irish stood up with a big grin. "You know, if Windy gets in trouble in the bull ring, he can just lasso the bull and drag him to the nearest butcher shop."

"Doggone it, Irish, can't a feller even—" Windy started to say, but Tex announced, "OK, Riders, that's enough excitement for tonight. Tomorrow's Saturday and we've got a lot of work to do then. It's time to hit the hay."

They all said their goodnights to each other, and Pokey Johnston, and all the occupants of the B-Bar-B Ranch headed for a soft pillow.

Saturday morning arrived, accompanied by a cold drizzle that did not seem to dampen the spirits of the ranch hands or their guest. Breakfast had been late due to Tia Maria oversleeping, the first time the cowhands could remember such a lapse. After breakfast, Pokey rode off again toward Cougar Mountain, singing to her mules. Most of the cowboys were hard at work about 11 AM when the telephone rang in the ranch house. Tia Maria answered it and then she ran out to the tool shed where Tex Mason was working.

"Senor Mason, come aprisa! Sheriff calls! Mucho trouble at bank!" she cried as she ran toward him, her colorful skirt flapping in the wind.

Tex hustled across the yard and into the house. He listened carefully for several minutes on the telephone, asked a few succinct questions, and then hung up the telephone, thoughtfully tugging on his chin.

"What was that all about, Tex?" said Bobby as he came into the foyer where Tex was still standing by the telephone.

"Well, son, the bank in Cactus City was broken into. Go get all the hands together on the front porch and I'll give them the details," Tex replied.

The young lad quickly complied with the instruction and a few minutes later, Tex was speaking to all the Riders and Tia Maria. His face was serious as he related the following:

"I want you all to know I just got off the phone with Sheriff Bancroft in Cactus City. He told me that the bank was entered, through the roof, last night and a large amount of cash and some silver bars were stolen. The thieves used an acetylene torch to cut through the roof and then the interior vault. The bank is still assessing the loss, but it could run over $ 40,000. The Sheriff and his deputies think three burglars were involved; at least they found the hoofprints of three horses in back of the bank were the loot was transferred from the roof to horseback. They followed the tracks only about half a mile but the trail disappeared on a gravel road. The Sheriff isn't sure whether the thieves continued on horseback from that point or whether they put the horses in a trailer and drove off."

"Glory be! Does the Sheriff want us to help look for them?" asked Irish.

"No, he was just alerting all the nearby ranchers to be on the lookout for any suspicious men, especially if there are three of them," Tex replied.

"Tex, do you think one of us should ride out and warn Miz Pokey to be careful?" Bobby inquired.

"No, I think the burglars will try to stay away from anyone they happen to encounter out here, and besides, I get the feeling that Pokey Johnston can handle just about anything," Tex said.

At the end of the day, just as the Texas sun was sinking in the west, Pokey returned to the B-Bar-B Ranch and joined the rest for supper. Windy and Irish took turns filling her in on the Cactus City Bank burglary and she took the news calmly. "I'll shore keep my eyes peeled for those sidewinders, and if I spot 'em, you can be sure I'll sic the law on 'em," she promised.

After supper, Bobby and Irish played checkers, Harka was whittling, and Windy was in a corner by the fireplace, studying his bull-fightting course materials. From time to time he would read a passage aloud, and getting no response, would resume in silence. "There are three different passes executed with the small cape: goovera, rebolera, and chicuelina," he read once with excitement, but since the rest ignored him, he continued studying quietly.

Sunday on the B-Bar-B was always appreciated by the Riders since it was their only day off in the week. However Pokey announced that she would be out prospecting again, promising to finish examining the government land near Cougar Mountain within another day or two. "You fellers probably want me out of your hair anyway," she grinned. "My ol' pappy always said, 'Fish and company smell after three days.'"

As she rode off, they all assured her that she was welcome to stay longer, and they cautioned her to be on the lookout for the three bank burglars. When she left, Bobby started playing a game of marbles by himself, failing to get anyone else interested in this game. Windy went to a nearby ravine where he could practice with his small cape, without the others teasing him about bull fighting. Irish and Waco were pitching horseshoes with two other cowhands at an adjacent ranch, the Lazy X. Harka went hunting for small game in a stand of prairie grass a few miles south of the ranch. Tex drove Tia Maria to see her elderly mother. The cowboys would be on their own for midday meal on Sunday, as was the custom at the B-Bar-B.

Shortly before 10 AM, the Cowboy Kid saw an automobile approaching the B-Bar-B; it was the tan squad car, with the gold badge painted on each door, that Sheriff Bancroft drove. Hero barked a welcome and Bobby walked down the entrance road to greet the sheriff. "Howdy, Sheriff," Bobby said, "Had any luck catching those owlhoots that burglarized the bank?"

"Not yet," Sheriff Bancroft admitted. "But we'll get 'em. I'm just checking some of the back roads and asking any of the local ranchers if they've spotted anything suspicious."

"Well, nothing to report from the B-Bar-B," the young lad said, "but we'll keep on the alert."

"Good, I appreciate that, son," the sheriff said. "You know, at first I thought we had a crime wave going on here Friday night. Not only was the bank broken into, but also Laredo Tate, the owner of the Circle 5 Ranch, which is about half way between town and the B-Bar-B, reported one of his horses was stolen late Friday night. But then he called me back on Saturday morning and advised me that the horse was back in the pasture with the rest of his mounts. So at least I don't have to worry about hoss thieves at the same time I'm trying to corral some bank burglars. So long, Bobby, I'll be in touch."

"Good-bye, sheriff; I'll relay to Tex Mason what you told me."

The sheriff backed up slowly toward the water trough, turned around, and then sped down the driveway to the entrance to the B-Bar-B, where he turned west and continued on the road toward the Lazy X Ranch.

Bobby turned around to pat Hero on the head, but he saw the dog running around the corner of the saddlery shop. Before Bobby had a chance to call him, Hero quickly returned, running to the boy with a stout stick in his mouth. Hero stopped at the feet of Bobby and dropped the stick gently on Bobby's boots. Then Hero barked sharply twice; it was his way of announcing that a game of fetch had begun. They played this game almost every day and both enjoyed it thoroughly. Bobby tried to keep the game interesting by throwing the stick in a place where it might take Hero a little time to find it and bring it back.

After several tosses, Bobby faked a throw toward the ranch house, and when Hero started running that way, Bobby quickly turned around and threw it in the opposite direction, accurately tossing it behind a prickly pear cactus. Hero was fooled only briefly.

His sharp eyes caught the movement behind him and he whirled around and scurried over in the direction of the cactus. His nose and eyes soon located the stout stick, but instead of picking it up in his mouth, he started digging at the base of the cactus with his forepaws.

"What are you doing, boy?" Bobby asked in bewilderment, "Did you find a bone you buried and forgot about?

By the time Bobby walked over to the cactus, Hero had dug out about three inches of the gravely sand, revealing a canvas bag. Bobby stared in amazement at the lettering on the bag: "Cactus City Bank; FDIC Insured."

"OK, Hero, good job, boy," he said. "Looks like you've found the bank loot." He pulled the canvas bag from the ground, and it revealed another one beneath it. A quick check of the contents revealed bundles of cash in one and some silver bars in the other.

He thought aloud: "Who could have buried this here?"

"That would be me," declared a familiar voice behind him. Bobby turned around sharply to face Pokey Johnston, a cruel smile creasing her face, her gloved hand holding a small pistol. Hero immediately sensed that a supposed friend had become a foe and he bared his teeth with a low growl.

"OK, lemme make it simple for you and your meddlin' mutt. He takes one step toward me and he gets a bullet between the eyes," Pokey said through clenched teeth. "And I'm just the gal to do it. If you want to stay alive, lock that flea-bag in the tool shed, and then you climb up on Sunny Jim. Don't pull any tricks or the B-Bar-B will have two graves in the back forty. Now move!"

Bobby was too startled to do anything but comply with her orders. He got Hero in the tool shed and shoved a spike through the door clasps, locking the dog in. He glanced around for help but there was none as he walked toward the two mules.

"And keep your trap shut, or the only thing you'll hear next will be this here pistol," Pokey growled. As soon as Bobby was on Sunny Jim, she tied his ankles together under the mule's belly with baling cord. Then she quickly scooped up the two canvas sacks, slung them into her saddle bags, climbed into the saddle on Gertrude, and rode off, with Bobby in tow behind on the other mule. Within minutes, they were out of sight, in the foothills of Cougar Mountain.

Windy was the first to discover Bobby's disappearance. He was roused out of the ravine, where he had his nose in his bull-fighting notebook, by the whining of Hero, confined in the tool shed. Windy released the animal who barked furiously at the old-timer, trying to convey the news of Bobby's kidnapping. Windy called for Bobby over and over and when he got no response, he telephoned Tex at Tia Maria's mother's house.

"You find Harka and Irish right away," Tex said. "I'll phone the sheriff's office with a missing person report before I leave here. I'll get back to the B-Bar-B as quickly as I can."

Windy had located Harka and Irish, and the rest of the cowhands by the time Tex Mason retuned to the ranch. Harka had already examined the immediate property for clues and he reported his findings to Tex.

"Tracks show Pokey's mules come back. Much easy to see, one mule have crack in one horseshoe. Little boots of Bobby-boy stop at mule tracks," the Indian said.

"Good work, campadre," Tex replied. "I had my suspicions about Miz Pokey, but now we know that she not only broke into the Cactus City Bank, but she also kidnapped Bobby."

"Doggone it, Tex, you're going too fast for me. How do you know she had anything to do with the bank burglary?" Windy asked, "The sheriff said it was three fellers."

"I'll explain later; right now we've got to rescue Bobby before Pokey Johnston does him any more harm. Saddle up, Riders, and let's go!"

Many miles away, Pokey rode her mule briskly, with Bobby behind on Sunny Jim, as they worked their way up the foothills of Cougar Mountain, toward the tracks of the Texas & Western Railroad which bisected the twin peaks of Sugarloaf and Aspen Tip. "I'm not gonna kill you, sonny, unless I have to. Looks like easy street for ol' Pokey now anyway. In a couple of hours, we'll reach the railroad tracks where I hop on the freight train that's coming through about that time. Of course, you and the mules will be securely tied up in the sagebrush when I leave, but with luck, your friends will find you before you die of thirst."

"I don't understand why you came back to the ranch so soon today," Bobby wondered.

"That's simple. I hadn't gone far when I heard the sheriff's car. I was on a bluff and watched him drive into the B-Bar-B. I couldn't be sure how much he knew, but I figgered it was time to grab the loot and move on to the next phase of the plan."

With that, she cruelly yanked on the rope attached to Sunny Jim and both mules moved a little faster in the direction of the railroad tracks.

Her pursuers were gaining ground. Harka seemed to have no trouble tracking the two mules and their riders.

"This must be the easiest trackin ' you ever did, campadre," Tex said.

"Si, El Tejano. Bobby-boy make trail more better for Harka. Him drop marbles for follow."

"I noticed that. He must have had them in his pocket when he was snatched and he can drop one every now and then, without Pokey noticing" Tex said, "And I see he's also been breaking small branches with his boots so he can't be tied too tight. "

"Doggone it, Tex," complained Windy. "We want to know how come you suspected Pokey."

"Well, Windy, I knew there was something wrong with her from the start. You remember she said that Sunny Jim was the colt of her mule, Gertrude. That can't be. All mules, male or female, are sterile and they can't reproduce. Anybody who's been around mules knows that. At first I figured she was just a dangerous liar, and therefore, someone to be watched."

"Glory be, Tex. So how did you connect her to the bank job?" Irish wanted to know.

"I didn't, at first. But then two other facts emerged. Obviously Pokey couldn't have left Tia Maria's room at night without waking her. So how could she get to the bank? Well, as you know, Tia Maria overslept Saturday morning for the first time ever. I guessed that Pokey had secretly given some form of sleeping pills to Tia Maria. So our cook slept soundly through the night, not knowing her guest had left for the Cactus City Bank, and when the sleeping pills still hadn't worn off, she overslept."

"Wal, shore, I could have figgered that out too, if I'd jist put my mind to it," Windy boasted, "but the sheriff said there were the hoof-prints of three horses by the bank."

"That puzzled me too, Windy," Tex admitted, "until I phoned the sheriff's office to file a missing person's report on Bobby. His deputy told me about the horse that Loredo Tate reported stolen from the Circle 5 Ranch Friday night, which had turned up back in his pasture on Saturday morning. That spread is about halfway between the B-Bar-B and Cactus City. Pokey must have rode there with her two mules and borrowed Tate's horse for the bank burglary, to make it look like a group, rather than just one person. After the burglary, she put the horse back in the same pasture on her return trip to the B-Bar-B. She probably hid the loot somewhere on our ranch. I'm guessing Bobby found it and she vamoosed, taking the loot and the only witness with her."

Dark afternoon shadows were stretching across the stoney trail when Harka raised his arm slowly and quietly. "We plenty close now," he whispered. "They be less than quarter mile, in scrub pines ahead."

Tex's voice was barely audible but none of the Riders missed a syllable. "This is it, Riders, get off your horses quietly and tie them here. We go on foot the rest of the way. Irish, you take Waco and Windy and sneak around to the north of that grove and get as close as you can without being seen. Harka, you and I will go with Slim and come in from the south. Bobby's life is in danger, so don't make the slightest noise. And when you hear Harka hoot like an owl, move in and move in fast."

"You sure you want Harka and me to split up?" Irish asked in a hushed tone.

"Yep, I do. Now let's get started," Tex said, putting his finger to his lips as a caution reminder.

The two groups slowly and silently moved up the trail and around the scrub pine grove, each man blending into the shadows, carefully measuring each step to prevent any sound that would alarm the devious prospector.

Unaware of the B-Bar-B Riders' soundless approach, Pokey was bragging to the Cowboy Kid, who was seated on a rock, his wrists tied together. "Wal, half-pint, I shore fooled those stupid cowpokes on your ranch. Nobody figgered me for that bank job so now I'm forty grand richer and that freight train that's a comin' will take ol' Pokey right into Mexico where I can live like a queen on all that dough."

As if to confirm her boast, the sound of the freight train was heard chugging along as it neared their position. Pokey took a swig of her canteen as an owl hooted nearby. "Wal, I guess it's time for our good-byes, you little squirt. Reckon I better tie your ankles too afore I leave."

At that moment, the six B-Bar-B Riders materialized out of the shadows and rushed her. But she moved as quickly as a snake. She threw her canteen at the nearest cowboy, drew her pistol with one hand and grabbed Bobby with the other. She held him in front of her, the pistol barrel at his temple, as she barked: "Stay where you are or the kid dies!"

"Easy, fellers, do what she says," Tex ordered the others.

"Mebbe you're not so dumb, Mason," Pokey chided. "Now here's what we're gonna do. You cowpokes throw them guns behind you into the brush and then git flat down on the ground. Any tricks and this kid gets it!"

"You leave us no choice," Tex started to say, but Bobby twisted his head quickly and fastened his teeth on Pokey's gun hand. Harka and Tex dove through the air, knocking her to the ground as they disarmed her at the same time. Waco and Irish bound her arms behind her with a lariat.

"Now, Bobby." Tex teased, "that's no way to treat a lady."

"She ain't no lady," Windy exclaimed. "She's a dag-nabbed lying, thieving, hoss-stealing, desperado who otta be locked up forever."

"Don't count on it, Grandpa," Pokey smiled viciously. "I broke out of the Women's Prison before and I kin do it again."

"Sorry, Claudia, but it appears your string of luck has run out. You'll spend your declining years in prison drab gray," Tex replied. "And by the time you get out, a governor from this very state will have been elected to the White House."

The next day, Claudia Johnston was in federal custody on charges of bank burglary and kidnapping. Local law enforcement authorities congratulated the B-Bar-B Riders on solving the case and capturing Johnston. When the Riders all returned to the ranch, Windy announced he would no longer be studying to be a bull-fighter. "Wal, fellers, when I finished Lesson 5, I learned that I supposed to not just fight the bull, but kill him. Killing, 'cept in self-defense, just ain't in my nature. How could I ever look my horse, Mabel, in the eye, after I had killed some poor bull, just to hear the crowd yell 'Ole.' T'aint right, I figger, so I'm gonna cancel this course and put the balance of the money toward another course that'll make you Riders even more proud of Walter Wellington Wales."

"Glory be! What course would that be now?" asked Irish with apprehension.

"It's called: 'How To Become a Millionaire in the Stock Market' and, after just 20 lessons, I'll be the Wall Street Wonder of the Big Bend Country," Windy exclaimed.

"That sounds great, Windy," Tex said. "I reckon all of us on the B-Bar-B will feel better with you fighting bulls, and bears, in the Stock Market, instead of our corral." ♦

RED RYDER

Little Beaver's Schooling
by Frank Bresee

One of the most interesting characteristics about Painted Valley is the rolling hills and the lush scenery.

Red Ryder, Buckskin and Little Beaver know every part of the valley, and have protected the area from con men and bushwackers for many years. Things have settled down, and Red decides it's time for his Indian companion, Little Beaver, to go to school. Red has a two-fold reason for this. Number one, Little Beaver will be growing into manhood in a few years, and number two, he is a bit sweet on the new schoolmarm, Mary Hawkins.

Red reckons that he will have an opportunity to visit Miss Mary more often if Little Beaver is in school. Red makes arrangements for Miss Mary to pick up Little Beaver at the Painted Valley ranch, and drive him to school in her new buckboard.

On the way, Miss Mary lets Little Beaver take to reins and as he is trying his hand, a rattler moves quickly on the path and spooks the horse, which panics, runs into the arroyo, the buckboard turns over, and the horse breaks free. Miss Mary's leg is broken and she is in great pain. Little Beaver, using all his skills and knowledge, gathers up stray pieces of wood and makes a splint for Mary's leg. Little Beaver is not big enough or strong enough to set Mary's leg, but he has arranged it in a way so that it can't move around and get worse.

He then uses more wood to start a fire in order to keep Mary more comfortable. Again he calls upon his Indian skills to start the fire by rubbing two sticks together over parched grass.

It is now late in the afternoon and night is approaching. So are some of the wolves that prowl Painted Valley. Little Beaver collects more wood, and builds up a large fire to keep the wolves away. After several hours

Little Beaver runs out of firewood and it's too dark to venture in the woods to find more.

The wolves close in, but Little Beaver again calls upon his Indian upbringing, and gives the wolf cries himself. He gets down on all fours and pretends to be a wolf himself to confuse them. Fortunately, just at the crucial moment, as night fades into sunrise, an antelope runs across the horizon, and the wolves take off after it.

After an all-night vigil, the first light of dawn breaks in the East and Little Beaver is able to find more wood. He starts a fire and sends smoke signals. Red, who has been worried, sees the signals, and he and Buckskin arrive and rescue them.

Mary is very impressed with Little Beaver and the way he took charge of the situation, and also the fact that Red showed in quick order for the rescue. She invites them both to school the next day. Miss Mary realizes that she has a lot to learn from Little Beaver, while he has a lot to learn from her.

Red, for once in his life, has a lot to learn from both of them. ◆

THE MAN CALLED X

Crisis in Cairo
by Charles A. Beckett

Ken Thurston hurried down the hall to the Bureau Chief's office. His mind was still on his recent assignment as a trouble-shooter at the World Council Conference.

"Hi, Betty. What's the chief want to see me about?"

"I don't know, Mr. Thurston. But he seems upset. Go on in."

Entering the chief's office, Ken found him pacing impatiently back and forth.

"What's up, Chief?"

"Where have you been, Ken? I had Betty page you an hour ago."

"Sorry. I had some unfinished business to attend to."

"Well, never mind. Sit down. We've got a problem."

"Oh? And what would that be, Chief?"

"Frank Reynolds is unaccounted for."

"Isn't he in Cairo looking into that international antiquities smuggling matter?"

"That's right. Well, I haven't heard from him for over a week. That's not like him. He's always been dependable about reporting in on a regular basis. All our efforts to contact him have been unsuccessful. He seems to have dropped out of sight."

"That is odd."

"Odd doesn't start to cover it. I want you to get over there and find out what's going on. In my last contact with him, Reynolds indicated that he was on the verge of a breakthrough in flushing out a key player in the illegal Egyptian artifacts market. On its surface, this isn't ordinarily something the bureau would get involved in. But this operation is so big that it could have not only serious political implications, but could also affect the world money market, the balance of trade, and result in the funneling

99

of money into the hands of the free world's enemies. Betty's got you booked on the afternoon flight to Cairo."

"OK, Chief. I'm on my way." Just as Ken opened the door to leave, Pegon Zeldschmidt—the small, ferret-like snitch the bureau often used to obtain information from sources outside official channels—burst in from the outer office, nearly colliding with Ken.

"Pegon! What are you doing here?"

"Are you not happy to see me, Mr. X?" Pegon—a young man of uncertain ancestry—was one of the few people who still addressed Ken by the code name he had used when the bureau had a link to the FBI. In a peculiar way, Ken liked the little man, but had never fully trusted him—knowing of his reputation for working dangerously close to the other side of the law on occasion, when it was in his financial best interests.

"I just came by to pick up my ticket."

"What ticket?"

"Why, my ticket for our flight to Egypt."

"Our flight to Egypt? What do you mean, *our* flight to Egypt?"

"Ken, Pegon's going with you," the chief interjected.

"Oh, no he's not!"

"Oh, yes he is!" The chief's firm reply left no room for doubt or argument. "Pegon is familiar with Cairo and speaks the language, which could give you a hold card if you should need it."

Egypt is the home of the Sphinx, pyramids, the Suez Canal, and the Nile river—along which most of the country's population lives. Cairo, founded nearly a thousand years ago, is the largest city on the continent of Africa, and the capital of the country. Egypt is a land of history, mystery and intrigue—with countless secrets and treasures still buried beneath the burning sands of its deserts. Tomb robbers and other opportunists have preyed on the dead—and the living—since the first pyramids were built over 5,000 years ago. Assassins, cutthroats, men of all ilk, still exist—waiting for any opportunity to work their evil schemes on the unsuspecting and the unprepared—for financial gain and power.

The flight was long, but uneventful. It gave Ken an opportunity to read the case file he had been given. By the time the plane began its descent to the Cairo airport, he felt he had enough background information to begin an investigation. Among other things, he learned that Reynolds had been working undercover as an archaeology assistant at a dig in the desert being conducted by an archaeologist from an American university.

The lumbering twin engine plane touched down lightly on the runway. Looking out the window as the plane taxied to the disembarking area, Pegon remarked excitedly, "Well, here we are, Mr. X. Beautiful Cairo."

After a brief taxi ride, the pair arrived at the El-Azar Hotel. As they were checking in, Ken asked the desk clerk about Frank Reynolds. The clerk averted Ken's eyes, hesitated, and then said, "Oh, yes—Mr. Reynolds, the American archaeologist. He was with us for two weeks, but then he left unexpectedly—without taking his luggage or personal effects with him. I've stored them in the back, until he returns for them. He was easy to remember because he was often seen with a beautiful dark-haired woman. Odd, Ken thought, half aloud. There was no mention of a woman in any of Reynolds' reports, and he was not a casual ladies man.

"Would you know the woman's name?"

"It's here in the register. Let me see. Oh, yes. Miss Martine Ornet."

"Did she leave a forwarding address?"

"No need. She's still registered."

"What's her room number?"

"Room 203."

Ken wasted no time in appearing before her door and knocking. After a brief pause, the door opened—warily. The desk clerk had been accurate in his description. She *was* beautiful. Long dark hair, an olive complexion, and a figure that men only dream about.

"Yes?" she asked in a soft, cool voice. If the face didn't get your attention, the voice most certainly would, Ken thought. He was reminded of what a senior agent had once told him early in his career—"Beware of a woman with a luscious voice!"

"My name's Ken Thurston. I'm sorry to disturb you. But I've just arrived in Cairo, and understand that you are acquainted with an old friend of mine—Frank Reynolds."

"No, I don't believe so." Ken showed her a picture of Reynolds. "No, I've never seen that man before." There was no change in her expression or her tone of voice. Odd, Ken thought. A word he seemed to be using a bit too often, lately.

"The hotel clerk said he had seen the two of you together."

"He must have been mistaken," the cool voice countered. Ken decided not to pursue the subject further.

"How long have you been in Egypt?" he asked, changing the subject.

"Not long. I come and I go. I enjoy the travel, the history, the culture and the people."

Ken was eager to find out more about her, but that would have to wait. This obviously wasn't the time. She wasn't going to open up to him easily. He thanked her for her time, then returned downstairs and entered the hotel dining room. There, as expected, he found Pegon busily attacking a large platter of food he had captured from the buffet table.

"Oh! Mr. X. I was just wondering where you were. I thought I would have a little snack while I waited for you."

"I'm going out to the dig, Pegon. You stay here until I get back."

"I'll go with you in case you need a translator."

"No, I would rather you stay here. The man in charge is an American. I don't anticipate any language problems."

Without further comment, Pegon turned his attention back to the food in front of him. Ken walked outside and approached the driver of a taxi parked in the waiting zone of the hotel. "Do you know where the American archaeological dig is—the one outside Giza, near Saqqara?" The driver rewarded him with a blank stare, and said something in Arabic.

Ken held up a hand, indicating he wanted the man to wait. He hurried back into the hotel restaurant, where Pegon was still busily bent over his food.

"Come on, Pegon," Ken said reluctantly, turning back toward the hotel entrance at the same instant. Pegon smiled slyly, quickly forked in two more bites of food, wiped his mouth, and followed Ken outside to the waiting taxi. Ken gave directions to his desired destination, which Pegon relayed quickly and easily to the driver.

A bumpy, dusty 35-minute ride later, the duo arrived in front of a large canvas safari tent situated among sand mounds, rubble, native workers, and excavating tools and equipment. A small, round, heavily bespectacled man rapidly approached them.

"Ah, visitors," he said, with obvious delight. "I'm Professor Hiram Langton. What may I do to be of assistance to you?" His description in the case file didn't do him justice, although no picture had been included. Getting right to the point, Ken said, "I'm Ken Thurston, and this is my..uh..assistant, Pegon Zeldschmidt. We're looking for an old friend— Frank Reynolds. We understand he's been working with you."

"Ah, yes. Strange young man, your Mr. Reynolds. A bright and capable lad, but he suddenly disappeared without any notice. Not very professional. No, sir, not very professional at all."

"That's why I'm concerned. He's usually very reliable, and I'm worried that something may have happened to him."

Langston shrugged his shoulders. "All I know is that the curator of the museum sponsoring this expedition sent me a wire saying that Mr. Reynolds would be joining my team as an administrative assistant—which I really have no need for. But…since the museum is funding this project, I was in no position to refuse him. However, it seemed that Mr. Reynolds was preoccupied with something else. He spent a great deal of time away from the site, wandering the desert, and talking to disreputable-looking types in Giza and Cairo. Or so I've been told. That's all I know. Perhaps my team leader, Abdulla, can be of some further assistance."

Abdulla El Gandor turned out to be a tall, thin, swarthy man with intense eyes and an expressionless, bearded face. Through Pegon, he told Ken that he knew nothing about the American's whereabouts—then abruptly turned and walked away.

"Well, now that's a friendly fellow, don't you think, Mr. X?" For once, Ken had to agree with Pegon, and nodded accordingly.

Arriving back at the hotel, they found a balding, middle-aged man wearing a rumpled and sweat stained khaki uniform waiting for them in the lobby. Pulling himself up to his full five-and-a-half-foot height, he proudly introduced himself—in heavily accented English—as Inspector Ramad Hagra of the Cairo Police Department. He had a somber, official expression on his face.

"I'm afraid I have bad news for you, Mr. Thurston. Your friend has been found—in an alley behind a Cairo bar, with a knife in his back. He died on the way to the hospital."

Although Ken had dealt with death many times in his career, it never got any easier.

"Did he say anything before he died?"

"No. But he had written M-A-R in blood, on the wall beside him," the inspector explained.

M-A-R? Of course, Martine, Ken thought to himself. He returned to the desk, where the clerk was attempting to look busy, shuffling and sorting papers.

"Is Miss Ornet in her room?"

"No sir. She checked out about an hour ago, right after I came on duty."

"Did she leave a forwarding address?"

"No sir. Sorry."

"You say you still have Mr. Reynolds' suitcase in the back?"

"Yes sir. I'll get it for you."

Ken did not expect to find anything in the suitcase that would be helpful, but it was worth a look. He carried the bag up to his room and examined it thoroughly. Nothing unusual. Going through the pockets, however, he discovered a matchbook with a picture of a pyramid and the words "Golden Pyramid Bar" and an address embossed on its cover.

"Pegon, I want you to check this place out. Here's the address." He handed him the matchbook.

"At last. Some action. What am I looking for, Mr. X?"

"Just go there, have a drink or two and observe what's going on."

After Pegon left, Ken placed a collect call to the chief from an outside telephone booth.

"Chief, there's some things I need you to check out for me." Ken gave him the information.

"Are you sure this is important, Ken?"

"I don't know yet. But I have a hunch it might help answer some questions I have."

"O.K. I'll get back to you."

"Thanks, Chief."

With Pegon out of his way for a while, Ken was able to do some serious thinking. Something was not the way it should be, and he did not know what or why. He mentally reviewed everything that he had learned from the case file, and everything he had seen and heard since he arrived in Egypt. His concentration was broken by Pegon's high pitched voice.

"I'm back, Mr. X."

"Learn anything?"

"No. Everything looked the way it was supposed to in a bar. Oh, one thing. I did see Miss Ornet in a corner booth, talking to a man."

"What did he look like?"

"Like the desk clerk. Actually, it *was* the desk clerk. Not the one on duty now, but the other one."

"Could you hear what they were saying?"

"No. They were talking real low, with their heads close together. But it must have been something important. They both looked very serious."

"Good man, Pegon. Stay here."

Ken approached the desk and asked where the other clerk was. He was told that it was Raoul's day off. As Ken started back to his room, a phone rang in the background. Over his shoulder, he heard the clerk's voice.

"Mr. Thurston. You have a telephone call."

"Hello? Oh, hi, Chief. What did you find out?"

Ken listened intently to the chief's report—then hung up the phone and started up the stairs. He met Pegon coming down.

"I got worried, Mr. X. Thought I better check on you."

"Get the inspector, Pegon. We're going back out to the dig site."

Within minutes, Pegon appeared back in the lobby with the inspector.

"What is the urgency, Mr. Thurston?"

"Do you have your car nearby, Inspector?"

"Of course."

"Good. We need you to go with us out to the archaeological encampment. I'll explain as we go."

When they arrived at the site, the workers were sitting idly under a large tent flap, in a futile attempt to escape the blistering afternoon sun. The professor and El Gandor were nowhere to be seen.

"Where's Professor Langton?" Ken asked, in the general direction of the resting workmen. At that moment, the little man appeared from around the corner of the tent.

"Ah, Mr. Thurston. How nice to see you again."

"Maybe you won't think so, when I tell why I'm here...Mr. von Behren!"

"Why, what do you mean?"

"You can drop the phony act. I know who you are. You're Otto von Behren, trader in illegal antiquities, gun smuggler, and revolution financier. My suspicions were first aroused when I asked you about a certain tomb. You told me that it was a typical example of the 18th Dynasty, built for the pharaoh Horenheb. Professor Langton would have recognized it as the 19th Dynasty tomb of Tia. What have you done with the real Langton?"

"Too bad for you, Mr. Thurston. You will never know." von Behren pulled a pistol from his field jacket pocket. "You are just a little too smart for your own good. Unfortunately, the arrival of your Mr. Reynolds caused me some inconvenience, and I had to alter some of my plans. I began to suspect that he was sent here to spy on me. So I had to have him removed before he learned too much. In Cairo, such matters can easily be arranged.

There are always men around willing to do whatever needs to be done—if the price is right. Stand still! You too, Inspector! Do not move, or I will have to shoot you." With that said, von Behren began backing toward a Land Rover parked nearby.

"Drop the gun!" All eyes immediately focused on El Gandor, who had stepped quickly out from the shade of the tent. A rifle was cradled in his arms and pointed at the escaping man. With surprising agility, von Behren turned his weapon from Ken and the inspector and fired at El Gandor. Before he fell, the Egyptian managed to fire back a single shot. Von Behren slumped into the sand.

The inspector rushed to von Behren and removed the pistol from his hand. At the same time, he placed his fingers on the fallen man's carotid artery. He was dead. Ken had gone to see about El Gandor, who was on the ground next to the tent. Fortunately, his wound was superficial, the bullet having only grazed his side.

Later that day, after El Gandor had his wound attended to at the hospital, he, Ken and the inspector discussed and reflected on recent events. Now speaking in fluent English, El Gandor revealed that he was a member of the Egyptian secret service, and had been working with Reynolds, gathering evidence on the theft and transportation out of Egypt of the country's natonal treasures. He apologized to Ken for being so rude at their first meeting. He said that he had not known who Thurston was working for at the time.

Initially, no one had been suspicious of the phony professor. He had killed the real Langton before anyone else had seen him. Then he took his identity, hired some local workers, and had them randomly digging in the sand and clearing stone rubble. It had been a perfect cover for his black market activities. He had been serving as a fence for tomb robbers who needed an outlet for their stolen property—and who were willing to take pennies on the dollar for their valuable loot. It had been a very lucrative venture—while it lasted.

Shortly after the shootings in the desert, the inspector dispatched a squad of police officers to search the archaeological encampment and surrounding area. They had discovered the professor's body, half buried under sand, among a pile of stones and other debris.

Pegon, quiet to this point, asked, "But what about Miss Ornet and the hotel clerk?"

"I can explain that," Ken said. "They were go-betweens for von Behren, making contacts and arrangements to move items out of the country, sell them, and transfer the money to a group of international revolutionaries. Frank Reynolds befriended Miss Ornet in the hopes of getting a line on von Behren's operation. When his questioning began to arouse her suspicions, she informed von Behren, and he arranged to have Reynolds killed. Then, when we arrived and I started asking questions, Miss Ornet began to get nervous. She convinced her partner, Raoul Bressen, that it was a good time for them to leave the country."

"So they both got away?"

"No, Pegon. When I called the home office, I asked the chief to run background checks on Professor Langton and Martine Ornet—also known in international circles as Simone Bornet. As soon as she and Bressen dropped out of sight, I had the inspector place surveillance on all departing flights from the Cairo Airport—since that was the fastest and most likely escape route for the pair. When they boarded a plane, the Italian police were notified that the two were headed for Rome. They were arrested by the police when they landed. Bresson hadn't been aware that the professor and Reynolds had been killed. When he found out, he was more than willing to cooperate with the Italian police. He told them the whole story of the operation—in hopes of receiving a reduction in his punishment.

"So that's the end of it, huh, Mr. X?"

"Unfortunately, no, Pegon. It's the same old story and the same old game. Anything for a crooked dollar. It's a treacherous game that's being played all over the world by treacherous people. You just have to keep winning, that's all," Ken said, with a touch of sadness in his voice. "You just have to keep on winning!" ◆

NIGHTBEAT

A Dancer, a Soldier, a Villain
by Bryan Powell

Hi, this is Randy Stone. I cover the night beat for the Chicago *Star*.

My stories begin in many different ways. This one began with a desperate girl and ended with an even more desperate man.

If you've ever worked a night shift, you know it's easy to feel out of step with the rest of the world, like you're swimming against the current. You're going to work while most of your neighbors are coming home. You work while they sleep, and hit the rack while their coffee is brewing.

This is not a complaint. I like my beat just fine, but on some nights, especially the bone-chilling variety for which our Windy City is famous, it takes a little extra juice to get the old motor to turn over.

It was just such a night, so I was bound for the Crescent Moon, an all-night beanery where I'm known to stop in for a cup of joe and a bear claw, or maybe a full-fledged bacon 'n' eggs breakfast.

I was just turning the corner toward my destination, my mouth already watering with thoughts of that sweet pastry topped with sliced almonds, when my reverie was broken by a ruckus inside the diner.

Through the double-glass doors burst the figure of a waifish young girl making a mad dash out of the place like ol' Enos Slaughter headin' for the barn.

"Stop her! My money! Call the police! Come back here!" It was Pops McNulty, who ran the joint, yelling frantically. He was dressed in his apron and paper hat, crisp and white like any good counter man would wear it, and he was chasing the girl out of the door.

Sure as sunrise, the girl had a fistful of greenbacks in her left hand. She turned in my direction, still at full gallop, and I turned to tackle her like a Bears linebacker moving in for the hit. As I reached for her, though, she spun, twisting quickly from my grasp, and scooted past me toward the intersection behind us.

She ran into the intersection, apparently oblivious to the risk she was taking, and darted right in front of a car. As luck would have it, it was a prowl car, a police cruiser, and the black-and-white made a nose-down stop just inches from the young girl's kneecaps, tires and brakes squealing in protest.

The girl was stunned for a moment by the near miss, and froze in her tracks. Before she could bolt away again, a police officer emerged from behind the wheel of the car and pointed a snub-nosed .38 at her chest.

"Stop right there," the policeman said. "Don't you move an inch." There was a nervous edge in his voice. Fear? Nah. Couldn't be. In any case, he was holding the gun.

The girl stood perfectly still, mortified, her hands up beside her head, the money still protruding from her hand.

"Don't shoot me!" she pleaded.

I was standing next to the cruiser by then, as the policeman moved toward the girl.

"I saw her coming out of McNulty's place," I explained. "I think she must have snatched the money from the till and made a run for it."

"Quiet," the cop said.

"Now wait a minute, I'm only trying to—"

He had the girl by the collar now, and he turned and pointed the gun at the space between my eyes.

"Shut up and get in the car," he said. There was something manic in his eyes now. I started to protest, but I could see the rounded points of the bullets in the chambers of his revolver, and I decided to do what he said. Shut up. Get in the car.

Something was wrong with this picture. It began to register as I moved toward the rear passenger door. His uniform coat wasn't buttoned fully. He needed a shave and maybe a bath as well. I didn't know what to make of it.

He prodded me into the rear seat with the gun and shoved the girl in on top of me.

"You make a lovely couple," he said.

The girl recoiled from me and sat straight up in the seat.

"Are you all right?" I asked her.

She gave me a fleeting, wild-eyed glance. She was small, maybe five feet three, dressed in a floppy hat, a loose white shirt and dark overalls. Her blonde hair, which she wore in a bob that barely reached her shoulders, was in need of a good washing. Still, it was plain to see at just a glance that there was a beautiful young lady lurking incognito under her boyish attire. Her complexion was rosy and smooth, and her eyes were brown and radiant, her lips full.

She didn't answer my question. She was looking for a way out, but the rear doors of the prowl car didn't open from the inside. That fact registered with her in short order. Then she fixated, with a puzzled expression, on the man sitting in the passenger seat in front of her. My eyes followed hers, noticing the second police officer for the first time.

I took one look at him and the tumblers started to fall into place. He was a small man, but stocky and muscular, with disheveled black hair, a lock of which was hanging in an unruly curl over his forehead. He was not wearing his uniform cap. He had a gun, a bigger one than his partner's, and he waved it carelessly in our direction.

Three-point-six million souls in the Windy City and this had to happen to me.

"Well, look-ah here. It is your lucky day," he said, in an accent that was clearly Eastern European. "You just hitched a free ride. And are we not the city's finest boys in blue?"

No. They were not.

"Who are you?" I asked. "You're obviously not policemen. What do you want from us?"

By now the other officer—or the man I had thought was a police officer—had climbed back behind the wheel. He put the car into gear and we sped away from the intersection.

"We have ourselves a tiny bit of a problem," said the man in the passenger seat. "We robbed a bank this afternoon, then a couple of hours ago we shot a couple of police mens," he said with affectation. "POE-leese-menz," he snarled. "But we have their beautiful handguns, their uniforms and their car. Ha! Then we made a little detour to…what's the phrase? Yes, an ol' Mom 'n' Pop just down the road. Stocked in some necessary provisions. The proprietor he didn't like that, but his protesting days, they are finished. Protect and serve, isn't that what they say?"

"So what's the problem?" I asked. "What do you want with the girl, and with me?"

"Now what *would* I want with the girl?" he answered, giving her a carnivorous leer. "But first, we need to get out of this city, and a hostage or two might be quite useful."

The driver took a right turn, sharply. We were heading south now, along the lakefront. The man in the passenger seat considered me for a moment.

"You look like you might know your way around, yes, pretty boy? Do you know Chicago?"

"Why?" I answered.

My defiance apparently enraged him. He cocked the gun and pressed the end of the barrel against the girl's forehead.

"You will answer my question!" he ordered.

"Okay, okay, just take it easy with that thing," I said gently, motioning to the gun. "It just might go off, and then what have you got? One less hostage, right?"

He pulled the gun away slowly and eased the hammer back into its resting position.

"I am waiting," he said.

"Yes, I know the city. I know every side street, short cut and alleyway from here to Kenosha. Or would you prefer Kankakee? Kalamazoo?"

"You talk too much," the driver interrupted. There was a quiver in his voice. "Stan, get me another one," he said.

There was a rustling sound as the passenger reached into a crumbled brown bag in the floorboard and pulled out a bottle of Pabst Blue Ribbon. The bottle glistened with condensation. He used an edge of the dashboard as a bottle opener, popped off the cap and handed the bottle to his partner.

"To your health, Mr. Boone," he said to the driver. He looked back at us. "You Americans, with your weakness for beer. It will make you fat and lazy. A good vodka is always a much better choice."

It was plain that ol' Stan had a snootful of something under his belt. Vodka it was, then. At that moment, I could have used one myself.

"Look, Stan, right? We have something in common," I told him. "We all want to get out of this alive. Let's use our heads. We can do it, together."

"What do you have in mind, pretty boy?"

"My name is Stone. Randy Stone. I'm a reporter for the Chicago Star. And if you think I'm pretty, you need your eyes examined. Or maybe you've just had too much of that potato juice."

He took the measure of me, slowly, but I'm not sure I would trust his arithmetic at this point. Then he glanced at the girl.

"Well, surely you are pretty enough. What is your name, missy?"

She didn't answer. The man took the gun barrel and used it to flick the girl's cap off. He looked at her and waited.

"Andrea," she said softly. "Andrea Turner."

"Ahn-DRAY-yah," the man repeated in a childlike sing-song. "My name is Stanislav Vladu, but you may call me Stan. We will be good friends, yes?"

"Leave her alone," I said. "We'd better pay attention to getting out of town. How far do you think you'll get in this police car?"

Vladu leaned over to Boone and mumbled something I couldn't hear. They conferred quietly for a moment, ignoring us. I slid over toward Andrea.

"Guess the old saying is true, huh?"

She stared at me blankly.

"You know. 'Crime does not pay,'" I continued. "What were you doing running out of McNulty's place with his money?"

"I needed it."

"Don't we all?" I said.

"This is all your fault. If you hadn't chased me..."

"McNulty's my friend. I should let someone rob his place?" I answered.

"I hadn't eaten in two days, and I didn't have money to afford a place to sleep tonight."

"You're not from around here, are you? Have you been in Chicago long?"

"No. I'm a dancer, also an actress and singer, but a dancer most of all. I came down from Saginaw five weeks ago. My father died last spring and my mother and I don't see eye-to-eye. I had a friend here in a theater production. I thought he had gotten me a part, but he really had other things in mind. I've had to pawn some of my clothes, even a ring my father gave me. I loved that ring." She paused. "Are they going to kill us?"

"Not if I can help it," I said.

"Enough!" Vladu said. "Alright, Missssster Stone, we have a plan. We need another car, one that the police will not recognize. And you and my girlfriend are coming with us. You understand clearly?"

Within a mile, we saw a garage and turned in. Boone flashed his badge at the night man as we entered. It was easy enough. We found a shiny '49 Chevy Fleetline, a crisp little four-door torpedo of a car, with the keys under the floor mat. Vladu dragged Andrea into the vehicle, pushing her in the backseat and following her in. I could easily have escaped while this was going on, but I wasn't about to leave her behind.

At the garage exit we plowed through the gate without slowing down. It shattered like glass. The night man, who appeared to have been asleep in his chair, jumped with a start. He would no doubt phone the police immediately. Whether he had a good look at our vehicle, I couldn't say.

We passed the stockyards, still heading south. I guided Boone away from the areas where we'd most likely see prowl cars. I wanted to get out of this in one piece, and get Andrea through it as well, and I didn't believe that would happen in a shootout with the police.

In the backseat, Vladu was whispering to Andrea, and trying to nuzzle at her neck. She didn't like it. He seemed to prefer it that way.

"I will *not*," I heard her tell him, resolutely.

"Stan, leave her alone," Boone said. "This is not the time."

"Who are you to tell Stan what is a good time? I want a good time now."

Suddenly, Boone jerked the wheel to the right, knocking all of us off balance. The right side tires scrubbed the curbing, climbed the sidewalk momentarily before sliding back down as the car came to a stop.

Before I had gathered my bearings, Boone had turned, leaning and reaching into the backseat. He stuffed his .38 into Vladu's mouth. As he held the gun, I noticed that his left eye was twitching, and he was perspiring, despite the cold.

Vladu looked him in the eyes calmly, but with resignation, and nodded. Boone moved the gun back, just a half inch or so.

"I was just kidding, my friend. We will wait," Vladu offered.

I exhaled, and realized that I hadn't been breathing.

"You take chances, Boone. You know that?" Vladu continued. He sighed and stretched. "I need to sleep now. Should we kill them before I sleep, or do you think they'll behave?"

"We'll behave," I volunteered.

"And what about you, Precious?" he asked. "I have this gun. Will you try to take it from me if I sleep?"

The gun was pushed firmly into his waistband. It would have been extremely dangerous to try to take it from him, even if he were passed out from drinking.

"Go to sleep, Stan," Boone said. "You're safe."

In a moment, Vladu was snoring quietly. Andrea relaxed a little and studied him. Then she spoke to Boone.

"Why can't you let me go? You don't need me. You need him," she said, pointing in my direction.

"I need you both," he answered. Perhaps, I thought, but with Vladu asleep, Boone was vulnerable. Maybe I could hit him, steer the car off the road so we'd crack up. But then, that could be dangerous, too. I chose another approach.

"So, Boone, tell me the truth. What are you doing here? Somehow, you don't seem like the criminal type."

"Mind your own business," he answered.

"What have you got to lose?" I asked him.

Boone sighed heavily and looked in the rear view mirror.

"Look, Stone. It's Stone, right?"

"Yep."

"That bank we hit today? I used to work there. Before the war, that was *my* bank. I was the branch manager. Had thirty people working for me. I also had a wife and a daughter and a nice house…"

His voice trailed off.

"What happened?" I asked.

"I was in the Marines. Had a platoon of men under my command in the South Pacific. I was captured, along with most of my men. I spent two years in a Japanese prison camp. I watched my men die, one by one, in that camp. Tortured, skewered with bayonets, shot, beaten to death. Others died from starvation, dysentery, malaria, dengue fever…I came home. Not one of my men did."

"Boone, I'm sorry," I said. "But it was the war, and—"

"And I survived, and I came home to find that my job at the bank had gone to another man, and that my wife had taken up with a 4-Fer. Can you imagine that? My wife, Joanne, my daughter, Marie, and a man who didn't serve his country because he was color-blind. And they sing about 'When Johnny Comes Marching Home Again.' Ha!"

"That's tough, Boone, really tough, but—"

"So I met Stan yesterday, drinking in a bar downtown—he's a hard man, you'd better not cross him—and after a few too many vodka shots we decided I was going to pay them back at the bank. Going to have the last laugh, make a little withdrawal. And I was going to show Joanne. She had tried to come back to me, you know, but it was too late. How could I forgive her?"

"People make mistakes, Boone," I said. "That's what makes us human."

Andrea leaned forward. "If she loves you, it's never too late," she said.

Boone started to speak, but suddenly the wail of a siren erupted behind us, accompanied by the flashing lights of a prowl car. Ahead of us, another police cruiser emerged from a side street and slid into position, blocking our path.

Boone mashed the brake pedal on the Chevy and the car skidded sideways to a stop. The prowl car in front of us was probably thirty feet away. The trailing car pulled into a parallel position behind us, roughly twenty feet distant.

The commotion woke Vladu suddenly, just in time to hear a policeman speak through a bullhorn.

"Walter Boone! Stanislav Vladu! Let the hostages go now, and come out with your hands up!"

Vladu swung the rear passenger door open, grabbed Andrea, wrapped his burly arm around her neck in a choke hold and put the gun to her ear. He climbing out, lifting her forcefully by the neck. She clawed at his arm in an effort to breathe.

"You go away now, or she will be dead," Vladu shouted.

He knew the cops wouldn't dare take a shot at him. They were armed only with handguns, maybe a shotgun, none of which would let them shoot him without grave risk of harm to Andrea.

What Vladu underestimated was the determination—or perhaps the desperation—of Andrea, the little dancer from Saginaw. As I watched from my seat in the car, helpless, Andrea arched her back and kicked Vladu's shins hard with both of her heels. It was a foolish maneuver, because he very well could have squeezed the trigger of his gun in spontaneous response to the pain. He didn't, though, and in that moment as his knees buckled, Andrea was able to twist away from his grasp, falling and rolling underneath the Chevy.

Before Vladu could recover, at least five well-placed shots struck him front and center, knocking him backward over the curb, his body toppling a large wire trash can as he collapsed into a twisted, dead heap.

I became aware of several more shots being fired, coming from the area of the prowl car in front of us. I thought of Andrea, under the car. Vladu couldn't hurt her any more, but Boone still could. I turned to him and was shocked to discover that the driver's side door was open and he was gone.

Somehow, in the fracas, with the police momentarily focused on Vladu and Andrea, Boone had made it from the car to the buildings across the street as gunfire peppered the pavement around his feet. Most of these buildings were condemned and unoccupied, slated to be torn down in the wave of new development in the city.

Boone kicked open the door of the nearest building and fled inside, disappearing up a flight of stairs just inside the door. In a matter of moments, a half dozen policemen were in the building in pursuit.

I got out of the Chevy and helped Andrea to her feet. She was shaking, but she was not crying. I put my arms around her.

"It's okay now," I said. "That was a brave thing you did. Foolish, dangerous, but brave, and you're alive and safe because of what you did, because you had the courage to do it."

A policeman gave us a first-aid kit. I helped Andrea tend to scrapes on her elbows and palms where she'd fallen from Vladu's grasp. An ambulance arrived, but she refused to get in.

"I'm okay," she said. And indeed, she was.

A police detective, just on the scene, was beginning to ask me questions about our ordeal when another officer approached me.

"You're Stone?" he asked.

"Yes, I am."

"We've got this man Boone trapped on the roof. We could take him, I'm sure, but we might lose a man or two in the process. He says he wants to talk to you."

"Me? Why?" I asked.

"I don't know. My sergeant sent me down here to get you."

In less than a minute, I was standing on a dark, flat roof with at least ten police officers behind, all with weapons trained in the general vicinity of my back. Boone was at the southeast corner of the rooftop, tucked in behind a massive exhaust vent and a smaller brick partition. I approached his position slowly, my hands away from my body, palms up. My shoes crunched over the small white pebbles that covered the rooftop.

"Boone, it's me. Randy Stone!" I yelled.

"Are you alone?" he shouted.

I replied that I was.

"Stone, come here slowly. I won't hurt you. I want to talk to you."

I slowly walked around the vent. Boone was resting heavily in the corner where the vent met the brick partition. He'd been hit at least twice in his sprint to the building, and was bleeding from his right shoulder and lower leg. His breathing was labored.

"Stone, I need you to do something for me. It's important."

"What's that, Boone?"

"I'm never getting off this rooftop alive. You know that, don't you?"

"Boone, I can walk you right out of here, right now. Just put down the gun," I told him. "There's an ambulance waiting at the street. You can be at the hospital in a matter of minutes."

"Then what?" he said. "Life in prison? I've already spent all the time in prison that I ever care to spend. I can't do it. I won't. Do you understand?"

I paused. "Yes. I think I do," I said. I knelt down in front of him. Beads of perspiration covered his forehead. His shoulder was bleeding profusely.

"Stone, I need you to tell my story. First of all, I didn't kill anyone. Stan shot both of the cops, and the old man at the grocery store. Make sure the truth is told."

"I will, Boone."

"And tell people what happened to me, when I came home from the Pacific. Make them understand—"

He took a great gasp of air, and another, before continuing.

"—about the bank, and about Joanne. Tell my story, all of it. I'm sorry for what I did, but I'm not ashamed. Tell the truth."

Boone gulped another breath of air, more shallowly this time, then slumped, motionless. He was dead.

There are some people you can save, and some you cannot. But I am here to see to it that the true story of Walter Boone is told, right here in the Chicago *Star*.

As for Andrea Turner, she's pursuing her dream of a life as a dancer. It turns out that Stanislav Vladu was no small-time hood. He was a gun smuggler, and there was a federal reward for his capture. I was able to convince the authorities that Andrea was entitled to some of that money. It was enough to square things with McNulty and enough to buy her a bus ticket to New York. It was enough to ensure that, with any lucky breaks at all, her dream would have a chance to come true. That's all we can ask for, isn't it? She wouldn't need to pawn her clothes, or the ring her father gave her, a ring she was able to buy back from the pawnshop just before she boarded the bus to New York.

That's the story, true to the last word.

Copy boy!   ♦

THE JACK BENNY PROGRAM

The Fred Allen Murder Case
by Laura Wagner

"Jack Benny is so cheap he won't eat in the sun. He's afraid his shadow might ask him for a bite."

"If Benny keeps making pictures he's going to make fresh-air fiends out of a lot of theatergoers."

"He squeezes a nickel so hard the E Pluribus laps over the Unum."

The audience attending comedian Fred Allen's radio broadcast was howling with laughter. Allen smiled to himself, waiting for the final applause of the evening to die down. He loved heaping these verbal potshots on his famous rival Jack Benny. The difficulty between them had started a few years back, during the 1936-37 season to be exact. It was Jack who started it all, Allen thought. It was Benny who poked fun first in a skit called "Clown Hall Tonight," which lampooned Fred's "Town Hall Tonight." It built on from there—each trying to match the other jab for jab, never letting bygones be bygones.

Satisfied with his weekly dig at all things Benny, Allen finished up his show and made his way back to his dressing room. The usual crowd was milling around backstage. Then he heard it: "Allen, you no good swine!"

It was the familiar voice of his favorite person, Jack Benny—who looked *mad.*

"Allen, what's going on here?" Jack demanded. "I came here to invite you to a party I'm having tonight. We called a truce just last week. Portland was there."

119

Jack turned to Portland Hoffa, Fred's co-star and wife, for support. "Right, Portland?"

But Portland was smarter than her radio persona suggested, and she was quickly through the door to her dressing room.

"Well!" Jack exclaimed.

"Well, nothing, Jack," Allen countered. "Yes, we had a deal—but what about what you said on your last broadcast about the bags under my eyes?"

Jack played innocent; he was good at this.

"You said that my face reminded you of 'a short butcher peeping over three pounds of liver.' What do you call that?"

Jack smiled. "I said *two* pounds, not three!"

Well, that did it! The two were at each other's throats. Several people ran over to separate them. Andy Devine, a friend of Benny's and a former cast member on his show, who had guested on Fred's show that night, chastised the pair with his inimitable raspy delivery. "You both should be ashamed of yourselves! You should get along." Then, winking at Jack, he added, "Besides, Buck, Mr. Allen can't help it if he's so pale that if he slept between two sheets, the bed would look empty."

With that, Fred stormed into his dressing room, slamming his door to the gales of laughter. "Hmm, that's the first time I've seen Fred Allen without a comeback," Benny mused. "Oh well, I'm leaving, but he hasn't seen or heard the last from me!"

Jack left the building, almost skipping. "That Fred Allen—he's going to miss a swell party...great food...great music...and only a $5 cover charge..."

Jack's happy thoughts were interrupted by the screeching of a horn. "Rochester! Where have you been?"

Rochester Van Jones, Jack Benny's valet and chauffeur, rode up to the curb to the symphony of the worst clanks, clinks and bonks—it didn't sound like a car as much as a wreck on wheels. Benny's old Maxwell groaned to a halt.

"Sorry, boss, but I ran those errands for you. I had trouble in one store—they wouldn't accept those wooden nickels."

"Quit kidding, Rochester. Let's get home, we're late for the party."

The noise of the Maxwell was deafening as it started up again. "Here we go, boss—hold on to your toupee, I mean, hat!" Rochester shouted over the noise, as the pile of junk lurched down the street.

On the way home Jack recalled the start of his and Allen's feud. It all began when Allen had that ten-year-old violin prodigy on his show, belittling Jack's prowess on the instrument. Jack bristled at the memory, but, no, Fred Allen wouldn't ruin tonight. Tonight was Jack's own "surprise" birthday party for himself. 39 years old! He couldn't believe it—nor could anyone else.

The party was in full swing when Jack arrived. It didn't seem to matter to anyone that the guest of honor just seemed to stroll in and mingle with the guests. Jack's announcer, Don Wilson, was the first to spot Benny.

"Hi Jack, where have you been? I wanted to read you the opening I wrote for next Sunday's show. This one's a dilly—listen to this…"

"Don, not now. I wanted to check the money at the door…"

Without missing a beat, Don launched into his intro. "And now, ladies and gentlemen, I bring you a man I thought wouldn't last—Jack Benny! He…"

"Don, I know you're trying to be clever, but seriously, how could you possibly think I wouldn't last? After all, a man my age is just in the prime of life."

"Sure, Jack—they've been priming you for ten years." Amusing himself, Don started to guffaw: "Oh, Wilson, you may not be from Boston but you certainly use your bean!"

Don's hysterics at his own quip propelled Jack to move away in disgust. "I have to remember to look up Harry Von Zell's phone number," he mumbled to himself.

Everyone was at the party: George Burns, Gracie Allen, Bob Hope, Connie Moore, Walter Tetley, Barbara Stanwyck with her husband Robert Taylor—all good friends of Jack, all wishing him well, and wishing he wouldn't play his violin. Dennis Day was the underpaid entertainer that night, plus doubling as a waiter—and Jack got 10% of his tips. He was singing "Bei Mir Bist Du Schon" as Benny passed by.

All manners of show business were there that night, including Jack's proteges Jake and Luke Vichnis, a sensational song/dance/comedy act he found while traveling through Maine looking for scrap metal. They were just kids, but had terrific possibilities—besides, they washed his Maxwell for free on weekends. Jack was featuring them on his next show.

"We heard Fred Allen tonight, Mr. Benny," Jake growled.

"Yeah," Luke piped in, "he's a dirty rat, Mr. Benny."

Jack patted their heads—oh yes, these kids certainly had wonderful possibilities.

The evening was still young when a knock at the door, interrupting Jack's under-duress encore of "Turkey in the Straw" on the violin, produced a Western Union man. The guests all gave a collective sigh of relief at the disturbance.

Jack took the telegram. The messenger's outstretched hand indicated that he wanted a tip. Mary Livingstone, Jack's wife, who was nearby, eyed the messenger with amusement.

"Optimist!" she chuckled, as she fled to safety.

Jack looked at nine-year-old Luke Vichnis, who emptied his pockets, unearthing only a guitar pick and a penny.

"That'll do," Jack brightened, as he handed the cent over to the man.

The telegram, ill-timed considering the "Turkey in the Straw" performance, unfortunately came from Fred Allen: "Roses are red/ Violinists are blue/ all over the country/ on account of you."

Jack was *steaming*. "That Fred Allen! Wait until I get my hands on him!"

Jack was even more annoyed when he heard his guests applauding Jake Vichnis' violin playing in the other room. "So the kid can play 'Holiday for Strings,'" Jack grumbled.

The next day Jack was due at Paramount to start a movie with, believe it or not, Fred Allen, and Mary Martin. At an earlier script conference several weeks before, the two were literally at each others' necks—with only Mary Martin in between trying to retain order. Both men had nursed black eyes for several days. *Miss* Martin, which is what they decided to call her after that run-in, was tougher than she looked.

He wasn't exactly looking forward to working with Allen, nor could he let Fred get away with insulting his musical ability. I mean, so what, thought Benny, if my violin teacher ran away? He didn't appreciate art when he heard it.

Something was wrong on the lot when he arrived. A crowd was congregating in front of the dressing rooms, and one in particular. Benny made his way through the throng and came across his friend Dorothy Lamour. "Dotty, what's happening?" At the sight of Jack, Lamour backed away in horror and quickly disappeared.

"What's wrong with her?" wondered Jack. "I mean, the movie we made together wasn't *that* bad."

But, in fact, everyone seemed to disperse, amid whispers, from the door at the sight of Jack.

"Well!" Jack exclaimed. He was puzzled. Whose dressing room was this? What was going on?

The answer became very apparent when the door suddenly flew open and the Chief of Police stood in the doorway glowering at Jack.

"So, returning to the scene of the crime, eh?"

"Scene of *what* crime?" Jack was understandably baffled at everyone's offbeat behavior.

He was ushered into the dressing room—Fred Allen's, as it turned out. It was pretty fancy. "Hmm...*my* furniture is made out of porcelain," Jack glumly muttered, until he was ordered to shut up by the gorilla-like Chief. Policemen were scattered all over the room searching. For what, Jack didn't know, but everyone seemed to be looking over at the couch. Benny moved across the room to get a better look, and discovered what looked like a body, under a white sheet.

"What's this?" Jack naively inquired.

The Chief moved over to Benny's side, as he handcuffed the surprised comedian. "As if you didn't know. Jack Benny—I arrest you for the *murder* of Fred Allen!"

Fred Allen—*dead*? Oh, this was too good to be true, Benny reflected. Or was it? *He* was being arrested for a murder *anyone* could have—should have—committed. Jack was in a daze: "Maybe it was his sponsor," he wailed as they hauled him away.

It was a very tired Jack who welcomed his lawyers Harrington, Harrington, Harrington and Droop, in his jail cell that afternoon. The men approached Benny's cell.

"Mr. Benny?" they asked in unison.

"What do you think I am in this cage, a canary?" Jack snapped.

After the sarcasm, his lawyers informed Jack that the prosecution had a pretty solid case against him. Witnesses at Fred Allen's radio broadcast and the Paramount story conference recalled their coming to blows, and guests at Jack's party the night before described Jack's reaction to Fred's telegram and his prophetic words that night: "Wait until I get my hands on him!"

The history of Fred and Jack's dislike for each other was a major factor in Benny being the main—*the only*—suspect. A trial was set for the following day and, in a rare occurrence, it was being broadcast live over the radio.

What was the rush? "More importantly," queried Jack, "where did these lawyers come from? And why are they talking in harmony?"

The next day the courtroom was packed, which really disheartened Jack, who was escorted in with chains on his arms and shackles on his legs, no less. Orson Welles was assigned MC duties for the somber broadcast, accompanied by Carmen Cavallaro and his Orchestra. Jack was in awe of the jury: Jerry Colonna, Larry Fine, Van Heflin, Baby Rose Marie, Ruby Dandridge, Alice Faye, Charles Coburn, Iris Adrian, Charlie McCarthy, Leon Errol, Jack Oakie, and Lassie.

Was this a nightmare? It certainly seemed so: "Oh great, I'm being convicted by dummies, animals, children—*and* Colonna," Jack sputtered in panic. "What are my chances? And where the heck is Edgar Bergen?"

None of this seemed real, and it was downright strange, Benny grimly surmised. He waved to Jane Frazee, whom he had known in vaudeville, but she just looked right through him. Not a good sign, thought Jack.

Everyone rose as the Judge came into court. His name was bizarre: Myron Proudfoot. Well, at least it wasn't Johnny "Scat" Davis, Jack sighed with alleviation.

"This is Orson Welles and we are broadcasting live at The Los Angeles Courtroom where famous comedian Jack Benny is being tried for his cold-blooded slaying of the equally famous comedian Fred Allen…"

"I object!" Jack yelled. "First of all, I am *beating* Allen in the ratings!" After a short tussle, his lawyers persuaded him to sit down.

The Judge was livid. "One more outburst like that, Mr. Benny, and this court will hold you in contempt."

"But, Judge, we don't even know each other," Jack reasoned as the gavel rang out to silence the room. Jack sensed something peculiar about Judge Proudfoot. Did they know each other? His manner and particularly his voice sounded awfully familiar to Jack.

The trial was under way. Judge Proudfoot's repeated attempts to curb Lassie's incessant barking were for naught. After Larry Fine was bitten, however, something had to be done. A short break to take the dog for a walk—volunteered by Gloria Blondell, who was in the audience—helped matters considerably.

To the surprise of many, Charlie McCarthy asked some sharp, perceptive questions during the trial, but to no one's surprise Jerry Colonna was a handful.

"Pardon me, gate," Colonna asked the prosecuting attorney, Douglas Parsons, on one occasion, "could you please illuminate that last remark?"

Jack thought the trial was turning into a circus—heck, it *was* a circus! Embarrassing details about his personal life and spending, um, non-spending habits were brought up excessively. His lawyers were doing nothing for him, except they did sing the commercial well over the air and, at one point, they appropriately serenaded Jack with "The Prisoner Song."

Orson Welles colorfully narrated the proceedings, while also attempting to run the whole trial, much to Judge Proudfoot's annoyance; one of Welles' most inspired ideas was recasting Benny's lawyers with Ray Milland, since Milland's speaking voice was more adaptable to radio, but that idea was nixed since the actor couldn't sing. Carmen Cavallaro did some piano solos during Lassie's frequent breaks, including one well-received version of "I Get the Neck of the Chicken." Yet for Benny, the end seemed to be very near.

It was revealed that Allen was killed by being hit on the head with a blunt instrument—a violin, of all things. Mary Livingstone, who had remained silent throughout the trial stood up, announcing to the Judge, "Your Honor, there's nothing blunt about Jack's violin—except his playing." Jack rolled his eyes. Mary sure must like the May Company to be talking like that.

Various witnesses were called by the prosecution, including Benny's own bandleader Phil Harris, who complained that Benny was not as good looking as he; one of the jurors, Alice Faye, agreed. Benny's writers Ed Beloin and Bill Morrow testified that Benny was jealous of Allen's ability to ad-lib. Singer Kenny Baker, a former Benny cast member now on the Allen show, brought the house down with a lovely rendition of "Why Shouldn't I?" This was followed by his comment that working for Allen was more profitable, monetarily and artistically, than working for Benny. Also, Allen didn't make him mow the lawn.

"Little things mean a lot," added Baker, tearfully.

Benny's lawyers could only muster two witnesses: Samuel Goldwyn and S.Z. "Cuddles" Sakall, a faithful friend who no one could understand. Goldwyn was also no help, stating that he "regretted not producing *Gone With the Wind*." When asked what that had to do with the case, he seemed puzzled. "Nothing, why do you ask?"

Jack was finally called to the stand to be cross-examined by Douglas Parsons. Everyone held their breath—Parsons was known for being a ruthless, no-nonsense interrogator, a sharp contrast to Jack's happy-go-lucky quartet of attorneys, who kept breaking into song throughout the trial. Jack was sworn in and the barrage of questions started:

"Mr. Benny, where were you on Sunday evening around three a.m.?"

"I was home depositing some money into my vault. It takes a good twenty minutes to get down there."

"Do you have any witnesses to back up this statement?"

"Yes sir, Ed, the man who guards my vault."

"And why isn't he here today?"

"Are you crazy?!" Jack was incredulous over the lawyer's notion that Jack should leave his vault unprotected. Besides, Ed was down there so long he still thought Lincoln was president.

At the mention of Benny's vault, Mary stood up again. "Jack, why don't you stop being so stingy?"

"Mary, I'm not stingy—and you know it."

"You're not, eh?…Last year when you were going to have your appendix removed, you wanted Rochester to do it."

"I DID NOT," Jack insisted. "I merely asked him if he knew how."

Parsons proceeded, after the Judge threatened to clear the courtroom if an exchange like that took place again.

"What was the problem between you and Fred Allen?" demanded Parsons.

"Well," considered Jack, "he had the same old show, the same old jokes…"

"I object!" shouted Van Heflin from the jury box. "I happen to think Fred Allen had a very funny show."

"Mr. Heflin," Jack answered, "I realize you are an Oscar-winning actor, and I wouldn't have minded if Allen's jokes just laid there—but they crawl out of the radio and stain your rug!"

Laughter in the courtroom was abated by Judge Proudfoot who, grudgingly, had to admit that Jack was good at ad-libbing. The interrogation started again.

"Everyone knew you hated Fred Allen, Mr. Benny. Why don't you just come clean?"

"Come clean? That's easy for you to say. I just realized yesterday, after seeing Allen's dressing room, that Paramount has me changing in the bathroom!"

Lawyer Parsons could see nothing was to be gained by questioning Benny, so he proceeded to spend most of his time flirting with Jane Frazee in the jury box.

After securing a future date with the singer, Parsons, filled with re-newed vigor, went into a long tirade about Benny's faults and dislike of Fred Allen. The prosecution rested. The incompetent team Benny hired, though loaded with showmanship and impeccable vocal skills, were de-cidedly inept at the law, and they too rested.

It was all in the hands of the jury, but to Jack it was an open and shut case. Jack realized he was in trouble—*I mean, Van Heflin is a Fred Allen fan and Jane Frazee is enamored of Douglas Parsons. Who picked this jury and what's going to happen to me?*

The jury deliberated for about ten minutes, since air-time was get-ting close to the top of the hour. Orson Welles, in those ten minutes, had inspiringly delivered a poem about "Paul Revere's Ride." Mercifully, the jury came in to read their verdict.

"Jury," the Judge soberly inquired, "have you reached a verdict?"

Jerry Colonna, the foreman, cracked, "Yes, we have, gate." Then, smoothing out his mustache, he prepared to read, complete with flour-ishes, the jury's statement: "We the jury, find Jack Benny guilty offffffff…" Colonna held the note at the top of his lungs, until Baby Rose Marie poked him in the ribs, "murder…in the eighth degree!"

Eighth degree?! Everyone in the courtroom went crazy. "Eighth de-gree? Eighth degree? What's that?" Benny was in a whirl. "Is this some-thing new created to punish me?"

The Judge hushed the room, as he started to explain. "Jack Benny, you have heard the jury's verdict. I can understand your puzzlement. But you are hereby sentenced to ten years…of silence."

"Of *silence*?" Jack demanded, "What kind of sentence is that?"

"It's a sentence that will make it easy on radio listeners, I trust," the Judge chortled as he ripped off his mask—it was *Fred Allen*! He wasn't dead—and this wasn't a real trial! "The joke's on you, Benny!"

Everyone, including, thank God, the jury, was in on the joke—all except poor Jack, who, recovering from his disappointment that Fred wasn't really dead, was furious.

"Allen, this is the last straw! Why go to all this trouble? For what?"

Fred smirked a bit. "I was auditioning my new show—*Celebrity Jury*—and who better to test it out on than Jack Benny? I don't really hate you, Jack, but this was too good to pass up. You should have seen your face. No hard feelings, right?"

Dejected, but glad he wasn't going to be hanged for murder by Charlie

McCarthy, Jack decided to just leave. Reporters were everywhere covering the story. Benny declined all interviews, but then he heard Fred Allen make a statement: "Jack Benny is so anemic that when he cuts himself the cut doesn't bleed, it just puckers and hisses."

"Allen, you no-good swine!"

And here we go again. ♦

LUM & ABNER

Murder in Pine Ridge
by Donnie Pitchford

And now…let's see what's going on down in Pine Ridge. Well, as we look in on the little community today, we find Abner alone in the Jot 'Em Down Store. This is a condition the old fellow has known all too well as of late, since Lum has discovered the charms of Miss Earline Biggers, county seat librarian. It seems Lum has finally recovered from the sorrow of losing his longtime sweetheart, Evalena Schultz, who married newcomer Spud Gandel not too long ago. Lum's new flame has put a bounce in the old fellow's steps, one that poor Abner can scarcely match! It looks as if Grandpappy Spears is just entering the store:

"Well, hidey hidey hidey!"

"Hidey, Gran'pap! Come on back!"

"Where's that dad-blame partner o' yourn, Abner?"

"Aw, Lum's on his way back from the county seat."

"Still a-courtin' that' li'l lie-berrian, huh?"

"Yeah. Doggies, Gran'pap, he's actin' like a kid of a boy, all gigglin' an' sangin' an' carryin' on!"

"He's in love, Abner, that's his trouble."

"Well, he's too happy! He ort ta git married an' settle down an' be miserable like us!"

Suddenly, the screen door of the old store swings open, its bell jingling, as Lum Edwards fairly dances through. "The game is on somebody's foot!" he sings, "It's elementary school, my dear Watkins! Thank you so much!"

"Lum Eddards!" a disgusted Abner scolds, "You git yore grade school hide in here an' git ta work! We got grocery orders ta put up!"

"Abner, I ain't got time fer sich prittle prattle. I got book-larnin' ta do!"

"What kinda book larnin'?"

"I done dis-covered my true callin'!"

"Oh, you have, have ya? An' jist what is it?"

"I'm a-gonna be-come a dee-teckatif!"

"Fer the land sakes! What air you a-talkin' about?"

"Abner, ever since I started sparkin' Miss Biggers, she's been larnin' me about all the great dee-teckatiffs in these friction books. You know, fellers like...oh, what's his name..."

"Well, if you don't know him, I shore don't!"

"Aw, you've heered of him, Abner... Oh, I re-collect! Sure-luck Homes!"

"Huh?"

"I reckon they call him that 'cause he's 'sure lucky' the way he solves them cases. You know, he's gotta partner named Dr. Watkins."

"Huh? Oh, I know him, Lum! He's that feller who makes that Watkins Vaniller Extract!"

"No, no...Homes an' Watkins went ta elementary school tagether...Homes is always re-minded him of it."

"Lum, we got a store ta run here!"

"No, Abner, my mind's made up. I'm a-gonna be-come a dee-teckatiff. All I need now is a new name."

"New name?"

"Yessir, Abner, all them dee-teckatiffs got fancy names. Like...uh...Mr. Motto. Er, that Zero Wolfe, I b'lieve his name is. Er, that Shadder feller on the raddio...Yeah! Whut does he say? Oh yeah: 'Them snakes in th' weeds eats bitter fruit...'"

"Fer pity sakes!"

"My favor-rite is that Chinese feller. I seen him in a new movie in there at the Lyric Theatre with Miss Biggers. Grannies, there's a great dee-teckatiff!"

"Miss Biggers is a great dee-teckatiff?"

"No, ya eediot, I mean that Chinese feller...Can't re-collect his name, but he was a reg'lar genus at solvin' crimes an' murders an' sich as that! Grannies, I b'lieve he's my he-ro."

"An' ya don't even know his name?"

"I wish I had me a Chinese name. Grannies, I'd be th' best dee-teckatiff in Polk County iffen I had a Chinese name!"

"Yeah. Too bad you got sich a plain ol' American name like Lum."

"Wait a minute, Abner, I got it! I'll use my name Lum, but I'll change it around...I'll call myself Bulldog Lummond! How's that?"

"Sassyfras!" Grandpappy Spears comments, "Sass-ee-fras! Lum Eddards, that's the biggest buncha huskin' shuckins I ever heered! I'm goin' over to th' barber shop. Mose Moots is gotta new 'Po-leece Gazette' that's more innerestin' than this pish-posh. I'll be back when you grow up, Bullfrog, er whatever yer callin' yerself!" With that, the old timer storms through the creaking, jingling screen door, waving the ever-present summer flies from his face as he stomps along on spindly legs.

Friendly general store competitor Dick Huddleston has been busy as well, renting and preparing his Ouachita River fishing lodge for a newcomer. He has just departed one of the cabins as a strikingly beautiful woman inside smooths her raven-black hair and begins touching up her rather exotic makeup. She is interrupted by a dull, thud-like knock. Peeking through the shade, she smiles and slowly opens the door. "Well," she coos, "I see you made it—big boy!"

The oversized figure of Cedric Weehunt begins to shuffle and squirm "like a feller bein' pestered by a wasp" as the embarrassed lad giggles. "Er, uh," he stammers, "ya said ya wanted me fer sump'm, Miss Carver!"

"Oh, that I do, you big handsome creature! I want you! I've got plans for us! Come right in..."

"Lum Eddards!" scolds Abner two days later, "Yer gittin' later and later ever dad-blame mornin', an' I ain't a-gonna..."

"Couldn't hep it, Abner, I was too busy half the night doin' head work."

"Head work?"

"Yeah, I was studyin' these dee-teckatiff books...bonin' up!"

"Well, you got the head fer that!"

"Abner, lissen ta me...Cedric Weehunt's done disappeared an' ain't nobody seen him fer two days!"

"Oh, he's might nigh went fishin'..."

"Nossir, his fishin' tackle is all over ta th' place—ain't been tetched."

"Why, Cedric's been tetched ever since he got kicked by that mule!"

"Fer pity sakes, I meant his fishin' tackle..."

"His fishin' tackle got kicked by a mule?"

"Hesh up, Abner! This is a real mystery! One fer me ta solve as Bulldog Lummond! Now lissen. Dick Huddleston's tole me that the last he seen o' Cedric was when a missa-terus womern rented a cabin at his fishin' lodge an' asked fer a big, strong young feller ta help her out! So, Dick sent Cedric down there! I think the poor boy's been kidnapped!"

"Well, if that don't beat the bugs a-fightin'!"

The old crank telephone begins sounding the familiar store's ring and a disgusted Abner resigns himself to his position of sole storekeeper for the time being. Shaking his head, he walks to answer the phone while Lum searches for an old magnifying glass and other items he intends to use as detective gear. "I doggies, I hate this phone," Abner fusses, "Orta have it took out! Hello, Jot 'Em Down Store an' Hound Dog Lum's dog-house or some sich prittle prattle! Huh? Who? Yes mum…Hey, Fleabag Eddards, hit's yore true love, Miss Biggers!"

"Abner!" a flush-faced "Bulldog Lummond" barks through clenched teeth, then whispers, "Don't never talk like that! Give me that ree-ceiver!"

Adjusting the mouthpiece to his greater height, the Pine Ridge psuedo-sleuth croaks, "H-hello?"

"Why, Mr. Edwards!" the honey-voiced librarian replies.

"OH! Miss Biggers! Grannies, I couldn't see ya! Er, I didn't know my own voice! Er…"

"Mr. Edwards, there's a wonderful new detective movie showing at the Lyric tonight…"

"Well, y'see, Miss Earline, I'm gonna solve a big dee-teckatiff case myself! Cedric Weehunt's done disappeared, an' we think some missa-terus womern's done kidnapped 'im!"

"Oh, this is too, too thrilling! I wish I could be there to witness your bravery as you capture the evil woman!"

"Well, I gotta go now, an' do some dee-tecktin'! Bye!"

"Well, goodbye—Bulldog…dear!"

"G—goodbye!" Lum hangs the ear piece on the hook before adding, "Honey!"

Frogs, crickets and owls sing a nocturnal trio as Lum and Abner creep slowly about the outside of one of Dick's cabins. An old oil lantern flickers as it sways in Abner's hands, creating eerie shadows on the side of the building. Abner speaks, and much too loudly for Lum:

"Lum, I don't see why…"

"Abner! Hesh up, ya eediot!"

"Why, ya got a headache? Must be that silly-lookin' hat yer a-wearin'."

"This is sump'm all dee-teckatiffs wear. It's called a deer-squawker."

"Looks like two o' Cedric's ol' baseball caps, and one of 'em's backerds."

"Well, it is, but don't tell nobody."

"I won't. They kin see fer theirselves. Lum, why in the world did we hafta come down here so late? Doggies, hit's past my bedtime!"

"'Cause, silly, we had ta wait till this womern was gone! Tom Foster at th' fillin' station said he filled up her car with gas an' said she told him she had ta spend the night at the county seat. Somethin' about pickin' up some kinda supplies off th' train. She's s'posed ta come back early in the mornin'. Come on, let's git inside this room here an' inna-vestigate! I'll crawl through this winder first...right after you do!" Lum, taking the lantern in his left hand, uses his other to push the unwilling Abner through an open window. The yelping fellow quickly stumbles over a nightstand, sending a lamp to the floor with a noisy crash. "Be quiet!" demands Lum, adding, "What do ya see?"

"Lum! Lum!"

"I'm inside now, Abner, hesh up!"

"Lum, this womern must be a killer!"

"Hot dog! My first case, an' hit's a real murder mystery!"

"Lum, look...see them sheets? Looks like...like folks is under 'em!"

Abner's voice quivers with fear as Lum passes the light of the lantern over several still forms covered with cloth.

"Oh my goodness!" gasps Lum, "Yer right, Abner! Tetch one!"

"I ain't goin' near them things!"

"We gotta see if they's shore 'nuff dead!"

"Let's ask 'em!"

"No, Abner, here, go on, tetch that one thar!"

"Lum, don't push my arm!" Abner shoves back, knocking the lantern from Lum's hand, its flame extinguishing as it hits the floor.

"Dad blame it, Abner, you coulda set this place on far! Now the wick's all out...I ain't got no more matches...Lucky fer us this thing didn't flame up...Now we ain't got no light!" The moon shining through the window casts a faint glow over parts of the cabin. As the old fellows' eyes adjust, Lum pushes his unwilling partner toward what appears to be a body. Just then a breeze blows through the room, uncovering an arm. Abner's foot slips on something unseen on the dark floor and the poor little fellow pitches forward, his arms brushing against the partially covered figure, whereafter he shrieks.

"Wh-what is it, Abner?"

"L-Lum, that feller is stiff an' cold!"

"Oh my goodness!"

"Let's git outa here, Lum! The sheriff kin solve this!"

"Nossir, this case is gonna be solved by Bulldog Lummond!"

"I cain't stand this no more, Lum!"

"Abner, we gotta find the murder weepins! Look! Over thar! All kinda knives!"

"Oh, me!"

"An' here's some kinda wire with little sticks o' wood on each end—like sump'm she might use around a feller's neck ta cut off…"

"Oh, don't say it, Lum!"

"We don't wanna rurn the fangerprints…Abner, see that cabinet thar? Open it up and git some towels out so we can wrop up some o' this evidence."

"I'm gonna wrop one around my eyes so I cain't see no more o' this…"

"Come on, now, hand me a towel…"

Abner, trembling, opens what he hopes is a cabinet full of linens and bath towels, but instead sees the grisly shape of a human head covered in thin cloth. "Lum! Lum!" he squeals in terror, when suddenly, the object lurches forward, landing with a sickening thud in the sink below. There, staring up at them, is the face of Cedric Weehunt.

Abner sits wearily in his old rocking chair the next morning, slowly swallowing a cup of thick coffee brewed in a battered pot atop the old store's pot-bellied stove. Lum, sprawled about in a wheelbarrow parked in the middle of the floor, slowly awakens with a low groan. "Grannies, what a dream…" He lifts his head, realizing he is not in his comfortable bed at home. "Abner, what in the name of…" His movements throw the rusty wheelbarrow off-balance and he tumbles to the floor. "Oh, Abner, how in the daylights did I git in that wheelbarrow?"

"Lum, hit was the only way I could carry you back here after you fainted!"

"Fainted? Why, I didn't never do no sucha thing!"

"You did done it, right after poor Cedric's head fell outa that cabinet. They's been a murder! Pore ol' Cedric… bless his heart… er, bless his head…buh-less his lit-tul head!"

"We shoulda brang that back as evi-dence!"

"Oh, Lum, don't say sich a thang..."

"I shore wanted Miss Earline ta be here when I dragged in that mysaterus womern..."

"You ain't a-gonna git that chance, Lum, 'cause I done called th' sheriff."

"Aw, Abner, I can solve this case myself, er my name ain't Bulldog Lummond!"

"And it ain't! Besides, here comes the sheriff now." A stocky, middle-aged officer of the law, his boots striking the old floor boards with a clomping sound, strides through the doorway, allowing the sweet smell of morning to temporarily mask the odor of stale coffee. A second gentleman, a stranger, waits outside on the porch. "Come on back, Sheriff!"

"Howdy, Abner!" the armed official grunts, "How're you, Lum? What're you doin' on the floor?"

Embarrassed, the stiff-jointed Lum struggles to his feet, lamely answering, "Er, I was jist lookin' fer footprints."

"Boys," the sheriff chides, "Don't y'all ever try to investigate a situation like this on your own again! Lum, I know you're the justice of the peace, and Abner, you've served as constable, but honest, men, this business is over your heads!"

"Naw," Abner interjects, "Hit was Cedric's head!"

"Abner, when you called me this mornin', I was just about to leave on a search for this woman. Her name is Ima Carver, and a big city detective come to Mena searchin' for her. He's outside now, lookin' around the buildin'. The woman is from New York, and he thinks he's spotted her footprints. She wears some real expensive New York shoes. He thinks she might have snuck around the back of your store."

Suddenly, the feed room door swings open, and the svelte form of Ima Carver walks briskly into the store proper. "Doggies, Lum," Abner warns, "She's got a knife!" Whereafter "Bulldog Lummond" sinks to the floor in another faint!

"Git up, Lum," pleads Abner, "she ain't even stabbed ya... yet!"

"Oooohhhh..." moans Lum, regaining consciousness. "What happened? Hey, Lady! P-p-put down that knife!"

"You hayseed boob," Miss Carver growls, "this is a fettling knife!"

"Well, let's fettle this like gennlemen!"

"You simpleton, I just came to your feed room to use your whetstone to sharpen it!"

"Sh-sharpen…"

"I've got some heads to work on!"

"Oooohhhhh…" sighs Lum, his body again melting to the floor.

"Okay, lady," the sheriff orders, "I'm placing you under arrest."

"Curses!" she shouts.

"She ain't no lady!" Abner exclaims, "She's cursin' at us! It's bad enough she's a murderer!"

"Murderer?" chuckles the sheriff, "Miss Carver isn't a murderer, Abner."

"Ohh…wh-what's 'at?" groans Lum weakly as he struggles to stand.

"She ain't no murderer? But we done seen people and heads all wropped up in sheets!"

"Nope," explains the lawman, "Miss Carver is a talented artist! She makes statues! Y'see Lum, a fettling knife is used in carving clay! Miss Carver is under contract to produce this stuff for a big art gallery in New York."

Her eyes blazing, Carver adds, "But those fools didn't appreciate my talent! They dared dictate my subject matter and place me on a schedule! They treated me like a loathsome, ignorant, despicable grocery clerk!"

Abner mumbles, "I ree-semble that ree-mark!"

"You see," the sheriff continues,"this New York gallery lost thousands of dollars due to this disappearance of Miss Carver! They sent this big time detective down to find her."

"So…" Lum slowly drawls, "them bodies and heads…"

"All clay sculptures, men!"

"That's right, you old geezers!" hisses the angry artist, "and I thought I'd found the best studio I could ask for! Peace and quiet, and dozens of primative hicks for subjects!"

"But grannies," asks an exasperated Lum, "Whur's Cedric Weehunt?"

"Oh, I'm right chere!" the lanky lad announces, emerging from the feed room, carrying a basket of clay sculpting tools. "I been workin' fer Miss Ima! She pays good, too! Boy!"

"That's right," she confirms, "I paid this big goof to wedge my clay and pose for me, and I sent him to hunt for food in the hills and sleep in the wild. For my next set of sculptures, I wanted him to look even more primative—if that's possible!"

Disgusted, Lum leans against a counter and exclaims, "Well I'll be dad blamed!"

"But saaaaay…" Ima coos, stepping ever closer to Lum, "look at that forehead!"

"M-mum?" stutters a nervous Lum.

"Let me study those features… "

"Y-y-you want ta carve me? Er, make a statuary outa me?"

"My, my, my…those cheekbones…that jaw line…why, you're a perfect example of Lum-magnus Edwardus Imbecilus! "

"I always thought so," observes Abner.

"Let me get my hands on that beautiful face," Miss Carver continues with a lusty giggle, as she cups Lum's trembling jaw in her talented hands. Just then, the bell on the screen door jingles, as the dainty Miss Earline Biggers enters.

"Omigoodness!" gasps an embarrassed Lum.

"Lum Edwards!" Miss Biggers exclaims in a voice trembling with emotion, "Who is that hussy and why are her hands on your face?"

Without missing a beat, the sultry sculptress responds, "And who is this Southern simp, and why does she wear so much lace?"

Tearfully, the librarian explains, "Mr. Edwards, I came to Pine Ridge to be an eyewitness to the proud moment you clamped the hands of justice on that evil purveyor of crime! Now I see the roles have been reversed! Farewell! I shall leave you now!" Her dress whirls about her as she spins into as ladylike an about face as she can muster, while her gloved hand dramatically pushes the screen door open.

"Aw, Miss Earline," Lum pleads, "Wait, don't…don't…Grannies, she's comin' back!"

Proudly, Miss Biggers holds the door open, stands at attention, and announces, "And you own 10¢ for that overdue HOUND OF THE BASKERVILLES!" She departs, the door slams and each diminishing clop of the lady's shoes seems to stab at poor Lum's aching heart.

The sheriff breaks the brief period of silence that follows by commanding, "Come along, Miss Carver."

Her heavily lidded eyes narrow as Miss Carver purrs, "Oh, just when I was having fun…" As she is led through the door, she turns toward Lum

and seductively adds, "Goodbye, Bulldog Lummond…If you're ever in New York…or Monte Carlo…or Reno…or Rio…come up and see me sometime…"

Abner, noticing the "big city" detective rejoining the sheriff and taking custody of Miss Carver on the porch, makes an observation to his downhearted partner: "Lum, lookit that city dee-teckatiff! He's a Chineseman, ain't he? He's got a white suit, an' a li'l mustache and a li'l beard...He sorta looks like one o' them dee-teckatiff fellers in them movies you an' Miss Biggers likes sa much! Yessir, he does, he looks jist like..."

"Abner!"

"Huh? What is it, Lum?"

"Hesh up!" ♦

HAROLD LLOYD COMEDY THEATRE

The Maltese Omelette
by Michael Kurland

Starring Harold Lloyd as Spud and Jimmy Wallington as Dumpty

Picture a small office in a grubby downtown office building in San Francisco.

The sign on the door reads:

Spud & Dumpty, Private Eyes, Gumshoes,
And General All-Around Busybodies.

Fluffie, the office secretary, is on the phone when her boss Sam Spud walks into the office. She hangs up and turns to Spud. "Sam."

"Hi, Fluffie, doll."

"There was a woman here to see you," Fluffie says, "but she couldn't wait. She said she'd be back."

Spud pauses at his office door. "Do I want to see her?" he asks.

"Oh yes," Fluffie tells him. "She's a real looker."

"Well then, shoo her right in, Fluffie my darling. I have to type up my report on the Cock Robin Caper now, but don't wait. When she returns just shoo her right in."

Spud enters his office, takes a glass from the bookcase, carefully wipes it out, and pours himself two stiff fingers of chocolate milk.

"Let's see," he says, sitting at the typewriter, "the Cock Robin Caper." He begins his two-finger, hunt-and-peck typing.

A few minutes later Fluffie sticks her head in the door. "Miss Muffit is here to see you, Sam."

"Shoo her in, Sweetheart, shoo her in."

With a heart-shaped face surrounded by red hair that spills over her shoulders, a red, pouting mouth, and legs that go from here to a little past

139

there, Miss Muffit is everything Fluffie said, and perhaps a bit more. Her tight red sweater and black skirt that is just too short enough leaves no doubt as to just what little girls are made of. She sits on the edge of the client chair in front of the battered oak desk. "Mr. Spud," she says through her deep, full, red lips, "I need your help."

Spud looks her over thoughtfully. Just what his thoughts are is his own business. "That's what we're here for, sister," he says. "Tell me all about it."

"It's my sister, Mr. Spud. My little sister. She's run away."

"Run away?"

"Yes." She leans forward provocatively, a helpless look on her face. A very practiced helpless look. "We live with our parents in a small tuffit in Gotham. My little sister was always rather wild, Mr. Spud. She was going out with this gangster called the Spider. He used to take her to a curds-and-whey joint on the South Side. Our father didn't approve."

Spud nods. "What father would?"

"Yes, well. She ran off two weeks ago. We got a postcard from her on Monday. She's here in San Francisco."

Spud leans back in his chair. "With this Spider character?"

"No. You've got to understand, Mr. Spud, my sister's beautiful but naive, inexperienced in the ways of the world. She ran off with a gigolo – a fancy ballroom dancer named Lloyd Thursday. Everyone called him the Spoon."

"I see," Spud says. "So this dish ran away with the Spoon."

Miss Muffit leans even further forward. "Oh, Mr. Spud—Sam— you've got to help me."

"You're good, kid," Spud says, a grin spreading across his face. "You're real good. Just what is it you want me to do?"

The door to the inner office opens, and a large, rotund, egg-shaped man waddles in. "Hello, Sam," he booms. "Oh, sorry; I didn't know you had company."

"Come in, Humpty; this is a customer. Miss Muffit, let me introduce my partner, Humpty Dumpty."

Dumpty takes Miss Muffit's hand and raises it to his lips. "It's a pleasure, a real pleasure," he says. "You're a real looker, you know that, Miss Muffit?"

She pulls her hand free. "Mr. Dumpty."

"Call me 'Humpty.'"

"Humpty. Is that a tie or a belt you're wearing?"

Dumpty looks puzzled. "How's that?" he asks.

"Is that a cravat or a cummerbund, Mr. Dumpty?"

"Humpty, please. Call me Humpty. It's a…"

"Oh!" Miss Muffit cries, jumping to her feet. "I certainly hope you gentlemen can help me."

Dumpty leers at her in a friendly way. "I'll help you myself, Miss Muffit," he says. "What's your problem?"

Spud leans back in his chair and grins. "Her sister's missing," he explains.

"I see," Dumpty says. "You want us to find your sister?"

Miss Muffit nods. "She's with a fellow who calls himself 'the Spoon.' Mr. Dumpty—Humpty—I'm afraid. For my sister, I mean."

Humpty Dumpty nods seriously, his cravat, or possibly his cummerbund, jiggling up and down as he did. "I'll take care of this myself, Sam," he says. "You want me to meet this 'Spoon' character, Miss Muffit?"

"I want you to follow him when he leaves me and find out where my sister is. But be careful—I don't trust him."

"That's my middle name, Miss Muffit," Dumpty says. "Humpty 'Careful' Dumpty. Let's go talk about it, my dear." He turns to Spud. "I'll see you later."

Spud grins a non-committal grin. "Sure you will."

Time passes. A shot sounds somewhere in the distance, but it's a big city.

Spud is at home asleep when the phone rings. He gropes for it. "Hello? Who's this? Sprat? Don't you know it's"—he peers over at his alarm clock—"three o'clock in the morning? And don't say 'No, but hum a few bars and I'll fake it.'" Suddenly he sits up in bed. "What's that? Dumpty? Dead? Fell off a wall? Where? Okay, I'll be right down!"

A few minutes later Spud approaches the corner of Jackson and Durant. Sergeant Jack Sprat of the San Francisco Police awaits him. "Hello, Spud."

"Hello, Sprat. How's the wife?"

Sprat shakes his head sadly. "You know how it is. She wants me to quit the force. Live off the fat of the land, she says. But I eat no fat. The missus eats no lean. It's a problem. You want to see your partner?"

"What happened?"

"See that wall?" Sprat asks, pointing. "He's on the other side. Maybe he fell, and maybe he was pushed. Either way, he's crushed his big end."

Spud goes over to the wall and peering cautiously over the edge. "Why haven't you moved him? What are you waiting for?"

Sprat shrugs an expressive shrug, that carries with it the futility of all human endeavor. "You know, Sam: the king's horses and the king's men. You've got to go by the book in a case like this. Listen, Inspector Pumpkin wants to talk to you."

"You keep that Peter Peter Pumpkin person away from me," Spud says, the anger evident in his quavering voice. "He's always riding me."

Sprat shakes his head sadly. "Come on, Sam; he's not himself these days. You know he's got a problem with his wife. She still hasn't come out of her shell."

"Yeah? Well, we all got problems."

Just then Inspector Pumpkin arrives from the other side of the wall. "Spud—Spud—I want to talk to you."

"Yeah? What can I do for you, Pumpkin?" Spud says without turning around.

"*Inspector* Pumpkin to you, Spud. Your partner just got himself killed. Don't you want to help us clear it up?"

Sprat breaks in, "He was a good egg, Sam."

"Yeah," Sam says, staring down at the shell of what had been his partner. "He thought he was hard-boiled, but he was soft. And now he's been scrambled."

"What was he doing out here at this time of night, Sam?" Pumpkin persists. "Was he on a case?"

Spud wheels around to face the inspector. "*Mr.* Spud to you, *Inspector* Pumpkin. Yeah. He was working. He was tailing a fellow called Thursday. Lloyd Thursday. Calls himself 'the Spoon.'"

"Now that's interesting. That's very interesting. Tailing the Spoon, eh? Who was the client?"

"You know I can't give you that."

Sprat interrupts, "But he was your partner, Sam."

"Yeah. But it's my business and I'll take care of it my way."

Pumpkin grins an official grin. "Well, it's police business now. We'll be in touch with you. Don't get yourself mashed, Spud. And don't go looking for this 'Spoon' character, either."

"Why not?"

"'Cause we found him already. Half an hour ago. Someone put two bullets into his ticker in front of his hotel."

"Yeah, Sam," Sprat adds. "The spoon got wiped. Ha ha ha."

Fluffie arrives at the office the next morning to find Spud there before her. "I heard about Humpty," she says. "Maybe you shouldn't have come in today."

"Yeah," he says. "Well, there's a lot to do today. Got to take Dumpty's name off the door. Got to clean out his desk and send his stuff over to the widow. Got a carton, Fluffie?"

She looks in the closet. "Got an egg carton."

"It'll do." Spud grins a wolfish grin.

A short, round-faced man enters the office. His thinning hair is parted in the middle, and an overly-large handkerchief flops out of the breast pocket of his white linen suit. The handkerchief—and indeed the man himself—smells of lavender, and perhaps just a bit of sour milk. "Excuse me, miss," the man says, "this is the office of Spud and Dumpty, perhaps?"

Fluffie smiles at him. He might be a client. "Yes sir, it is."

"My name is Porgie," he tells her. "Georgie Porgie. I seek an audience with Mr. Spud."

Sam looks up. "I'm Spud."

"Ah, yes. I should have realized. I must speak with you on a matter of some importance and delicacy."

Spud opens the inner office door and gestures Porgie in. "Now, what can I do for you?"

"First permit me to say—" Porgie pauses and takes from his pocket a slim but oversized silver cigarette case inlaid with small ivory hippopotamuses. "Cigarette, Mr. Spud? No? Perhaps you won't mind if I have one. First let me say that I was sorry to her of your partner's untimely demise. He had a reputation as such a hard-boiled detective."

"Say," Spud interrupts, "what's in that cigarette you're smoking? It don't smell like tobacco."

Porgie takes the cigarette from his mouth and waves it slowly under his nose, breathing the fumes in with a dreamy expression on his face. "Creme de menthe," he says.

"I should have guessed."

"Try one?" Porgie asks, taking out the cigarette case once more.

Spud shakes his head firmly. "I think I'll pass."

"Very well. On to business. You and your partner—were you close? He confided in you? You, perhaps, worked on your cases together?"

"That's right," Spud agrees.

"You perhaps met his client?" Porgie asks. "You are aware of the object of the investigation he was engaged in when he, ah, met his great fall?"

Spud turns the question over in his mind, examining it carefully from all sides. "You should know I can't discuss my clients with you."

"Yes, yes, how silly of me. Then let us leave the young lady out of the conversation. Let us just say, Mr. Spud, that I would like to employ your services in a—" he gave a moist chuckle "—totally unrelated matter, of course. Totally."

"What matter is that, Mr. Porgie?"

"I will pay you well to locate a certain—object—for me."

"What object?"

"Come. Let us not beat around the bush, Mr. Spud. Let me just say that a bird in the hand could be worth five thousand dollars to you."

"A bird?"

"*The* bird, Mr. Spud, *the* bird. And if you don't understand my reference, then perhaps I am wasting both of our time."

Just then Fluffie calls from the outer office. "I'm going to lunch now, Sam."

"Okay," Sam yells back. Then he turns to Porgie. "All right now, let's try to reach an understanding…"

As the outer door closes Porgie reaches under his coat and pulls out a strawberry-rhubarb pie covered with a thick layer of whipped cream. "Don't move now, Mr. Spud," Porgie says, holding the pie in a threatening manner. "Put your hands on the desk where I can see them. I'm not playing around—this pie is loaded."

Spud sighs and puts his hands on the desk. "Sure, sure, Georgie Porgie," he says. "Don't get your pudding in an uproar. What's all this about?"

"I intend to search your office, Mr. Spud," Porgie says, moving around to the side of the desk. "Now, just move aside—"

With a sudden leap, Sam knocks Porgie to the floor, deftly catching the pie as he does so. "There," he says. "That restores the natural balance of the universe. Now you just lie there, Porgie; I'll take that pie!"

"That," Porgie says, rubbing his jaw and glaring up at Spud, "was most unkind, Mr. Spud."

There is a perfunctory knock on the office door. It opens, and a large man stands in the doorway. Did I say large? I meant massive. Although not over five foot three, he is larger than life in every other dimension. His suit could have been styled for a hippopotamus, and it fits him well. His shoes could have been lived in by a family of cats. His perfectly round head protrudes from the collar of his jacket with no visible neck, and makes the rest of his body look petite. "What's all this, what's all this?" he demands in a booming voice, his eyes sweeping the room. "Porgie, get up off the floor; you look ridiculous!"

"Who are you?" asks Spud.

"Ah, you must be Mr. Spud. It is a privilege, no, may I say an honor to meet a man of your repute. As for myself, I am Wee Willy Winkie, at your service."

"Wee?"

"Ah, yes. An attempt at jollity on the part of my compatriots." Winkie chuckles. "As you can see, I am anything but 'wee.' But I have not come here to discuss my, ah, girth. There is an object in your possession that I am interested in obtaining." He waggles one huge finger at Porgie. "Georgie, get up! It is most unbecoming of you to spend the afternoon on the floor."

Porgie gets up and dusts himself off. "It wasn't my idea," he announces plaintively.

"Ah, I see. Up to your old tricks again." Winkie turns back to Spud. "Porgie will sometimes get ideas of grandeur, Mr. Spud, and attempt things for which he is constitutionally incapable. Kissing the girls is about his limit. He seems to get some strange, perverse pleasure in making them cry."

Porgie glares at the fat man. "Now Mr. Winkie, I act only in your interest, Mr. Winkie. And if we are to start telling tales out of school—there are a few things..."

Winkie raises a plump hand and barks, "Enough! Back to the affair at hand. You have the bird, Mr. Spud?"

"I haven't said so."

"You have the bird, Mr. Spud. But do you know what it is that you have?"

Spud grins. "Frankly, Mr. Winkie, I do not."

"Well, Mr. Spud; this is an object of incredible worth. And I shall not be stinting in my reward, of that I can assure you."

"Generalities, Mr. Winkie. Let's get down to facts."

"Of course, Mr. Spud. The facts themselves are incredible—but indisputably true. I shall relate them."

"But Mr. Winkie…" Porgie begins, looking horrified.

"Shut up, Porgie. There's enough to go around—no need to be greedy. Mr. Spud, are you familiar with the legend of Goosy-Goosy Gander?"

"It's a kid's nursery rhyme."

"Humph! A nursery rhyme indeed!" Winkie shakes his massive head to refute the very notion. "It is much more than that. Let me relate it to you:

"Goosey-Goosey Gander, whither shall I wander?
"Up stairs and down stairs, and in my lady's chamber.
"There I met an old man who would not say his prayers
"I took him by the left leg, and threw him down the stairs.

"Well, what do you think, Mr. Spud?"

"I think I'll go to lunch now."

Winkie chuckles. "Understandable. You have listened, but you have not comprehended. Now I will tell you the story of that ancient rhyme. There was an emperor, Mr. Spud, in the seventh century, called Carlus Magnus. We know him better today as Charlemagne. The name, perhaps, rings a faint bell?"

"Charlemagne? Sure, I've heard of him."

"Sarcasm! You have heard of him? The ruler of perhaps the greatest empire the world has ever seen. Well, at any rate, Carlus Magnus had a mother, Mr. Spud; that is indisputable. And his mother, perhaps because of her profession, this is unclear, was known as Bertha, the Goose Girl. This is historical fact! Because of this, Carlus was called 'Carl the Goose' by his close friends."

"Is that so?"

"Yes, Mr. Spud, that *is* so. In honor of the annexation of Ruritania, the Grand Knights of the Order of the Maltese Goose—named in honor of Carlus's mother—presented the emperor with a small statuette, some three feet high and a foot and a half across. This tiny bird, Mr. Spud, was encrusted with gems more precious than those that Jack gave Jill, that Punch gave Judy, then Tweedledum presented to Tweedledee—but we won't discuss *their* relationship."

"Must have been some rocks."

"Yes, of course Mr. Spud. In the year 1274, when the Mongols over-ran Ruritania, this precious goose disappears, leaving behind only a vague, mysterious poem to explain its whereabouts. I will not tell you of the years I worked to decipher that verse; of how I traveled to Budapest to establish the identity of the 'old man.' Of the time I spent living in a shoe—a shoe, Mr. Spud—to find out why he wouldn't say his prayers. The layers I had to penetrate to discover why it was the *left* leg. But finally, Mr. Spud, it all came together. I almost had that fabulous goose in my grasp when it was snatched from me by a cruel twist of fate."

Spud leans back in his chair and grins up at the fat man. "Sorry to hear that. These cruel twists of fate are hard to take."

"Was that more sarcasm, Mr. Spud? I admire a man who isn't afraid to use sarcasm. A man who uses sarcasm can be depended upon to employ alliteration, simile, and onomatopoeia."

"Get on with it, Winkie!" Porgie growls. "Try to stay on one subject for more than twenty seconds!"

"You're right, Porgie. Well, Mr. Spud, as I said, I will pay well for the recovery of this little statuette."

Spud lets the chair fall back down and puts his hands flat on the desk. "I may be able to get my hands on it, gentlemen. Give me a few hours and I'll get back to you."

"A few hours?" Porgie asks, managing to sound insulted. "How do we know what you will do in a few hours? How can we trust you?"

"You haven't got much choice, have you? You don't think I'm going to trust you two birds."

Winkie chuckles, a massive, booming chuckle. "You're a forthright man, Mr. Spud. I admire a man who says what he thinks. A forthright man can—"

"Winkie!" Porgie cries.

"Oh, sorry. We'll go now, Mr. Spud, but we'll be back. Let us say at six o'clock?"

"Sure, let us say that," Spud says, grinning a wolfish grin.

After they leave Spud remains at his desk, not doing anything. Perhaps he is deep in thought. Perhaps not. A short while later Miss Muffit knocks at the front door.

"Mr. Spud—Mr. Spud—are you there?"

"In here, doll."

"Oh. Here you are," she says, coming into his office. "I got your message. Listen, I'm very sorry about your partner, Mr. Dumpty. I can't help feeling responsible."

Spud waves Miss Muffit into the client chair. "No need for that. He knew what he was getting into. He fell off that wall with both eyes open."

"I'm glad you feel that way, Mr. Spud – Sam."

"Yeah. Your friend Georgie Porgie was here earlier."

"Georgie?—Porgie? What did he—that is, did he say anything about—anything?"

"He wants the bird."

"The bird. Ah, the bird. What bird is that, Sam?"

"You *are* good. The fat man was here too."

"Wee Willie Winkie? The pair of them here? What did they say? You're not going to sell me out, are you, Sam? You're the only man I can trust."

The wolfish grin appears on Spud's face. Where else? "Trust? Hah! That's a good one. You haven't told the truth since we met."

"Why, whatever do you mean?" Miss Muffit asks, her hands going to her mouth, her eyes wide with astonishment.

"You have no sister, sister. And your name isn't Muffit. I checked it out."

Miss Muffit, or whoever she is, drops her hands to her side. "You're right. I lied. I shouldn't have, but I needed your help so desperately I was afraid to tell you the truth."

"What is the truth?"

"My name is Mary. Mary Q. Contrary."

"I see. And is that the truth?"

"Yes, I swear. Oh, you must believe me, Sam."

Sam Spud nods. "Tell me about the bird."

"Just a bauble, Sam. A family heirloom."

The wolfish grin reappears, and then disappears, to be replaced by a deep frown line above his eyebrows. "They offered me five thousand dollars for it, sweetheart."

"Oh, Sam, you *don't* trust me. You *are* going to sell me out."

"That's funny, that is, Mary Mary. What have you ever given me but fairy tales?" Spud rises and comes around the desk. "If you want me to help you, you're going to have to tell me what's happening, no matter how screwy it sounds."

Mary Mary takes a deep breath. "All right, Sam. It's this way, Sam. The fat man hired me to get the goose for him. A fellow named Simon had it. Simple Simon, they called him. But he wasn't as simple as they thought. I tried silver bells, and I tried cockle shells, but he wouldn't fall for it. Then I went all the way."

"Not— "

"Yes." She nods, a blush spreading across her face. "Little maids. All in a row."

Spud considers this. "Some people will do anything for a goose," he says finally.

"I admit it, Sam," Mary Mary says, giving Sam a practiced wide-eyed stare. "I haven't been a good girl."

"The way I hear it, you've been very good."

She winces. "I deserved that, Sam."

"Who has the goose now?" Sam asks, sitting on the edge of the desk.

"Bo Peep."

"Bo Peep?"

"Yes. A charming girl. She's a shepherdess. She promised to deliver it as soon as she found something she was looking for."

"And what about this Lloyd Thursday? Where does he fit in?"

"The Spoon? He was working for Simple Simon, trying to get the statue back. I wanted to keep an eye on him. The Spoon was a slippery character."

"I got it now." Spud nods thoughtfully. "Quite a story, but I think you're telling me the truth. Who do you think killed him?"

A shrug. "Winkie? Porgie? It's hard to say."

"Do you think one of them killed my partner, too?"

"Oh, yes!" Mary Mary says, giving the wide-eyed stare another work-out. "Don't you, Sam?"

"It doesn't much matter what I think. The police would sure like to pin this on someone."

There is a knock at the door. Spud turns. "Come on in, it's open."

Porgie enters. "Mr. Spud, I am, perhaps, a trifle early?"

"Hello, Porgie," Contrary says quietly.

"Mary Mary, of course you'd be here. Keep away from me, I don't trust you. Bad things seem to happen when you're around."

"Just sit down, Porgie. Don't get your pudding and pie in an uproar. Where's your friend?"

"Wee Willie? He will be along directly."

And another knock on the door.

Spud sighs. "This is getting monotonous. Come on in!"

A young girl, dressed the way Marie Antoinette imagined shepherd-esses dressed, enters. She has a sheep under one arm and a large object wrapped in brown paper under the other. "'Allo, 'allo," she says in a lilting French accent. "'As anyone seen—oh, zere you are, Mary Mary."

"Baa, baa," says the sheep under her arm.

"Hello, Bo Peep," says Mary Mary. "Did you find what you were looking for?"

"Baa, baa." (The sheep again.)

"Yes, thank you. I have your package for you. Frankly I was getting tired of lugging it around. I'll just set it on the desk here." She does so. "Well, I have to run."

"Baa, baa." (You know.)

"Thanks a lot, Bo, you've been a real help."

"Glad to help." she waves gaily. "Bye now."

And a last distant "Baa, baa," is heard as she heads down the corridor.

"Well," says Spud, "let's look at this thing."

"Yes, yes; get the wrappings off. It's been so long," says Porgie.

"Wait!" Winkie bellows, wobbling into the room. "You'll excuse my undue haste, but I did not wish to miss the, ah, unveiling."

Spud nods. "Understandable, Winkie. Sit down, we'll all watch."

"Ah, yes, thank you." He turns and bows to Mary Mary. "Good day, Miss Contrary." And then seats himself in one of the client chairs. It is a tight fit, but he makes it.

"Now," says Spud, "settle down everyone. Let's not get excited. Go ahead, Mary Mary."

"All right, Sam. If you say so."

Mary Mary rips off the brown paper wrapper. A strange looking object is unveiled. "Ah, there it is—look!"

Georgie Porgie leans forward, his eyes bulging. "But that—it's—Mr. Winkie, look!"

Winkie pushes himself up from his seat and leans forward. "Say," he says, is voice quivering with emotion. "Is this some sort of joke?"

Sam Spud peers at the object. "What is that supposed to be?"

"It's a goose, of course," Mary Mary says, sounding puzzled at the uproar. "I admit it's not exactly representational. It's a sort of surrealist goose. The way I see it, this brass piece here is the beak, while the wooden sort of toilet seat is—"

"If this is a jest," Winkie interrupts loudly, "it is in very bad taste. Mr. Spud, I suspect the Contrary girl is attempting to gull us."

"It looks like you're the goose, Mr. Winkie," Porgie snaps, an undercurrent of petulant anger bubbling to the surface of his voice.

"Shut up, Georgie. Miss Contrary, where is the real goose?"

"But this is it!" Mary Mary insists. "I mean, this is the package I took from Simple Simon."

"Ha! Simple Simon, indeed!" Winkie snorts a fine and rounded snort. "He has taken us. I, for one, do not propose to be made a fool of. Goosy Goosy Gander may wander, but I shall see that he is brought home." He buttons his jacket. "Are you with me, Georgie Porgie?"

Porgie rises, looking dazed but game. "Yes, yes. It has taken this long— what's another hundred years or so?"

"And what of you two? Miss Contrary has shown herself to be quite resourceful in the past. And you, Spud, I could use a man like you."

"No, no," Mary Mary says sadly. "I don't think I'll come. I've had enough of this running around. I have a garden to tend."

"Mr. Spud?"

Spud shakes his head. "No thanks, Winkie; I have plans for the next hundred years."

"A pity." Winkie places his hat (Did I mention that he has a hat? Well, he has a hat: An oversized straw boater.) firmly on his head. "Well, we must be off."

He and Porgie go out the door, arm in arm. "First to Istanbul," Winkie tells Porgie as they head down the hall, "then to Gotham."

Their voices trail off as they start down the stairs. "You think the three wise men—"

"Perhaps, perhaps. Old Mother Hubbard, on the other hand…"

…And their voices fade away, and they are gone.

Mary Mary clutches Sam's hand. "Oh, Sam, I was so frightened."

"Yeah, baby, I'm sure you were." Spud picks up the phone.

Mary Mary stands up, her hand to her throat. "What," she asks, a quaver in her voice, "are you doing?"

"Calling the police."

"The police?"

"You got it, baby. Hello, headquarters? Give me Inspector Sprat.

Hello, Jack? This is Sam. I'm at my office. Get over here right away, will you? I've got something for you. Right. I'll be here." He hangs up.

Mary Mary drops her hands to her side. "Oh, Sam," she says helplessly, "what are you going to do?"

"It's time for a little honesty, baby."

"Whatever do you mean?"

"It was you, Mary Mary—you poached my partner. He may have been cracked, but you're the one who scrambled him."

"How can you say that, Sam?"

"No one else could have done it. He never would have gone onto that wall with Thursday. But with you? He'd follow you right up there, licking his lips and loosening his cravat."

"I thought it was a belt."

"And then you pushed him. He fell twice, you might say. You didn't kill Thursday, some gunsel killed Thursday. But you pushed the egg off that wall!"

After a long pause, Mary Mary says in a low and quavering voice, "What are you going to do, Sam?"

Spud straightens his tie. "I thought maybe you and I'd run off together."

"You don't want me to take the fall?"

"Nah!" Spud shakes his head. "Humpty took the fall. I never liked him much anyway."

Inspector Pratt pushes open the office door. "Sam," he says, "I got here as fast as I could. What have you got for me?"

"I want you to be my best man, Jack," Spud tells Sprat. "Mary Mary and I are getting hitched."

"Say, that's great, Sam."

Mary Mary clutches Spud by the arm and goes up on her toes to kiss him on the cheek. "Oh Sam, Sam," she says, the vibrato doing overtime in her voice, "you're a prince!"

"Yeah." Spud grabs his coat and they head out the door.

Sprat pauses at the door and looks behind him. "Say, what's that thing on your desk?" he asks.

"Oh that?" Sam Spud shrugs. "Just a goose." ◆

HERMIT'S CAVE

Last of the Legares
by T. Wayne Clay

"Ghost stories! Weird stories! And murders, too! The Hermit knows of them all. Turn out your lights. Turn them out! And listen to my hounds howling…as I tell you the story of…Last of the Legares."

Virginia stepped forward and gazed down into the casket. He looked just like he was sleeping, she thought. The reddish rays of the late afternoon summer sun crept through the burgundy drapery and into the study where the wake was being held. The few mourners, mainly servants of this old plantation house, waited in silence as she paid her last respects. Old Raylo, the family's devoted black butler, had excelled himself in preparing the body for burial in the best backwoods bayou tradition.

Gaston was still a handsome man in his middle years, dressed in his favorite white suit and dignified by the pencil-thin moustache he always sported. With his immaculately groomed thick, dark hair and lean facial features, he was the epitome of a bygone Louisiana gentry. What bothered Virginia most was that subtle sneer on her dead husband's face—for, even in this somber repose, that cruel streak so attributed to his lineage shone through to the end.

Virginia backs away now from the bier to be comforted in this sorrowful time by Wesley, a distant cousin recently arrived from Natchez—or so he had introduced himself to this small gathering just this very afternoon—a tall, striking young man dressed appropriately in black.

Raylo now steps forward and closes the top of the mahogany coffin. Three other black men, all locals who abide in the nearby swampland of this isolated region, assist him in lifting the polished wooden box, carrying it out of the study and through the portal of the front door.

The young blond widow, clinging to Wesley, follows the group while

153

Preacher Simms, an elderly black minister with Bible in hand and moving along with a touch of rheumatism, is the last to emerge from the antebellum manor as they make their way toward the family crypt - an old, decaying stone structure a few yards away from the garden. The walkway leading to the crypt is shaded by tall oak trees garnished with the ever-present Spanish moss so familiar to this particular and picturesque locale.

The procession approaches the mausoleum which has withstood the dank humidity of the climate for well over two centuries...before that time when echoes of gunfire from the strife known hereabouts as the War Between the States rang through the dense forests. The pallbearers with the utmost care enter the crypt, placing the wooden coffin on the stone centerpiece. The grating sound as the casket comes to rest is eerie in its effect. The four black men now exit the structure as Raylo, being the last one, closes the rusty iron gate behind him.

The young widow, her face veiled by black, watches in silence along with Wesley.

Preacher Simms, with reverence, faces them and opens his Bible.

"Man that is born of woman is of few days, and full of trouble. He comes forth like a flower and withers."

Wesley, with head bowed, manages to glance at Virginia as Preacher Simms continues.

"He flees like a shadow and continues not. Let us pray."

Virginia closes her eyes - but sheds no tears.

"Almighty Father, may you take into your caring arms the soul of our dearly departed...and give comfort and strength to the living. Amen."

Virginia and Wesley join in together. "Amen."

Near the swamp's edge and partially obscured in the shadows of a large tree stands a beautiful young black woman shabbily dressed. She observes the goings-on with keen interest.

Preacher Simms steps to Virginia and comments, "There rests the last of the Legares—descendant of a long line of troubled and wicked men. I pray that he finds peace."

Virginia adds, "No one wishes that more than I, Preacher Simms. I thank you for comin' here today." She starts back toward the white mansion which, now in the setting sunset, has taken a grayish pallor.

She continues to offer her own explanation for her dead husband's legacy.

"Poor Gaston was not to blame. His mother sheltered him here with her odd beliefs. I did my best to console him…and change him…for the short time we were married."

Preacher Simms disagrees. "No, my child. I doubt if there was anything you could have done to change him. The old tradition was bred into them. Speakin' for myself, Mrs. Legare…I don't think it was fair of him to take such a young bride and keep her shut away here like he did."

Wesley joins in. "As soon as the estate is settled I'm goin' take Cousin Virginia away from this dreary place. A trip to Paris will do her a lot of good."

Preacher Simms looks about surveying the surrounding swamp and shaking his head.

"Folks 'round here say that when the Almighty made this here world, he turned His back on this bayou. Superstition still hangs over it like a dark cloud. If only it could die as easily as men do. I'll stay on preachin' the Good Book and fight that curse to my dyin' day."

The warm summer wind suddenly gushes against them.

Preacher Simms remarks, "Be dark soon. Looks like a good rain comin' up. I'll be getting' on. You take care of your cousin, young man."

"Oh, I will do that, sir," Wesley adds with a smile.

"Goodbye, Preacher…and thank you," Virginia replies as she eyes the clouded skyline.

Preacher Simms joins the pallbearers in his old black Pontiac sedan. The young pair watches as she car departs out the huge gate at the end of the long driveway and onto the muddy dirt road.

"He was right, Wesley. We may get a good rain tonight," says the young widow as she leads him now into the front door of the aging mansion.

Wesley slams the large wooden door shutting off any remaining sunlight. Inside the dark hallway the overhanging chandelier adorned with candles looms above them. Virginia now tears off the cumbersome mourning veil and bursts into gleeful laughter.

"We did it! WE'RE RID OF HIM!"

She rushes to Wesley, throwing her arms around the handsome man as they now swirl about happily. Wesley gives her a passionate kiss, then replies, "Oh, you are the most beautiful widow I think I have ever seen…'Cousin' Virginia!"

"I do declare, I thought I was just goin' to bust out laughin' watchin' you try to keep a straight face, Wes honey!"

"Well, just dreamin' of all that money your departed husband's leavin' you is enough to tickle any man's fancy, ain't it, sugar?"

Virginia becomes serious for a moment.

"You don't reckon anyone's goin' suspect somethin', do you?"

Wesley moves into the study where moments earlier her husband had been resting quietly in his coffin. He pours himself a good slug of bourbon in a tumbler as Virginia watches him from the doorway.

"How could they, darlin'? I think havin' that little black witch cook up that poison was a marvelous idea."

He takes a gulp.

"Mixin' it in with his nightly glass of port was perfect. Why, no one will ever know."

He savors the liquor as he winks at the lovely widow.

"And then your persuadin' that drunk doctor to sign the death certificate showed considerable expertise. But he always had an eye for beauty, didn't he?"

"Oh, yes. Ever since I first arrived here. But he was way too shy to flirt with me…at least while Gaston was around."

"That's a man after my own heart, I'd say."

Virginia smiles while she adds, "It was always Gaston's wish to be interred right here on the estate without a formal service or outside fuss. Why should a bunch of strangers dictate how a man should be laid to his final rest anyways? Keepin' it 'just fam'ly' made it so much easier."

"Well, let's drink to dear Gaston's memory. A man with foresight," laughs Wesley.

"No, don't, honey. That ain't right. He's dead. Let's just let him rest in peace," she says with the hint of superstitious uneasiness. "It's hot and I'm sticky all over. I think I'll slip out of these clothes into somethin'…more comfortable."

Wesley's eyes follow her as she now prances out of the study and up the staircase.

"You know, Virginia…I think black's your color."

Virginia turns and smiles back at him coquettishly.

"Why don't you come on up and help me undress?"

Wesley, drink in hand, hurries after his shapely lover.

At the top of the stairs Virginia can hear the distant rumble of the approaching storm. The rain will cool off this old house, she thinks. Gaston had always lived in the past, like the rest of his breed, without the comfort of modern conveniences. That old Creole aristocracy...proud and stubborn...would not have let him be otherwise. She can remember him saying, almost like his ghost was there in the hallway with her...whispering in her ear...that such contrivances were the work of Yankee minds. It was always Yankee this...and Yankee that—so immersed in their infernal Southern thinking were these Legares, she thought.

She remembered that old story that he used to tell her. During the great war against the Northern invaders a group of Yankee soldiers had trespassed onto the Legare plantation. Gaston's great-great-grandfather had lured these hapless men into that immense swamp and, with a new Henry rifle, then tracked them down one by one. A man lost in this seemingly endless green maze had no chance at all pitted against avid hunters like the Legares, for this was one of the few hobbies they clung to. Such tales as this the young children hereabouts relished hearing on many a rainy eve.

Besides, men should live with what the Almighty had given them...nothing more. Even though he was freshly laid in his tomb he was still with her. Gaston was one of those rare men, so intense in his bearing and with such a lack of fear of anything, that the average mortal might wonder if death would ever dare knock at his door. Wesley was correct when he told the old reverend that Paris would be good for her. There she would be finally free of her husband's everlasting possessiveness...and free to spend his money. This was money, of course, invested in solid Southern enterprises.

In the large master bedroom Virginia undresses and tosses the black dress into the arms of a nearby chair. But there, on the dressing mirror, sits a photo of Gaston and her on their wedding day. That was a mere six months ago. It seemed like six years! Now she can throw it away. Or better still...she would burn it.

The photo distinctly shows Gaston's physical handicap that she so detested. Where his right hand should be is the steel hook he had worn since childhood. He had once described the incident in detail to his young wife. As a youngster he had been warned by his stern mother not to play with the alligators that shared the habitat of the Legare estate. Often the creatures would be tossed the leftovers from the evening meals and they would eagerly away the delicious morsels of discarded meats. Gaston, being a curious child, liked to pet animals...and once, while caressing a seemingly docile 'gator, the beast had, in one quick instant, viciously snapped off his hand!

Gaston recounted the story to his pretty bride of how his mother had severely reprimanded him...even as the blood was gushing freely from the stump. Gaston still had fond memories of his dear mother and he looked for similar attributes in young women...her beauty...her poise...her strength.

His mother was indeed strong. For, according to Gaston, she was ever so faithful to his father. There was talk among the swamp folk that the Legare men had yet another family tradition. They had kept mistresses—black women...quadroons—what the people hereabouts would describe only in the most secret of places as "voodoo queens." For the Legares were feared among these common folk. If anyone stood up against them or even complained of unfair treatment these swamp witches would...and could...place a curse of ill fate upon them. And so, with this, the Legares remained powerful to the last.

But Virginia was not one of these backwood illiterates. She was a woman of breeding—or so she proclaimed—and made no effort to dissuade her handsome husband. She was from New Orleans miles away and possessed the etiquette of a woman of means. How good an actress Virginia was, she thought. How gullible Gaston must have been to believe the stories of her upbringing. Of course, he was prone to overlook them by his fascination with her bedside charms. To Gaston she was a passionate angel. His marriage to her was the pinnacle of his life, he often remarked to her.

He had worshipped Virginia from afar the first time he watched her riding her horse in that beautiful park near New Orleans. It was on one of the few trips he had made off the plantation. She remembers that day well, too. She hardly noticed the horse-drawn carriage under the shade of the looming trees as her steed galloped by. While she came to a brief stop to turn the sleek stallion, a black servant hailed her down and asked that she come over to the coach and meet his benefactor. With curious fascination Virginia did so and first heard the deep, commanding voice of the mysterious man inside.

"I have been watching you, my dear. Forgive me for perhaps imposing upon you...but I see no other way to make your acquaintance. You are indeed beautiful."

Virginia was used to the flattery of men, but his seemed so honest...so sincere.

"Thank you, sir."

She looked into the dark corner of the carriage, but could not see his face...only the large brim of his white hat and the puffs of smoke emitting from his cigar. Then he leaned forth out of the shadows and she saw him. By those handsome features and his finely woven white suit she knew he was a man of means.

Never had Virginia been so impressed by a gentleman. He was careful not to reveal his right hand, she now recalls to herself. He was sensitive about it and rightly so. For many a swooning young belle the mere sight of it must have caused alarm. Virginia was different and this stranger sensed it. She had courage. Rarely do beautiful women possess so many fine points, his eyes seemed to say, as he gazed upon her ravishing good looks. Virginia was in complete accord.

"May we dine tonight?"

"I would be honored, sir."

And that is how the romance started. So simple, so direct. Even from their first meeting, though, Virginia was soon to become his master.

For all of his strange life Gaston had stayed close to his mother. His private schooling had taken place in that large mansion and in the garden. His mother mistrusted outsiders, he told her. Perhaps it was fortunate that she had not lived to witness his happy wedding day—for she had passed away only a few months prior to their meeting. It was certain, Virginia pondered, that that wise old patriarch would have seen through her and her motive for marrying her only son. His mother would surely have found out the truth about her...and she hated the old lady even to the grave. How would she have explained her working in those dingy dives of Bourbon Street? She was little more than a woman of low repute, Virginia admitted to herself.

But all that was past and she could take a deep breath of relief knowing that this night she had all she had set out to obtain. No one...not her dead husband...or his dead mother...would interfere with her right to live a long and leisurely life on the money they had for so many years hoarded to themselves. The Legares had always lived in the past. Let them stay there.

Suddenly Wesley pounces into the bedroom and Virginia snaps out of her mental daze. She now turns her attention to him. He spies the photo of

Gaston on the dresser and turns it over. His only thought now is making love to this beautiful woman and the thought of her late husband eyeing them, even in a photograph, in their heat of passion would spoil all the fun.

"I want you to burn it, Wes."

"Tomorrow's soon enough, honey," he remarks while finishing his glass of bourbon.

He tosses the glass into a corner and kisses the blushing widow. They fall onto the large bed and enjoy the sweet intimacy they have long awaited.

An hour passes. Thunder is heard coming nearer to the large house and it echoes down the dark hallways. Virginia stops kissing Wesley and becomes silent. For once…in well over two centuries…there is no Legare in this mansion. It is strange to her. The dead cannot be shut out so easily and so quickly, she thinks. For the presence of those who have lived, laughed, celebrated holidays and the coming of children in this place cannot simply cease by such an ordinary thing as death. How naïve for even her to think such a thing.

"What is it, Ginnie, dear? Are you tirin' out so soon?" Wesley asks.

"It's just that I don't belong here. I never did. And now I feel so aware of it."

"One more night here won't be so bad, dear. Then, tomorrow, if you want to, we can head back to New Orleans. The lawyer can settle ev'rythin' for us."

"I guess that'll have to do," Virginia agrees.

A sound abruptly comes from downstairs. They both hear it and turn quickly to the door.

"Must be one of the servants come back for somethin'," says Wesley, who for a moment is shaken by the sudden noise.

"Let's go see," Virginia adds as she gets up and hurriedly scurries into a nightgown.

Wesley likewise puts on his bathrobe and leads the way out of the bedroom and into the darkened hallway.

They look down from the upper stairway into the hall below. It is dark now and they can see nothing. They begin descending the steps and can hear the rustling of bottles in the kitchen.

Wesley gets up the courage to push open the door as Virginia looks over his shoulder. Inside the kitchen is the young black girl who had watched the burial.

Virginia is both relieved and aggravated by her intrusion into the sanctity of her home.

"Ravenique! You scared the life out of us!"

"What are you doin' here anyway, girl?" Wesley snaps.

Ravenique is not shaken by their appearance or the question.

"I came for my things," she quietly answers.

"What things you talkin' 'bout? You got no business here anymore," Wesley says as he pushes his way into the kitchen.

"My things," Ravenique repeats.

Virginia calms him and explains. "She means her bottles…those herbs and potions."

"She couldn't have waited 'til the mornin' to get that stuff? Hell, you're the woman of this house now, Ginnie. Set her straight."

"I get my things and go," Ravenique adds politely.

"Very well. Get them." Virginia replies while eyeing the lovely quadroon.

Virginia walks into the study and opens an ornate cigarette container that had been passed down to her husband from another generation. She lights up and takes a good puff.

Wesley starts up the staircase, turns and addresses Virginia. "You comin' up?"

"In a minute."

She takes another puff on the cigarette while watching her collect the bottles from a cabinet. Virginia is curious. She never really got very close to this mysteriously quiet black girl. This was the servant that her husband had always spoken of before they were married.

Ravenique. How that name suited her. She was dark and beautiful…perhaps more beautiful than she. Virginia could see how this younger woman might attract a man like Gaston. And he might, too, have a penchant for her…simply for pleasure and nothing more. Ravenique was primitive and full of dark passion. She had no pretense. Material wealth had no place in her world for she was used to servitude as had been her mother and her mother before her. They had all bowed before the Legares. They were part of this remote world, this swampland the rurals called Black Bayou.

In this land time had stood still…and so had the age-old traditions of her people. They believed deeply in things most whites would not bother to ponder. Yes, the white folk might even scoff and laugh at such words…voodoo…gris-gris…charms and potions and the like. These were things of folklore. To Ravenique they were as much a part of her as the dark blood running through her veins.

For many years past these swamp dwellers had gathered to celebrate their voodoo rites. A beautiful young quadroon, not unlike Ravenique, would dance under the full of the moon. Her ebony, sweaty flesh glistening in the flickering flames of the bonfire, the gaze of the fanatical onlookers intoxicated with the unleashing of savage emotions…these were forbidden, raw images a modern woman like Virginia could never conjure in her mind.

Virginia recalled Gaston telling her the story of how once he was stricken with what the locals called "swamp fever," a malady that had put many a strong man in the dank earth before his time. But Ravenique, with all her herbs and potions, had him up and on his feet in only a few days. She was indeed valuable here…for the Legares placed no trust in modern doctors educated in far-off cities. They had survived quite prosperously without them.

As Virginia smoked she wondered what Ravenique thought of her - this pale, blue-eyed woman, this stranger - the one who had come into her world and married a man whom she served.

Virginia approaches her directly.

"Did you come for money?"

Ravenique is silent and only looks at her.

"Is it more you want?"

Ravenique only stares and a faint smile crosses her face as Virginia questions her.

"Well?"

Very deliberately and simply the quadroon answers.

"What I did was not for money."

Virginia does not understand. Was it not the fatal brew that this girl concocted that put her husband in his grave?

"Then for what earthly reason did you do it?"

"Because I loved him, too. He was mine…before you came. He belonged to me."

Virginia's suspicions now come to light.

Ravenique continues. "He was the only man I have ever loved. I was angry that he brought you here. He was not for you. But he will be mine now."

Virginia does not understand her meaning. It sounds so strange. For he is dead. She can only see the humor in it and nothing more.

"Then take him. I give him back to you," she says coyly as she crushes the butt of the cigarette in an ashtray and now starts back up to the bedroom.

Ravenique stoically watches her ascend the staircase.

Another hour passes and the rain comes down in a cloudburst. The drops hitting the roof of the old house make a sound that puts one to sleep on such a night. It is a much-deserved baptism from heaven. This is what Virginia thinks as she lies next to Wesley, both tired from their bout of lovemaking.

Virginia has sinned indeed, and has much to answer for. She planned her own husband's demise. But like Preacher Simms said—the Legares were wicked men. She tries to console herself that the world is better off without him and, someday in the future, she will be forgiven for her prime transgression.

Gaston, with that steel hook of his, looked menacing, but when he made love to her in the quiet sanctum of this same bedroom he was such a gentle mate. That cold metal caressing her hair and the soft flesh of her back was a distinctly different thrill for even her. He had described to her how he had procured the services of a local Cajun blacksmith to create that polished work of horror. This surely cost him a pretty penny, but it was a masterwork! With it he could hold his favorite pen or an expensive cigar with ease. But the end of the hook was profoundly sharp and tempered.

Virginia saw the steel appendage at its worst one night while they dined at an exclusive restaurant in Baton Rouge. A drunken patron from the bar had made a foolish and wanton remark to her within her husband's earshot. The dress she had worn that certain evening was particularly revealing and her supple breasts had caught the eye of every man in the establishment. In an instant, like a springing cougar, Gaston was upon him. The poor man escaped with only a slashed coat. If the man had not quickly sobered and dashed out of the dining room…Gaston promised to leave a scar on his face. This is an incident Virginia would long remember. Here she saw the two things her new husband carried with him constantly—his possessiveness of her and the shiny weapon he wore to defend it.

But the one fault she profoundly despised so much about Gaston was that he put her on that silver pedestal. He worshipped her. To him she was perfection personified. This was his only offense. Because inwardly she knew she deserved no such adulation. No woman did.

Gaston recounted once to her the first love of his life, his dear cousin Angelie. As a mere child he could not wait for the summers when she would come to visit them at the plantation and they would play in the garden. Then one day this little cherub dashed his fantasy of marrying her when he grew up. She told him that her family was moving far away…and she would not be spending her summers there again. Gaston was crushed. He loved her.

In a sudden moment of rage he shoved her into the nearby pool where they were sitting. Before his mother could rush from the porch of the mansion the 'gators had done their worst. His mother, of course, had the difficult task of informing her own sister of that horrible accident and that her dear Gaston was in no way to blame. After that fateful day, however, Gaston's playmates were limited to servants.

Virginia sometimes wondered if this story was indeed true. Could it be that Gaston was simply spinning a yarn or was he using this parable to warn her of his insane jealousy? Virginia had to be very careful in her meetings with Wesley. For she was the stranger on this isolated plantation and there would be no one to help her if Gaston would find her out. Then his wrath would be unleashed in all its fury and she, too, would see him with that awesome fear as all the others did.

Yes, he is better off now. And so is she. He had the comfort of the grave where no memories of the past can reach forth to tinge with the pain of life. He had an eternity of peace before him and would forever be spared the knowledge that the wife he had held so dear was, in fact, as tainted as black as the darkness which now covered the crypt within which he slept. This was her consolation—that death was eternal. No earthly power and no backwoods voodoo chant would ever awaken him. With this in mind she dozes quietly next to her lover.

It is about midnight and the rain has stopped. Ravenique walks softly along the path leading to the family crypt. She does not wish to arouse those inside the old mansion and carries an unlighted lantern. With a quick jerk she pulls open the iron gate leading to the mausoleum and enters. The match she strikes now throws eerie shadows on the graying walls which are then made more grotesque in shape as the lantern comes to full brightness.

Ravenique hangs the lantern from a protruding stone piece on the wall and gently opens the lid of the casket. The croaking of frogs from the nearby swamp and the chirping of crickets fill the night air. She gazes down at the body of Gaston Legare not with fear, but with a remorseful tenderness. Her petite hand strokes his face and a smile comes to her lips...like a mother caressing her sleeping baby. She mutters just three words...

"I love you."

From under her cloak the black girl takes a small glass vial from one of the pockets and removes the cork. She then places the vial over his closed mouth and a few drops wet his lips. With the utmost tenderness she kisses him.

"Gaston...my love, I have come for you."

Slowly, his chest rises and falls. Then again.

In the faint light of the hovering lantern she can see his eyes open and stare at the ceiling of the tomb. The sound of his breathing fills her ears.

A few moments pass. In the master bedroom Virginia is awake. With the rain stopped the summer humidity creeps in at the open window. She is thirsty and summons Wesley.

"Honey, would you be a darlin' and go downstairs for some port? My throat is so dry."

Wesley rolls over on his side to face Virginia. He was sleeping so soundly, too, he thinks to himself.

"Ginnie...at this late hour?"

"I've worked up a horrible thirst, Wes. Please be a dear and fetch it."

Wesley figures he must get accustomed to Virginia's whims. After all, he cannot afford to get on her bad side at this stage of their affair.

He stumbles out of bed and puts on his robe in the dark.

"You know where it is, don't you, sugar? On the table in the study."

"I'll find it."

He stumps his big toe in the dark and lets out a groan.

"Ouch! Oh, that hurts."

"And hurry back, sweetie. This rain's given me a crick in my neck. You can work it out."

"I'll be right back, don't you fret."

Wesley opens the door and goes into the dark hallway. From there he finds the handrail of the staircase and goes down it slowly in his bare feet.

Virginia rubs her sore neck. It has been a busy day in many respects and the tension has mounted for her. She will be glad when the daylight comes to this dreary manor. She ponders to herself while her lover is out of the room. He will make a nice companion to travel the byways of Paris. There will be many wealthy man there and, once shed of Wesley, she may obtain the status she has coveted for so long.

Wesley was her partner in this dark little enterprise. He would be a fool to talk about their little plot because that would implicate himself as well. Virginia rests securely with the knowledge that he will be easy to toss off when the time comes.

Down in the study Wesley has lit a candle and finds an unopened bottle of port and two glasses which he grabs. The door leading to the garden has blown open from the storm and the wooden floor is wet. He uses his shoulder to force it closed again. He is careful not to slip on the beads of water. Wesley starts back upstairs again with his bottled booty.

Virginia rests now on her stomach looking out the rain-stained window. The port will help her drift back off to sleep. She has filled herself to the brim with love this night. Now Wesley must get back. The crick in her neck is more bothersome and she will get no rest unless he loosens those muscles with a good massage.

From the hallway downstairs she can hear a noise. That clumsy gigolo has bumped into something for sure. Hopefully he won't spill any of the port. With all the servants dismissed she will have to clean up any mess he makes in the morning. Maybe she should have kept Ravenique on…at least for one more day. It is too late now to worry about that.

Now the bedroom door slowly swings open. Virginia still looks ahead at the window. She can hear the bottle of port being placed on the dresser.

"My neck is really botherin' me, sugar. I need your gentle touch to work it out."

The bed shifts with the extra weight as her lover climbs in with her.

"The port can wait 'til you get this crick out."

Wesley is unusually silent. She feels his chilled hand begin to rub up and down on her neck.

"You're cold. To the right a little."

His hand moves over a bit and finds the spot that troubles her.

"That's it. Ooooh. That feels so good, honey."

His grip becomes firmer.

"Not too hard, Wes dear. Gentle now."

She moves her head to the side to expose the sort spot of her neck.

"That feels much better. Massage my back, too, and let me drift off to sleep right here."

The center of her back now chills with goose pimples as cold steel runs down her spine.

Virginia's heart freezes with stark terror.

This is not a nightmare for she is still wide awake. Virginia's throat becomes even drier in this moment which seems like an eternity.

She hears a tune humming behind her. It was Gaston's favorite - "Mama Dit Moi," a French melody he often intoned while reading in the study below.

Virginia is afraid to turn around, but must. The door is the only portal of escape.

She whirls to see now standing in the room his tall figure illuminated in silhouette by the faint yellowish rays of the moon.

Still in the white suit he had worn to the grave is her husband Gaston. That metal hook hangs by his right side. He is silent.

Virginia can only hear the pounding of her heart as she imagines his piercing eyes and that one thought now burning in his mind. To a man like Gaston she had committed the unforgivable.

In these quarters that he had kept as her nightly shrine, Virginia screams with all the life that is still in her. It is a harsh, long scream.

Outside the mansion near the stillness of the crypt stands Ravenique. She listens as the scream echoes across the bayou and then dissipates into black, eternal night. The chirping of crickets and the croaking of a few frogs fills the air as a smile beams on the face of the voodoo girl.

Her magic has proved triumphant. In her heart Ravenique knows that Gaston is hers…forever. ♦

A Witch's Tale

The Peltonville Horror
by Richard A. Lupoff

The Hudson-Terraplane roadster's electric headlights cut twin channels of brilliance through the swirling fog of the Peltonville Turnpike. The hour was late and traffic was almost nonexistent, save for the sporty little car's sleek, bright blue form.

The shrieking voice that had come from the automobile's custom-fitted Stromberg-Carlson radio gave way to the less disturbing and more polished tones of a staff announcer. "Tune in again next week for another *Witch's Tale*," he urged listeners. "But for now, sit back and relax, put your feet up and enjoy the melodic musical stylings of the Stan Sawyer Orchestra."

"What a relief!" Delia Davis managed a quiet little laugh tinged with a suggestion of nervousness. "I never did like those spooky programs, Paul darling. If I didn't love you so much I don't think I could ever put up with them."

"But Delia," Paul Carter reached across the seat to pat his sweetheart's hand, "it's all just make-believe. You don't think there's really an old witch named Nancy who's more than a hundred years old, and lives with a wise black cat named Satan, do you?"

"No." Delia hesitated. Then she repeated, "No. I guess not." Paul released her hand and she tightened the scarf over her head. Her hair was jet black; by candlelight Paul Carter said that it showed bits of midnight blue that matched the color of her eyes. Delia had let her hair grow longer now that the boyish look and the bobbed hair of the previous decade had been abandoned for a more feminine look. "I do so love the feel of the wind and the smell of the fresh air out here in the country. But it's getting awfully cold now that the sun is down. Feels more like winter than spring."

Paul laughed. "Changing the subject, are you?"

"I guess so. When we crossed that bridge over the Beeton River a while ago, I could just imagine we were flying through the stratosphere."

Delia reached for the tuning knob on the dashboard. The signal had drifted and she brought it back so the sound of saxophones and trumpets filled the convertible's tonneau. "I guess I just don't enjoy being scared. Well, maybe just a little, like at those frightening movies. But then I know you'll put your arm around me and I feel all safe. I wish we were married, Paul. Then you could put your arm around me all the time and I'd never be frightened again. Oh, Paul, will we ever be married? Can't we even set a date?"

"As soon as this Depression is over and the economy picks up again," Paul replied. "You know, I'm lucky to still have a job at all, but since they've been cutting salaries every few months, I can barely pay the rent on a furnished room. There's no way I could afford an apartment and support a wife."

Delia lowered her eyes to the engagement ring on her left hand. "We could sell my ring." She toyed with the narrow band and its tiny, glittering stone. "And we don't really need a car. As much fun as it is, Paul, you could take the streetcar to work at the plant."

Paul shook his head. "I bought the car before the crash. Some timing, wasn't it? I couldn't get a quarter of what it's worth, now. And you'll never sell your ring, Delia, not as long as I can draw breath and do a day's work. Listen—"

Delia interrupted him with a gasp. "Paul—what was that?"

"What, Delia? I didn't see anything."

"Right over there, Paul. I thought I saw something moving in the woods, and then—then there was a flash. I don't know what it was. Something bright, a point of light, two points of light. No, there were more. They kept blinking on and off. I think there were eight of them. I—they were some color I've never seen before. Something like red, I think, but so deep, so powerful—so frightening, oh, Paul, what could it be?"

Paul eased up on the roadster's accelerator and the little car slowed. "I don't see anything, Delia. Through this fog, I don't know how you did. But maybe there was a momentary break. It might have been an electric power line or a radio tower. Or maybe you just caught sight of a couple of stars."

"No, Paul. It was nothing like that. It was—oh, never mind. It's gone now, whatever it was. Let's go on."

A distant flash lit the night sky above the woods to the west. Paul pushed the car to a higher speed. As he did so a low, distant rumble followed the lightning. "Uh-oh. I hope we're not going to get rained on."

"Maybe we should stop and put the top up." Delia looked around them. The fog had largely lifted but the night had actually grown darker than ever. A bright moon struggled to send its light through thick storm clouds, but only an occasional break in the clouds permitted a brief moment of illumination.

Lightning flashed, closer and brighter, a sinister greenish sheet silhouetting dark deciduous vegetation. "Look!" Delia exclaimed, "there it is again!" She pointed toward the east. "Those lights, blinking like terrible, hungry eyes!"

This time Paul pulled the little car onto the shoulder of the road. He turned off the engine, followed Delia's pointing finger with his eyes. "I don't see anything."

"No," Delia shook her head. "They're gone. But wait, Paul, listen." The radio had of course lapsed into silence when the roadster's ignition was cut, and the whisper of the gathering storm sounded through pines and oaks.

There was another flash of lightning. This time Paul counted the seconds until thunder boomed. "What's the saying," he muttered, "a mile a second? That storm is only a few miles away now. In fact, I think I just felt the first raindrops on my face. Help me, Delia, let's get the top up!"

Delia cocked her head, "Listen to that, dear."

Paul frowned. "I hear the wind and rain."

"No, there's another sound. A sort of piping and hissing and scratching. Like some incredibly gigantic—oh, Paul, I don't know. Something horrible. Could there be a spider so huge that it towers above the trees? Is it possible?"

Paul put his arms around her. "No, Delia. It's just the storm. The thunder and lightning and wind. Really, dear, it's just the storm."

Paul fumbled for the three-cell flashlight that he kept in the Hudson-Terraplane. It blazed into light and he used it now as a work-lamp.

It took the effort of a few minutes to raise the canvas top on the little roadster and button it in place. Even so, Paul and Delia were halfway to a good drenching by the time they scrambled back into the car and slammed the side doors that turned it into a snug refuge from the storm. With the optimism of youth they laughed off their wet condition. Delia undid her scarf and primped her raven curls with a brush she'd carried in her purse.

Paul ran his fingers through his own rust-colored hair. He was overdue for a trim; the hair was beginning to curl over his collar. He turned the ignition key and mashed down on the self-starter switch with his heavy brogan. The Hudson-Terraplane's six-cylinder engine coughed once as if clearing its throat of the falling rain, then purred happily. Paul switched on the headlights. The fog had disappeared now, and twin shafts of raindrops appeared before the roadster.

"What shall it be, darling?" he asked. "Shall we push on or turn back to Springfield?"

Delia hummed for a moment, a habit of hers while considering choices. "I could do with a cup of warm soup beside a friendly fireplace, dear. Isn't there a roadhouse somewhere along the Peltonville Pike?"

Paul's brow furrowed in thought. "I'm pretty sure there is. I've only been to Peltonville a few times, but I think I recall seeing one not far beyond the Beeton River bridge."

"Oh, let's push on then, Paul. It's such a miserable night, the ride home wouldn't be any fun at all with our clothes all clammy and cold as they are."

"No sooner said than done!" He pulled the car back onto the black-top highway. "It's a good thing they paved over the old dirt road, isn't it!"

The roadster's tires hissed over the rain-swept blacktop. Now a few unseasonable hailstones were mixed with the drops. They clattered and bounced off the Hudson-Terraplane's hood and began to accumulate on the road surface as well. Winds pushed the lightweight car sideways but Paul Carter's skillful hands kept the roadster on a steady course. He reached to switch on the Stromberg-Carlson, but the lightning's interference and the noise of the storm, which had now struck in its full fury, made it impossible to hear anything worthwhile. Paul switched the radio back off.

He felt Delia's head resting on his shoulder and patted her hand with his own. Soon a sign appeared beside the highway, advertising Daniello's Road-house two miles ahead. Paul pushed on. Soon there was another sign. *Daniello's,* it read, *Steaks, Cocktails, Dancing to Willie Moore's African Chili Seven.*

Daniello's Roadhouse was a pleasant-looking establishment built in the popular Tudor Revival style, with cream-colored stucco walls marked by half-timbered beams. At least, that was the way it appeared in the spot-lights placed to illuminate its exterior. There was a neon sign on the roof, and the windows of stained diamond-glass showed an inviting amber color.

"We're here, Delia." Paul placed a gentle kiss on his sweetheart's fore-head.

Delia smiled up at him sleepily, then leaned away and stretched like a contented kitten.

The roadhouse door was made of heavy wooden planks and swung heavily on old iron hinges. Stepping inside, the couple were enveloped by the pleasant odors of hot, hearty cooking. They made their way to a lounge and found space for themselves on dark leather barstools. They could hear the sound of music coming from another room. Willie Moore's African Chili Seven lived up to their name. A hot version of "Decatur Street Stomp" drifted into the lounge.

A red-jacketed bartender asked for their order. Paul ordered a hot toddy. Delia giggled and asked for a tequila sunset. The lounge was not crowded. A few couples sat at tables. The other barstools were mostly unoccupied. The bartender placed their drinks in front of Paul and Delia and remarked that they were fortunate to make it safely through the storm.

"Why is that?" Paul asked.

The bartender pointed over his shoulder. On the shelf behind him a cathedral-topped Capehart radio. "Can't get anything now, but earlier the news said that the bridge was out. Beeton River's rising and the bridge couldn't stand the gaff."

Paul and Delia lifted their glasses in a silent toast. Paul introduced himself and Delia to the bartender.

"Mustafa Cristopolous," the bartender identified himself. Now Paul realized that his speech was unusual, more an oddity of intonation than an actual accent. His voice was deep and sounded like a truckload of gravel. "I am half Greek, half Turkish," the bartender explained, "I was born in Izmir. I don't suppose you've ever heard of that place." His face carried the marks of past experiences. His nose had been broken more than once, an oddly appealing dimple marked the center of his chin and an old scar on one cheek had faded now but looked as if it had once been livid. The absence of hair on his skull was made up for by a huge black moustache.

"In the old country the Greeks hated me because I was Turkish and the Turks hated me because I was Greek. So I come to America. Here, everybody's everything."

"But what about the bridge?" Delia asked.

"Big storm," Cristopolous growled. "The boss don't like me playing the radio when the band is on, but I like to listen to news. I get stations from Springfield, Aurora, Littleton. News on the Springfield station says too much debris coming down the Beeton River, jammed up under the bridge, roadway cracked. They won't even have crews there till after the storm is over."

He looked toward the entrance of the roadhouse as if he could see outside. "How bad is it now?"

Paul said, "It got pretty nasty, Mustafa. Rain turning to hail."

The big bartender nodded his understanding. Paul had finished his drink now, and Delia's glass was mostly empty. Cristopolous asked if they wanted a refill but instead they left the lounge and moved to the dining room. The African Chili Seven were playing "Deep Bayou Blues." Paul and Delia found a table and a waitress took their order. Paul asked for a sirloin steak. Delia asked for chicken. Both requested soup before their entrees.

While they ate they discussed what to do next. Clearly there was no point in trying to return to Springfield. They would get as far as the bridge and have to wait for repairs to be made.

"I'm afraid we'll have to continue on to Peltonville," Paul announced.

"But then we won't get back to Springfield until tomorrow at the soonest," Delia complained. "What will people think? Mother and Dad will be beside themselves. And all our friends, Paul—do you think it's right?"

He reached across the table and took her hand. "I'm afraid we don't have much choice. Besides, people will just have to think what they choose."

"I don't know." Delia frowned. "It's not as if we were married." Then, "Do you think there's an inn at Peltonville? If we got two rooms it might be all right. And if there's a telephone, I could call Mother and Dad and explain what happened."

"A good idea, darling, but in a storm like this one, if the bridge is out, you can be sure that the telephone lines are down, too. I'm sorry. But if your parents really love you and trust you, they'll stand by you. As for anyone else—well, we'll just have to see it through."

As they were leaving the roadhouse they stopped to speak with Mustafa Cristopolous once again. Paul asked how much farther it would be to Peltonville, and whether Mustafa thought the road would be drivable now. The bartender said it was only another dozen miles, and the road was a good one.

"I'm worried about the hail, though," Paul explained.

Cristopolous shrugged his massive shoulders. "Life is risky." He paused, then added, "But you be careful. Some bad things happen in Peltonville."

"What bad things?"

"Just bad things. There is an old synagogue there, people do not go any more. Good people, I mean. Good people have mostly left Peltonville. You be careful, Paul and Delia."

Cristopolous had remembered their names. Paul found small comfort in that. He asked, "What do you mean by that—about the synagogue, I mean."

A weary smile creased the bartender's battered features. He leaned across the polished mahogany and lowered his voice. "Did I tell you, I am myself a Jew?" He looked around as if worried that he might be overheard. "One more reason I left Europe. Bad enough to be both a Turk and a Greek. Being a Jew as well—that was enough to make everybody hate me. Here in America—well, no place is perfect, is it?" He nodded toward the African Chili Seven. "They still have to struggle. But if they were in Greece or in Turkey, they would have it far worse."

Paul was still concerned about the Peltonville synagogue. He pressed Cristopolous for information. Cristopolous told him that he had once been a member of the congregation. It was called Temple Beth Shalom— the House of Peace. But the old rabbi had been forced to leave and a new leader took control. The old rabbi, Yacoub ben Yitzak, Jacob son of Isaac, replaced by Yeshua ben Yeshua, Joshua son of Joshua.

Ben Yeshua was a kabalist. He introduced ancient Hebrew magic into the synagogue. Its name had been changed to Temple Beth Mogen, House of the Star. The old congregants had all left Peltonville, those who had not mysteriously disappeared before they could get away. Cristopolous was one of the lucky ones, he had avoided Peltonville ever since. Other Jews had come from far away to replace them and fill the ranks of Temple Beth Mogen.

"It's very bad, Paul. If you go to Peltonville, be very careful."

Once they were back in the car and Paul had the engine warming up, Delia turned toward him, the reflected light of the sign on Daniello's Roadhouse showing her worried expression. "Do you think we can make it to Peltonville, Paul?"

"There are other patrons. They didn't look too worried to me."

"But there's something else."

Paul turned and took her in his arms, comforting her. "What, sweetheart? Are you still worried about your reputation? I promise, I'll stand by you whatever they say."

"No, it isn't that, Paul. It's—remember those lights, those eyes, I thought they were. And that weird sound. They were real, you know. I could tell you didn't believe me, I know you too well to be fooled. There was something there."

"Oh, yes. A giant spider, was it?"

"I don't know. Maybe it was. Maybe something else. But there was something there, something alive. Oh, I don't like it. I don't know what it is, but I know it isn't nice at all."

Paul leaned back and looked into Delia's eyes. "If there was a monster loose in these woods, don't you think we'd have heard about it? Wouldn't there be stories in the *Springfield Courier* or reports on the radio? That's just the kind of thing they love to report. It's a nice change from weddings and Rotary Club meetings and high school basketball games. You haven't read anything about a monster, have you?"

"No," she admitted. "But still—I saw those lights and I heard that sound. You don't have to believe me but I know it was real, Paul, I know it!"

"Really, Delia—on a night like this, you were halfway asleep, we'd been listening to that spooky radio program, your imagination was playing tricks on you."

"But what about that evil rabbi? That whole story about the Jewish synagogue in Peltonville. I've been in a synagogue in Springfield. My friend Rebecca was married in a synagogue, I was in the wedding. It was a beautiful service. I don't see how it could be evil, any more than a regular church could be evil, but Mr. Cristopolous didn't seem to be making that up."

Paul shook his head. "Old World superstitions, Delia. Just look at the man. He's had a hard life. Heaven knows what terrible experiences he must have had in Europe. He was lucky to get out of there and come to America, from the things that are going on now. I don't think he was making it up either, but his head is so full of wild folktales, he could believe anything."

He turned on the headlights and backed the Hudson-Terraplane away from the roadhouse. In moments the little car was back on the highway. The storm had passed, the moon was bright and a black sky was dotted with colorful, distant stars that glittered like ice crystals in candlelight. The combination of moonlight, starlight and the roadster's headlamps showed the surface of the roadway, now white with crusted hailstones.

Paul reached to switch on the little car's radio. He twirled the tuning knob. On the Springfield and Aurora frequencies there was only hissing and crackling, but he managed to pick up a signal from Peltonville. He shook his head. "Is that music? Chanting? I can't understand a word of it. And it all sounds so weird."

Delia said, "I think it's Hebrew. The service at Rebecca's wedding was partly in Hebrew. I don't know what it means, of course, but that sounds like the service."

Paul tried to get a stronger signal but the best he could do was a faint chanting in an exotic tongue. He reached to turn off the radio but before he could do so the chanting faded into the background. Over it there came a hissing, piping, scraping noise, followed by the sound of voices exclaiming in ecstasy.

Even though the storm had passed, there was another flash of greenish lightning that seemed to come from all directions at once. The Hudson-Terraplane's engine sputtered into silence that was broken by an ear-shattering boom of thunder. Paul and Delia clutched each other's hands in alarm, then Paul managed a nervous chuckle. He grasped the steering wheel of the roadster and mashed down on the self-starter switch.

The little car's engine coughed once, then roared back to life. The orange light behind the radio's tuning dial glowed but there was no sound so Paul switched it off. He threw in the clutch, put the roadster in gear and set it to moving.

When they passed the Peltonville city limit Paul read the welcoming sign and population figures. Based on his recollection of his last visit he'd thought that Peltonville was bigger than the number indicated. Perhaps the latest census figures had shown a loss of population. Then he thought of Mustafa Cristopolous's words about Peltonville:

Some bad things happen in Peltonville…Just bad things. There is an old synagogue there, people do not go any more. Good people, I mean. Good people have mostly left Peltonville. You be careful, Paul and Delia.

It was hard for Paul or Delia to tell much about the character of Peltonville as the little roadster rolled into the downtown area. Every building seemed to be dark. Small houses in the style of the previous century loomed to left and right, but apparently Peltonvilliers retired early, for only the jagged silhouettes of the residences could be seen only against the backdrop of the night sky.

"Can you tell what time it is?" Paul asked.

Delia found the flashlight they had used earlier and shone its beam against her Elgin wristwatch. "It's ten-thirty," she announced. "I guess they keep going at Daniello's Roadhouse but people in Peltonville don't stay up."

After a few blocks lined by small retail shops the Hudson-Terraplane's headlamps picked out a building with a darkened marquee extending over the crumbling sidewalk. Paul pulled the car to the curb and Delia shone the flashlight on the sign.

Peltonville Inn, it read.

"Well, that's straightforward enough," Paul commented. "Let's see if they can put us up for the night."

"Paul." Delia took his arm.

He looked at her, waiting to hear what she had to say.

"Paul, you know I love you, dear. You do know that, don't you?"

"Of course, Delia. You shouldn't even have to ask. But—what's the matter?"

"Well—" She looked down. "Well, I'd really love to stay with you tonight. It would be—thrilling, Paul. But I know it would be wrong. I don't want to disappoint you, but would you mind if—if we took two rooms, dear?"

Paul shook his head. "Of course not. What sort of fellow do you think I am?"

He climbed out of the Hudson-Terraplane, walked around the car and opened Delia's door. "Come, darling, let's see what the management has to say to two poor travelers with no luggage to show for themselves!"

As Paul helped Delia from the car he realized that her breath was freezing in the air, as was his own. The wind had reversed its direction and brought the unseasonable storm back over Peltonville, or perhaps this was merely another front in a series. In any case, the wind had begun to howl unpleasantly and hail was battering both travelers.

Paul and Delia hustled to a place of shelter beneath the marquee of the Peltonville Inn. The hotel was dark. Turning back toward the street they observed that the town had not yet converted its street lamps to electric power from the older gas illumination. A few fixtures flickered feebly despite the icy wind that swept the street.

Paul searched his trousers for a coin. He found a silver dollar and used it to rap on the glass panel of the Peltonville Inn's main entrance, but to no avail. He called out but his voice disappeared into the whistling, howling gale.

Stepping to the edge of the sheltered space beneath the marquee he held Delia to him, gazing at the sky. Clouds like shreds of torn black cloth swept overhead; in the breaks between them stars glared down at the couple. Never had Paul seen them so cold and seemingly malevolent. To the east a new constellation appeared, a group of eight stars of a color he had had never seen before. If he had needed to name their color he would have called it red, but it was red of a shade and quality he had never previously experienced. The stars danced. Paul shuddered. An eerie auditory amalgam, part whistle, part hiss, part scraping, sounded faintly.

"There's nobody here," he muttered. "I can't tell, Delia, either the inn is out of business or it's closed for the night. Either way, we'll find no shelter here tonight."

"But Paul," she replied. Paul looked into her face. Clearly she was struggling to summon her courage but there were tears in her eyes and the corners of her mouth quivered. "What will we do? Is there anyplace we can go? We can't just sleep in the car, we'll freeze."

She was right, he realized. The wind whipped through their lightweight garments. Even beneath the marquee of the Peltonville Inn the hailstones bounced from the sidewalk and roadway and stung them like wave after wave of angry ice-hornets.

Across the street a faint light flickered in the windows of an old, two-story building. There was a momentary break in the screaming wind and a low chanting, barely audible, drifted to their ears. Paul stepped out from beneath the marquee, shielding his eyes from the pelting of hailstones as sharp and vicious as a bombardment of granite needles.

Yes, there was a light in the building.

Paul raised his gaze. The sinister constellation had disappeared from its previous location. Now it appeared once again, swooping and gyrating above the lighted building.

"There's somebody over there," Paul exclaimed. "Come on, Delia, they'll have to let us in!"

Hand-in-hand they ran from the Peltonville Inn to the lighted building across the street. The building loomed above them. The light they had seen flickered through a circular stained glass window. Its pattern was regular in shape, oddly suggestive of a sheriff's badge. Paul found himself wondering crazily if there wasn't a sheriff's station or town police headquarters here in Peltonville, if he and Delia should not have tried to find the authorities and pleaded with them for assistance against the cold and desolation of the darkness and the storm.

But it was too late for that.

Paul pounded on the heavy wooden door and found to his surprise that it swung open beneath his blows. He urged Delia in ahead of himself, then stepped into the shelter of the building, drawing the door shut behind them.

Clearly they were in a house of worship. The stained glass window behind them centered around a huge star formed of interlocking equilateral triangles. Paul had seen the pattern before, but there was something wrong with it this time. Each of the star's six points was surmounted by an image, a clutching claw, a hook, or some other disquieting image. And in the center of the hexagon formed by the major triangles he saw a face such as his most horrifying nightmare had never brought to him, a face whose inhuman features were exceeded in their fearsomeness only by the malevolence of their expression, a face surrounded by dripping tentacles that appeared for all the world to writhe and clutch even as he watched.

Hand-in-hand Paul and Delia advanced into the sanctuary. The chamber was illuminated by a series of gas mantles mounted on pilasters. There appeared now the massed congregants, robed figures of indeterminate gender. Human they seemed, but somehow and in some incomprehensible way, *wrong*. They stood in a circle, swaying rhythmically and chanting in what had to be Hebrew.

In the center of the circle towered a massive figure, broad-shouldered, bearded, wearing a skull-cap and fringed shawl embroidered with kabalistic symbols and horrifying images. The figure raised his voice and his arms, but where Paul expected to see hands emerging from the sleeves of his robe were frightening claws that clacked angrily, wreathed by tentacles wove and snapped like miniature whips.

The robed chanters surrounding their foul leader parted ranks. More quickly than Paul could follow they formed themselves into two rows. Those closest to Paul and Delia reached and took them by the hands. Paul's will was frozen. He stumbled forward, Delia at his side, passed from couple to couple of the frightening chanters, until they found themselves standing in the center of the newly reconstituted circle.

The leader loomed over them, far taller and more massive than any human being had the right to be. His arms were still raised, the claws and tentacles still performing their terrible gyrations. Involuntarily Paul raised his eyes, following the direction of the massive arms. Out of the corner of his vision he saw that Delia had done the same, and that even the monstrous figure before them had thrown back its head and was gazing in a state of spiritual rapture into the sky.

Yes, the sky loomed overhead. A retractable panel had been drawn back in the roof of the sanctuary. The hail had ceased to fall, but an icy wind howled through the aperture. The sound of the chanting rose, the leader began a strange and frightening dance, and in the blackness above the building, against the backdrop of faint, distant stars, the foul eight-pointed constellation appeared once more.

Only now Paul realized that the points of illumination were not distant stars but the eyes of a dreadful being, a being something like a huge spider, something like a frightening marine creature, something unholy and infinitely evil.

The eight red eyes drew nearer and the other features of the being became visible, fangs that dripped venom that steamed and sputtered as it struck the sanctuary floor, rope-like excrescencies that writhed and reached for the figures gathered beneath.

The chanting that surrounded Paul and Delia rose in pitch and urgency, the looming clergyman who stood before them lowered his arms and reached for Paul and Delia, seizing one of them in each arm, drawing them to his body that seemed to be more a chitinous shell than mere muscle and bone.

With immense and effortless strength he raised them, Paul in one horrid tentacle-circled claw, Delia in the other. Overhead the monstrous entity nodded and hissed, lowering itself toward the sacrifice that was clearly intended for it.

Paul reached for Delia, hoping in what must surely be the last moments of their lives to clasp her hand, but instead there was a monstrous crash and an icy blast as the massive doors of the building burst open and smashed to the floor. Paul was able to twist in the clergyman's grasp.

Standing in the doorway of the sanctuary was a figure he recognized at once as belonging to Mustafa Cristopolous, the Greek-Turkish-Jewish bartender that Paul and Delia had met earlier in the evening at Daniello's Roadhouse.

But now Cristopolous was transformed. No longer bent over a mahogany surface, no longer clad in a brass-buttoned, red service jacket, Cristopolous seemed to have grown to a height half-again his previous size. His shoulders bulged with muscles. His features, the broken nose, the cleft chin, had assumed a nobility they had not shown in Daniello's cocktail lounge. The jagged scar on his cheek was no longer a pallid reminder of a long-ago wound, but a blazing talisman of righteous rage.

The low, accented voice that Paul and Delia had heard at Daniello's now roared its challenge in words of ancient Hebrew. Among them Paul recognized the words that he had previously heard, *Yeshua ben Yeshua.* The evil clergyman, startled, dropped Paul and Delia. The entity that writhed above the sanctuary hissed and writhed in rage, deprived, at least for the moment, of its sacrificial prey.

The chanting congregants parted in terror, scurrying to cower among the pews and against the walls of the sanctuary.

Cristopolous strode froward, passing between Paul and Delia as he approached the clergyman. Cristopolous reached for the other, his massive hands clutching for the other's throat. The two were of a size and well-matched in strength. They bellowed imprecations at each other, both of them growling in the same archaic tongue that Cristopolous had used to issue his first challenge upon entering the sanctuary. But among the alien words of Yeshua ben Yeshua he was sure that he heard the name Yacoub ben Yitzak.

The clergyman and Cristopolous clutched each other in a dreadful parody of a lovers' embrace. The clergyman was clawing at Cristopolous's face and throat; Cristopolous held the other by his waist, lifting him from the floor by main strength.

From above a writhing, seething tangle of tentacles descended, dripping venom and slime. Ropelike organs wrapped themselves around the two struggling figures, then raised both, slowly, from the floor. Paul reached for Cristopolous's heavy ankles. For a moment he secured a grip on them and felt himself actually lifted from his own feet, but a burning blob of slime spattered on one of his hands. In agony he lost his grasp on Cristopolous's ankle with that hand; the other, alone, was not sufficiently strong to maintain its grip.

Paul collapsed back onto the floor. Delia knelt beside him, her arms around him, her tear-stained face pressed against his. Above them Paul saw Cristopolous and the clergyman, now wholly enveloped in a cocoon of writhing, ropelike tentacles, disappear into the gaping maw of the hideous entity that hovered briefly above the sanctuary, then rose with incredible speed until it disappeared once and for all into the starry sky above.

Again a cold wind swept into the sanctuary, and again the clatter of hailstones filled the night, this time pouring unimpeded through the open roof into the ancient building.

Taking Delia by the hand, Paul made his way from the building. The misshapen congregants whose chanting had earlier filled the building and the night had disappeared. Together, Paul and Delia made their way back to the Hudson-Terraplane.

Together, Paul and Delia turned back for one last sight of the desecrated synagogue. The monstrous creature was nowhere to be see; it had disappeared along with both Yeshua ben Yeshua and Yacoub ben Yitzak. But from the swirling clouds overhead a single lurid shaft of lightning crackled downward. It must have struck the gas line that fed the mantles in the synagogue. There was a deafening explosion and the building disappeared, fragments clattering down for city blocks in all directions.

"We can't stay in Peltonville," Paul announced. This assertion drew no objection from Delia. "And we can't get back to Springfield until the bridge is repaired. But we can press on. Aurora isn't too much farther, and we can find accommodations there." He paused. Then he added, "Even if we can only find one room."

Delia leaned her head against his shoulder and wrapped her arms around him. "One room is all we'll need, Paul," she murmured. ♦

LIGHTS OUT

Later Than You Think
by Christopher Conlon

Her breath was quick and shallow as she pulled the doll from its box. It was a simple thing, crudely made of brown clay, not more than ten inches tall. It wore an old gray rag wrapped around it like a miniature dress and its face was undistinguished, even undifferentiated: there was no more than the suggestion indented in the clay of eyes, nose, lips. It had hair, a few long, loose strands of it, pasted down on its head, helping lend an overall effect of femininity; it was a girl doll, it represented a female figure. But no girl would ever play with such an utterly charmless toy. It did not smile, it had no flexibility. It was not even pretty. It was, in fact, quite ugly.

But Betty didn't mind. She glanced around the dark apartment, listened to the distant city sounds beyond and below the window. A siren wailed somewhere far away. Betty lived alone in a fifth-floor walk-up; how her mother had exploded at her, years ago, when she'd told the old woman that she needed her space, her freedom, and that the certificate she'd received from the Secretarial College would get her a job in any city. Alone? her mother had gasped. All alone, in a *city*? Had Betty gone mad? She was much too young! Why didn't she marry, settle down as her sister Myrna had? Live right here in town, perhaps just down the block, like Myrna?

But Betty had always been different. She knew it. So did her mother; so did Myrna. Sometimes they chalked it up to Betty's having been so young when Charlie, her father, had died—only eleven. Myrna, ten years Betty's senior, was engaged to her high school beau, Jim Goldman, and they had married less than a year later. Myrna had been sad, of course, at her father's death, but not crushed in the way Betty had been. It had caused trouble between Betty and her mother for years afterward. Betty

183

became a rebellious child, then had gone through a wild period as a teen-ager, staying out too late too many nights with too many different boys. It was a dark time.

No, she and her mother were not close. There had been a time, though…Betty didn't often remember this, but now, holding the doll in her palms, she recalled her mother's fresh lemonade, her soft voice when reading a bedtime story, and learning to knit—difficult for her small child's hands—in the sitting room with her, to the sound of the Philco radio in the corner. They had listened to such programs together! *Jack Benny, Vic 'n' Sade, Fibber McGee & Molly*…but most of all, she remembered, the scary shows. *Inner Sanctum. The Whistler. Suspense.* And, best of all, *Lights Out.* She remembered the slow tolling of the bell at the top of each epi-sode, the gently-threatening voice warning, "It—is—later—than—you—think!" Betty would leave off the knitting then—she would have been nine years old or ten—and sit with her mother in her big overstuffed armchair, the one her mother always sat in to knit or read, and she would wrap her arms around the lady's big waist as the story came on: monsters that stepped out of movie screens, demonic fogs that turned you inside out, wives that changed into gigantic murderous cats…they were fright-ening, deliciously so, and her mother would smile indulgently as Betty held her.

All gone. Long, long gone. An entire world war since then, and a different kind of world now. Radio itself seemed to have lost energy, life; this new thing she'd seen in the department store windows, television, seemed poised to take over. Many of the old programs weren't even on anymore.

No, that time was past, dead. Betty could hardly even remember it.

What she remembered instead: endless marchings off to her room, in trouble for swearing or kicking or talking back; being picked up at the police station for shoplifting a compact and some lipstick when she was thirteen; her mother shouting at her, pleading with her: Betty, *why* do you do these things? *Why* do you stay out so late? *Why* are you so headstrong? And Betty having no answer, not really knowing herself, just wanting some-thing, something she couldn't define, that her mother could not give to her.

She took to reading strange books, books that appalled her mother: horror stories, accounts of the occult and bizarre, cannibals and devil-worshippers and the like. Her high school days became a blur of enraged words, running out the front door in angry tears, parking with boys she didn't even like, kissing them, feeling disgusted with herself and yet oddly thrilled too. Hearing words like *reputation* and *slut* murmured behind her back. Until, finally, she could take it no longer; she knew she would have to leave home. She was young—only eighteen—and her little secretarial certificate wouldn't guarantee her much beyond a low-paying job as a filing clerk or something of the sort. But she'd had to do it, and she'd done it. She'd moved to the city. She was free.

Or so she'd thought.

Because the frustration, the confusion, hadn't ended. She'd gotten just such a job as she'd imagined, a clerk in an office, a job that paid her little more than enough for her boarding-house rent and which held no future. She'd gone with many men, and gone too far with some of them, but none of it had assuaged this aching need within her. She felt miserable much of the time, depressed to the point of illness. And then there was mother. Mother, mother! The letters—whining, cajoling, begging her to come back. The phone calls she would be summoned downstairs for. Even telegrams, for God's sake! Betty had asked Myrna to try to get their mother to stop, but with no success. It was overwhelming, stifling, suffocating. Finally Betty simply refused to take the calls, threw away the letters without reading them. It had been over a year since she had any communication with her mother.

Over a year since…

Perhaps it was something inborn. Perhaps it started with the scary radio programs about monsters and demons. Perhaps it was her reading. Perhaps it was none of these. But slowly, Betty began to do research; she began to learn.

About voodoo.

She studied. She talked to people. She corresponded with experts. She made a long bus trip to New Orleans and hitched a ride out into a woebegone, swampy bayou, where an old Negro lady in a tin shack taught her things. Betty learned about the *kundalini,* or life force, the river which flows within everyone. She learned about *Legbra,* the spirit-interpreter who translates worshippers' prayers to the gods, and about *Baron-Samedi,* the god of sorcery, and about *Loa,* the ultimate being, God Himself. She learned that voodoo was the opposite of godlessness, that followers of voodoo were deeply religious, that the strands of the faith stretched back thousands of years to Africa, and that it was only rarely used for dark purposes. She attended ceremonies in that sultry Louisiana backwater, ceremonies held in a makeshift wooden *houmfo,* presided over by an ancient Negro man called a *houngan.* She watched the dancers, black and white, gyrating frenziedly to the manic drums that pounded to *Loa* all through the night. And finally, in a kind of abandoned ecstasy, she joined them. She became one of the initiated, the *kanzo.*

She was gone from her boarding house for weeks.

When she returned, she brought the doll with her.

She looked at it now, surprised at the floodtide of memory coursing through her. So much remembrance, so much *past* focused by the little doll she held in her hands. She tried to slow her breathing, to calm herself as she drew from under some shredded paper at the bottom of the box a heavy silver needle. She held it between her thumb and forefinger, and it reminded her of the knitting needles of all those years ago.

She held the pin in her right hand, the doll in her left. The doll was motionless, lifeless. Slowly, quietly, she said certain words she had learned.

Then, in one quick, decisive motion, she thrust the needle through the doll's body, in the exact spot, if it had been human, its heart would have been.

She dropped the doll then, fell back, and lay—suddenly exhausted—staring up at the ceiling. Her mind was completely blank. She waited there for what she knew would come next.

It took some fifteen minutes. Then, as she had known would happen, the phone began to ring downstairs. She stood up mechanically, crossed to the door, and opened it. Of course, no one was awake at this hour. She moved silently down the dark stairs and to the little alcove where the phone shrieked again and again. She picked it up, mumbled, "Hello, Myrna."

"What?" Her sister's voice was overwhelmed with grief. "Betty, is that you? How did you know it was me?"

"I guessed," Betty said quietly.

"Oh, Betty," Myrna wept, "it happened just a few minutes ago. She's gone. Mother is gone."

Betty closed her eyes. "I know," she said.

"It was sudden," Myrna said, not hearing her. "I was next to her, watching her sleep, and then she opened her eyes and said 'Oh'—just 'Oh'—and she clutched at her chest and then fell back and shut her eyes again. I ran for the doctors, of course, but she was gone. Just like that." The conversation stalled as Myrna cried for a moment. Then she said:

"Oh, Betty, it was the best thing that could have happened. It was so quick, so peaceful. After this past year—ever since she was diagnosed, that awful wasting-away…losing the house, unable to walk…by the end she was just—just skin and bones, that's all, skin and bones. The doctors couldn't do anything. The cancer had spread everywhere. And yet she just dragged on and on, for months…Who *knows* how much longer she might have…" Her voice grew tight with sobs.

"Yes," Betty whispered.

"God, I wish you two could have been closer this past year," she said mournfully. "It's so sad. But she always loved you, Betty. She did."

"I know."

"I just wish there could have been something…something you could have *done* for her."

The conversation stumbled on for a few more minutes. Betty agreed to come home to help with the arrangements. Finally they hung up.

In her room again, Betty lay on her back on the rug and stared up at the ceiling. She became aware that tears were streaming down her cheeks. It was over, finally, finally over. Praise be to *Loa*.

In the morning she would bury the doll somberly, with dignity and love, in a private place, and would speak a few words over it, as she had been taught to do.

She stopped crying after a while, when she noticed that purple sunlight was beginning to gleam through the window of the room. She realized that it was later than she'd thought; or, more accurately, it was earlier. The dark time had passed. It was morning, sunny and cool.   ◆

THE GREAT GILDERSLEEVE

Saturday Morning Paper
by Justin Felix

The alarm rang, for the third time, at nine. Throckmorton P. Gildersleeve awoke, for the third time, and stared at his clock by the bedside. He thought about grabbing it and setting the alarm for ten. He had already set the alarm an hour ahead at seven and at eight, however, and he decided that it was finally time to get up. Going to work was already out of the question for him, and Bessie, his secretary, was sure to call soon inquiring about his absence. Silencing the alarm with his right hand, he ran his left hand through his hair. He absolutely *had* to get up at seven tomorrow morning; when he walked home last night, he encountered Dr. Needham, and the pastor observed that Gildersleeve's little family had not been to church the previous three Sundays. Up to that moment, Throckmorton hadn't realized he had slept in so many Sundays in a row. Such was the consequence of being a bachelor: he was always out late Saturday nights, whether it was with Leila or Eve or any other single woman he built up the nerve to ask out.

Getting up and putting on a robe, the great man shuffled to the bathroom. Despite his grogginess, he was still careful enough to avoid his nephew Leroy's football and skates lying in the hallway. He was always after Leroy to pick up his things, yet the young boy never listened. While Gildersleeve wasn't a particular fan of corporal punishment, with Leroy, capital punishment seemed more attractive with each passing day.

Having gone through his morning routine, Gildersleeve, with a livelier spring in his step, took the stairway to the dining room, narrowly averting Leroy's toy cars at the bottom. He had a number of things to do: the fiscal reports that were due three weeks ago needed writing, the iron Birdie insisted was broken again needed fixing, and Leila needed placating (Gildersleeve said something to her Thursday night that she deemed offensive, though he couldn't figure what it was for the life of him). All that could

189

wait, though, he decided, preferring instead to read the Saturday morning paper. He didn't read the paper often now that the war was over, and he felt guilty about it. Keeping in touch with world events was still important.

His nephew Leroy, who had apparently been waiting for him to come down, walked into his path before he could reach the doorway and the freshly delivered paper that was sure to be waiting on the steps behind it.

"Hi, Unc," he said, in the voice that told Gildersleeve the little boy wanted something.

"Good morning, Leroy. I'm just getting the paper." Gildersleeve put a hand on the boy's shoulder and gently navigated him out of his path. He opened the door and looked through the screen door at the walk that led to their house. "Confound it, why isn't the paper here? It's nearly nine-thirty!"

"Oh. Here's a paper, Unc." Leroy handed his uncle a newspaper. Gildersleeve grabbed it without looking at the front page and thanked the boy while he closed the door.

"Have you eaten breakfast yet? I'm starved."

"Yeah, Birdie made up some eggs and toast." Leroy quickly changed subjects, as he was wont to do. "So I guess you're taking it easy today."

"I have a lot of work to do!" Gildersleeve lied, though he said it with mock indignation that the eight-year-old saw right through. They had been through this routine on many other weekends. Gildersleeve could see the knowing look on his nephew's face but he persisted in his ruse anyway. Habits were always hard to break. "It might interest you to know that your uncle has a lot of reports to draft. I just, um, brought them home so that I wouldn't waste time getting to and from the office. Bessie can handle things there."

"Hah!" Leroy belted.

Gildersleeve believed his nephew should apply for a patent for that exclamation, considering the frequency the little boy used it. The great man didn't much care for his nephew's insolence, but he wasn't really in the mood to go into one of his lectures just now, so he let Leroy off the hook with a warning. "Le-roy," he said, emphasizing each syllable.

"All right," the child replied, signaling he wouldn't push his teasing further. The boy remained quiet for a second or two, just long enough for his uncle to sit down at one of the dining table's chairs, before he changed subjects to what he really wanted to talk about. "Say, Unc," he hesitated for a moment before continuing, "Can you give me some money so that I can go to the movies?"

"The movies?!? You were just at the Majestic the other day."

"Yeah, they were showing *The Mummy's Revenge*." Leroy's enthusiasm, and perhaps nervousness, made him pick up the tempo of his speech. He wasn't sure if his uncle would be willing to give him a quarter. "You see, now they've got this movie starring Bela Lugosi. You remember Bela Lugosi. He was Dracula. Anyway, he's in this new movie and it's in color! Can you believe that? You see, Bela Lugosi, he's this guy with a dwarf. And there's this woman, see, and she gets scared to death! That's how she dies! Doesn't that sound neat? Piggy saw it yesterday and he says it's a real pip. He's going to see it again today and he wants me to see it too. You see, there's this scene…"

"Sss." Gildersleeve interrupted. So this was Piggy's doing. Leroy felt the need to do whatever his best friend wanted to do. *Piggy Banks*, the water commissioner thought, not for the first time, *what kind of mother has the audacity to name her son that?* Or more likely, she tolerated the other children nicknaming him that. He supposed he wouldn't hear the end of it if he didn't give the boy money to see the movie. He figured a little bit of dough in exchange for some quiet on a Saturday wasn't too much to ask for. "All right," he told his nephew, fishing in his pocket for some change and finding none. He grabbed his wallet instead. "I'll give you a dollar…"

"Yippee!" the boy exclaimed, as if they had struck oil or hit the jackpot.

"But Leroy," Gildersleeve said, taking the bill out of the wallet. "I want you to look into my eyes."

"Yeah, Unc," the boy said, following his uncle's instructions.

"I want you to give me back the change." He stared into the boy's eyes, emphasizing the seriousness of his demand.

"Okay, Unc." The boy accepted the dollar, then turned to flee the house, as if afraid his uncle would change his mind.

"Oh, Leroy."

The boy stopped at the front door and turned to face the great man again. "Yeah?"

"I want you to give me back *all* of the change this time."

"Okay. Okay, Unc." He flung the screen door open and went tearing across the yard to Piggy's house. The main door slammed shut against its frame with a resounding *wham!*

"And don't slam the door!" The dictate, of course, did not reach Leroy's ear. "Well, at least I'll get some peace and quiet around here," Gildersleeve said to himself. He opened the newspaper that Leroy had given him. He was about to read the headlines when Birdie stepped in.

An apron held in her heavy frame, and it was apparent that she had been about her chores for several hours already.

"Do you want some coffee, Mr. Gildersleeve?"

"Yes, thank you Birdie." Gildersleeve rustled his paper but the maid did not immediately leave the dining room, preferring, instead, to give him a disapproving look. "I won't be going to the office," he felt compelled to tell her. "I'll be working from home today."

"Yes sir." She said, out of habit but not quite sincerely. Sometimes Birdie had a way of making "yes sir" sound more like "yeah right".

Throckmorton shifted his eyes to the headlines but before any words registered, he thought of breakfast and called to Birdie in the kitchen. "Could I have some eggs too?"

"Sorry, Mr. Gildersleeve, we're fresh out."

"What? I thought you went shopping for groceries on Thursday."

"I wanted to," she replied, coming out of the kitchen with a half-full pot of coffee and a mug. "But you said to hold off until your paycheck came in, remember?" She poured him a cup and then set the pot on a coaster beside it. She knew he took his coffee black and hadn't bothered with cream and sugar.

"By George, that's right. I'm sorry, Birdie. I'll give you some money today. Will you have time to get to the store?"

"Yes, sir," she said, this time without the sarcasm. "Do you want me to make you up some toast instead?"

"No thanks, Birdie. Coffee will do for now." Gildersleeve's stomach grumbled at this, but he chose to ignore it. "I just want to read today's paper and sip my coffee."

"All right, Mr. Gildersleeve, I'll leave you be."

"Thanks, Birdie." As the housekeeper left him, Throckmorton enjoyed several tastes of her coffee. Birdie was a jewel; everyone said so and he couldn't agree more. Her coffee, he was convinced, was the best he ever tasted.

Gildersleeve topped off his mug before picking up his newspaper. He looked at its boldfaced title. *The Summerfield Indicator Vindicator.* He was about to read the headlines when the doorbell rang.

"The doorbell!" he heard a young girl exclaim from behind. It was his niece Marjorie. She obviously hadn't been at the piano, so Gildersleeve guessed she was at the writing table in the den, which housed both. God knew who she was writing to this morning. Gildersleeve had become quite concerned about his niece. She was nearing the end of high school, and she had definitely become "boy crazy," a fact he lamented to his fellow Jolly Boys during their weekly get-togethers above Floyd Munson's barbershop. He couldn't be sure, but he thought they took a little bit of pleasure out of hearing about his niece's running around with the likes of Jerry, and Walsh, and Keith, and that always smirking Marshall Bullard.

Marjorie ran to the door and opened it. "Oh, it's you, Judge Hooker."

"Indeed it is, young lady," Hooker responded, both hands holding his hat. "Sorry to disappoint you." He sounded insulted – Hooker was frequently insulted, Gildersleeve thought to himself. The old judge, who never married and lived alone, had in many ways "adopted" the Forrester family along with Gildersleeve, who came to live with his niece and nephew after their parents' untimely death. The judge was a good friend to the water commissioner, when they weren't ticked off at one another, but, more importantly, he served as a grandfather figure to the children, and on that count, he never failed. Marjorie's apparent disappointment thus probably justified the old man's reaction.

"Oh, it's not that," Marjorie rebounded. "I just thought you were Ben. He's coming over soon."

So it's back to Ben this week, Gildersleeve thought. That was a good thing. He liked Ben. Marjorie invited the elderly man in and directed him to the kitchen table.

"Good morning, Gildy," he said, placing his hat on the table and pulling a chair to sit upon without asking. "I dropped by the water department to speak with you and Bessie told me you hadn't come in yet. Skipping another Saturday morning from work, I see."

Gildersleeve folded his newspaper. "As it so happens, Hooker, I am very busy." Gildersleeve, like all the other residents of Summerfield, typically referred to Horace Hooker either by his title or his last name, or both. Gildersleeve tended to use Hooker's last name, however, when he was peeved by the man.

"Yes, so I see." The disapproval rang clearly in his tone, as did the sarcasm embedded in the statement. "Lollygagging another day away, are we? Gildersleeve, you are so lucky Mayor Terwilliger has bigger fish to fry in this town. If there were someone more powerful in office, I seriously believe you would be out of a job. I advise you to…"

"Hooker, the day I take advice from you will be the day I throw in the towel."

"Hmm."

"I was just going to take a look at today's paper and then get to work. It might interest you to know that I brought a lot of material from the office home last night. I have several fiscal reports to write, and I don't need an old goat like you interrupting me."

"What you need is for an old goat to give you a good kick. Didn't you tell me at the last Jolly Boys meeting that those reports were past due?"

"Well, yes. Maybe they're a little late, but..." Gildersleeve paused for a second. He studied the wizened face of jurisprudence for a moment. "Hooker, why did you really come here?"

"I actually came to tell you I won't be able to make it to the Jolly Boys next week. I have a convention to attend and I'll be gone for several days. Would you tell the other fellows? I didn't think I'd be free to go, you see, so I had to make arrangements post haste, as it were."

"Sure thing." Gildersleeve felt his combativeness fade away. He was a man of many moods, and they frequently shifted without much hesitation. "Anything else I can do for you? Do you want some coffee?"

"No, old man, I must be on my way. Thanks anyway." Hooker grabbed his hat and stood.

"Old man, look who's talking," Gildersleeve mischievously felt like rustling the judge's feathers. "Why that's funny coming from an old windbag like you."

"Windbag? Well, that's quite a statement coming from a lazy blowhard." Hooker began walking to the door, grinning.

"Why you! Do you know what Summerfield's problem is? Their judge needs to be taken out to pasture."

"At least Summerfield's residents can say their law is still in good hands. Their water department, on the other hand, is being run by an inefficient armchair plumber!" Hooker had been waiting to spring that one on Gildersleeve. He had thought of it just the other day, and when he told their mutual friend Chief Gates it, the head of the Summerfield police department laughed himself silly. The judge turned as he stepped outside and saw a flustered look on the water commissioner's face. Before the great man could muster up a reciprocal insult, the judge laughed his unique laugh, an unusual combination of a goat bleating and a machine gun firing, and slammed the door just enough to provide emphasis.

"Hooker!" Gildersleeve yelled too late. The old goat had gotten to him again. Of course, this was the kind of antagonism that only two old friends could engage in and, indeed, actually look forward to. Gildersleeve took a sip of his coffee, coffee which now seemed too warm for his thirst, and returned to the paper. He was about to read the headlines when the phone rang.

"Phone!" Birdie and Marjorie simultaneously yelled. Gildersleeve threw his paper down. He scolded each member of his adopted family a hundred times after they yelled when the phone rang, yet they continued the custom unheedingly. "I'll get it!" they both added. Marjorie raced from the writing desk to the telephone, nearly banging into Gildersleeve's arm along the way.

"Marjorie!" he exclaimed.

"Hello?" Marjorie had not registered her uncle's disapproval. She cradled the phone for a moment then turned disappointingly to her uncle. "It's for you," she said.

"Who is it?"

"I don't know. I didn't ask." She walked back to the den, at about a third of the speed that she stormed into the dining room.

"Marjorie" he called again, this time his voice lower than before, as he didn't want whoever was on the line to hear him lecture his niece. She hadn't heard him, though, and he could see her sitting down again at the writing table, her back to him.

"Confound it!" Gildersleeve stood to walk over to the phone as Birdie entered. She apparently knew it was for him as she didn't make a move to pick up the receiver. "I get no respect around this house," he told her.

"I know," she replied. "You just pay the bills around here."

"Hmmph." Gildersleeve said. She trumped him with one of his usual remarks, leaving the great man momentarily speechless. He picked up the phone. "Hello?"

"Hello? Is that you, Mr. Gildersleeve?"

It was Bessie. Gildersleeve figured she'd be calling eventually. He told the young girl yesterday afternoon that he probably wouldn't be coming in today, but his secretary was not the brightest of people.

"Yes, it's me."

"Why haven't you come in yet? It's nearly ten o'clock!"

Gildersleeve adopted the slow, purposeful tone he used to use with Leroy when the lad was five years old. "I told you, Bessie, that I'd be taking my work home for the weekend."

"Oh, that's right. You were taking that stuff home to do those reports. You said they'd be really hard. Is that why you call them physical reports?"

"Bessie, how many times have I told you? They're fiscal, *fiscal* reports. Oh, what's the use?" When he first hired the girl to be his secretary, she seemed to be a few pennies short of a dollar, as the expression goes. Yet, no one else answered his ad for the position, and he needed the efficiency and cleanliness a secretary provides an office. Now that he had worked with Bessie for a year, however, he was convinced she was missing not pennies but quarters.

"Oh, that's right. I'm sorry, Mr. Gildersleeve."

"That's quite all right," he placated her. At least she had gotten his telephone number right.

"Do you want me to close down the office? No one's come in yet today, and we're only supposed to be open another two hours."

"Yes, that's fine." Gildersleeve had hoped Bessie would stay in the office the whole morning, just in case Mayor Terwilliger decided to pop in to check up on his water commissioner. At least the door would be open with her inside. But, if she stayed, Gildersleeve imagined she'd just be on the phone yakking away to her girlfriends on the city's dime. He'd probably hear about it from the office responsible for the city's expenditures.

"Oh, good!" Bessie exclaimed. Then, in a much more subdued, breathy tone, she said "I'll see you Monday, Mr. Gildersleeve."

"Good-bye," he replied, wondering, not for the first time, whether his secretary had a thing for him. Deciding he didn't really care one way or another, at least right now, he hung up the phone and looked in on his niece. He thought about speaking to Marjorie, but her back was still to him and he decided not to bother her. "All I want to do is read my newspaper," he said to no one but himself. It was starting to sound like a mantra.

He sat back down at the table and took another sip of his cooling coffee. He picked up the paper and was about to read the headlines when the doorbell rang again. "Good grief," the great man said to himself. "What is this? Grand Central Station?"

As she had before when Judge Hooker visited, Marjorie bounced up and ran to the door. This time, she was not disappointed. "Ben!" she nearly cried as she let the Navy man in. Gildersleeve liked Ben. He was a little boring, of course, and bashful too. But, as a man in his twenties, Gildersleeve felt that Ben offered the maturity and stability that Marjorie's other teenaged boyfriends could not. Besides, he had recently returned from service in the war, and Gildersleeve admired that as a sign of character.

The young man came in, looked like he was about to kiss Marjorie, then decided not to, evidently because he noticed her uncle had turned to face the couple.

"Well, good morning, Ben. How are you today?" he asked.

"Oh, just fine, Mr. Gildersleeve," the shy man responded. He had a hard time establishing eye contact. "You're not at work this morning."

"No, I brought my work home for the weekend. Yes, sir. I have important work to get to. The job of a water commissioner requires a lot of time and sacrifice," he lied. "I just wanted to get a look at the paper before I start up."

"Well, I hope we won't bother you."

"What? You two aren't going out?"

"No, Unc," Marjorie answered. "Remember, I told you. Ben is going to help me with my lines for the school play. He's agreed to spend the whole day running through the play as many times as I need to memorize them. Isn't that wonderful of him?" She beamed the enthusiastic smile that only a teenager in love could smile. Ben alternated his gaze between her and Gildersleeve, and then chuckled his nervous chuckle.

"I suppose you're going to be working in the den," he said. This was his way of telling Marjorie that there was going to be no monkey business in his household, regardless of how he felt about Ben.

"Yes, Uncky. I hope we won't disturb you." With that, she took Ben's hand and half-led, half-pulled him into the den where she had been at work at the writing desk. Gildersleeve turned back to the table, took another sip of his ever cooling coffee, grimaced, and opened the newspaper. He began to read the headlines when Marjorie began rehearsing one of her scenes, with Ben reading the other characters' lines in an awkward, stuttering manner. "All I want to do is read my morning paper," he said, but found he could not concentrate upon it.

"Birdie!" he yelled, with equal parts resignation and annoyance. "I'm going out!" And with that, he donned his hat, tied his shoes, and walked out into the lazy residential streets of Summerfield.

The bell rang dutifully, as it always did, when Gildersleeve, newspaper folded snuggly under his left arm, pushed open the door to Peavey's Pharmacy. It was nearing noon, yet the druggist's store was empty save the old man himself, even though it was a Saturday. Peavey sat behind the counter next to a cash register and flipped a page of the comic book he had pulled from his newsstand. "Well, hello there, Mr. Gildersleeve," he greeted his good friend and frequent customer. "What brings you here on this fine young day?" He tried to subtly hide the comic book under the counter but was far from successful, and Gildersleeve wondered how Peavey ever ran a profit from his enterprise. It seemed like half the times he walked into the store, the old man was either in his chair propped against the wall snoozing or reading one of those confounded comic books that Leroy was so into when he wasn't wasting time with horror movies at the Majestic.

"Hello, Peavey," the great man said cheerfully. It was good to be out of the house, and the walk had elevated his mood. "I'm just here for a Coke." He sat down on one of the stools by the fountain.

"One Coke it is," said the pharmacist, grabbing a glass.

"I just wanted to get a look at today's paper, but I couldn't find any peace at home, so I thought I'd drop by here. This place is almost always quiet."

"Well now, I wouldn't say that," replied Peavey, his trademark remark brought a slight knowing smile on Gildersleeve's face, the smile that said *some friends are so comfortably predictable*. Peavey handed Gildersleeve his Coke. "That'll be five cents."

"Just put it on my tab."

"Okay. Will do."

Gildersleeve unrolled his newspaper and began to look at the headlines. He stopped, though, when he noticed that Peavey was still standing in front of him behind the counter.

"So what's the latest news?"

"I don't know, Peavey. I haven't had the time to read it."

"Oh."

Gildersleeve cleared his throat and glanced at the newspaper. He glanced back up almost immediately as Peavey hadn't seemed to take the hint.

"Did you see Judge Hooker? He says he can't make the next Jolly Boys meeting."

"Yes, I did see him. He gave me the impression that he hadn't told anyone else. Apparently, he had."

"Hmm." Peavey said. Gildersleeve thought that maybe this was the end of their friendly banter. He returned to his newspaper.

"Mighty nice day out there," the druggist said, trying to start a conversation.

"Yes it is," Gildersleeve replied curtly.

"The fellow on the radio says it might rain tomorrow."

"That's too bad."

"But then the other fellow on the radio says it might not rain."

"Well, that's not so bad then."

"Of course, we could use some rain. We haven't had some in a while."

"I suppose not."

"But then, it wouldn't be so bad if it just remained nice on Sunday. It's the only day I take off, you know."

"Yes, I do know." Gildersleeve placed his newspaper on the counter beside the Coke. "Peavey, I don't mean to be rude, but I came here so I could read my paper."

"Oh, I'm sorry, Mr. Gildersleeve. I won't bother you again." He began walking back to the cash register.

"Thank you, Peavey." Gildersleeve thought about tasting the Coke, but decided against it. He only ordered it as an excuse to spend some time at the pharmacy to read. He looked at the main headline and processed the first two words when he heard a metallic *ding!* from Peavey's cash register. He looked up.

"I'm sorry, Mr. Gildersleeve. I'm just getting a nickel."

"Yes. Yes."

Gildersleeve returned to the headline as Peavey walked over to the phone booth he had installed in the corner of the store. He slipped the nickel into the slot which made another *ding!* breaking Gildersleeve's concentration yet again.

Peavey dialed a phone number on the rotary, which produced a whirring sound that was peculiarly grating. Gildersleeve waited until Peavey finished dialing. He thought that perhaps after the number was dialed, he could return to the paper.

He was wrong.

"Hello, Mrs. Peavey? This is," Peavey chuckled for a moment, "Mr. Peavey." Gildersleeve frequently puzzled over the old man's relationship with his wife. Gildersleeve had only seen Mrs. Peavey a couple times over the years, as she rarely ventured out of their modest home. Her complexion was pale, but she didn't seem sickly. However, Mr. Peavey attended nearly all the Summerfield social functions that he could by himself, usually with a sly comment that things just wouldn't be as fun with Mrs. Peavey present. While there was a caginess with which the pharmacist explained his wife's absences, he was always extremely formal when talking with or about his wife. It was Mrs. Peavey to him, and Gildersleeve wondered if that was the product of a formality whose time had now passed or if there was tongue-in-cheek sarcasm buried within it.

"No. Not much going on here," Peavey said after a brief pause. "Mr. Gildersleeve is here enjoying a Coke. That's all." Another pause and then Mr. Peavey chuckled his nasally chuckle. "Oh, I could talk to you all day long, Mrs. Peavey."

"That's it." Gildersleeve said as he crumpled up his paper and got up. "Goodbye, Peavey."

"But Mr. Gildersleeve, you haven't touched your Coke." The pharmacist held one hand against the mouthpiece of the phone, expecting Gildersleeve to respond, but the great man left the store without saying another word. Peavey removed his hand from the phone and said to his wife: "That Mr. Gildersleeve. What a character."

Since a couple, probably a returning GI and his girlfriend, were passionately engaged with each other on the only bench in town, Gildersleeve decided to try his luck at Floyd's. His barbershop was open until five, and unlike Peavey's Pharmacy, Floyd had a customer. Summerfield's water commissioner walked in—the door was propped open—and nodded a greeting to his fellow Jolly Boy.

"Well, if it ain't the Commish." Floyd was the only person in Summerfield who called Throckmorton *the Commish*. "How's everythin' hangin'?"

"Just fine, Floyd. How are you?" Gildersleeve chose a seat and sat.

"Can't complain," he said, shaving the face of a man Gildersleeve couldn't identify.

"That's good. Don't mind me, Floyd. I'm just going to sit here and read my paper."

"Sure thing, Commish." The barber ran a straight razor down the man's chin. He remained silent.

Gildersleeve shifted his weight in the awkward chair and then reopened the crumpled newspaper he had tried to start reading since nine-thirty.

"So, you comin' to the Jolly Boys meetin' this Tuesday?"

"Yes, I am," Gildersleeve replied, then added, "Oh, but Judge Hooker says he can't make it."

"That so?"

"It seems the old goat has some law convention he wants to attend."

"Hmm" was the only response from the barber as he began to wipe away the remaining shaving cream from his customer's face.

"Yes." Gildersleeve agreed, then returned to the headlines.

"That'll be fifty cents, mister." The man gave Floyd a dollar and he handed some change back. They exchanged pleasantries and the newly-shaven man departed.

Floyd picked up a broom. "So you're not interested in a trim today, eh?"

"No. No trim today. I was hoping you'd be busier. To be honest, I was just looking for somewhere I could sit and enjoy today's paper."

"I see." Floyd swept the hair on the floor. "So what's Little Orphan Annie up to today?"

"I don't know, Floyd. I haven't even gotten a chance to read the front page."

"Oh." Floyd stopped for a moment, as if contemplating the tiles below. "So, Commish, do you think it will rain tomorrow?"

"Floyd, all I want to do is read my paper."

"Well, you sure picked a weird spot for it."

"Believe me, it wasn't by choice."

"Okay, Commissioner. I'll leave you alone."

"Thank you." Gildersleeve straightened the paper and began looking at the headlines.

"Yes, sir. Lots of men come to barbershops for idle talk, and that's fine by me. I can certainly talk a guy's ear off if that's what he wants."

"I dare say."

"But if someone wants some peace and quiet, hey, I can be as silent as a mouse."

"Then please do so."

"Yep, if someone wants me to be quiet, I'll be quiet."

"Uh-huh."

"I'm not one to go on and on if someone doesn't want to hear it."

"Good."

"I'm not like my wife's sister. Boy! Can she talk! Why, I remember one time…"

"Floyd, please! All I'm interested in is reading my paper."

"Of course, Commish. You're right. Here I am sayin' I'll be quiet, what with you wantin' to read the newspaper and not findin' a spot to do so, and what do I do? Talk, talk, talk. I'm sorry, Commish."

"That's okay, Floyd."

"Yessir. I'll just go about my business here sweepin' the floor."

"All right, then." Gildersleeve rustled his paper for emphasis and then returned to the headline, a headline he hadn't read despite umpteen attempts at doing so. Floyd swept up the hair into a corner.

"Boy, is my back hurtin' today! You know what, Mr. Gildersleeve?"

"That's it!" Gildersleeve crumpled his paper—yet again—in his fist and stood. "Floyd, you're worse than an old woman!"

"Commish! Is that anythin' to say to a fellow Jolly Boy?"

"Well, I suppose not. It just makes me so confounded angry that a man cannot be left to himself in peace and quiet in this town! Good day, Floyd!" With that, the great man barged out of the barbershop.

Floyd watched the heavyset water commissioner leave in a huff. After his form disappeared from the vantage point of Floyd's window, the barber shook his head. "Well, that's the Commish for you. What a character."

When Gildersleeve returned home, he walked up the walkway and the steps, carefully avoiding Leroy's bicycle which lay on its side and the boy's football helmet. Gildersleeve wasn't sure, but he thought he saw a turtle inside the helmet, nestled in a make-shift bed of dried grass. He probably had to lecture the boy again about taking in animals. At least this time, if that was a turtle in his helmet (and if it was still *alive*), Leroy had enough sense to keep it outdoors. The great man grabbed the screen door as he glanced down. There, beside the Welcome mat, was a fresh newspaper. Gildersleeve didn't think this was an afternoon edition of the paper; he only subscribed to the morning edition. The newspaper he had been carrying all day was still under his arm. He opened it and looked at it, really looked at it, for the first time. It was the *Summerfield Indicator Vindicator*, Morning Edition, Tuesday.

"Tuesday?!?" Gildersleeve exclaimed in a moment of realization. "I've been carrying around a paper that's four days old!" The water commissioner crumpled the paper into a wad with his fists. "That Leroy! Wait'll I get a hold of him!" ◆

BIOGRAPHICAL NOTES

JIM HARMON (James Judson Harmon) was born April 21, 1933 in Mount Carmel, Illinois. My mother, Valeria, was a housewife. My father, John Russell Harmon, was a building contractor. He had once practiced law but quit after only a few months. "This is not the sort of work for a decent man." Mount Carmel is on the Wabash River, and is mostly a farming community. It was also the home of a cousin, Brace Beemer, radio's Lone Ranger. This might have had some influence on me having such a great interest in radio drama. A sickly child, I had about everything going, except polio. I read a lot (and listened to the radio). I begin writing short stories when I was thirteen, and began selling them before I was out of my teens. I sold detective and Western stories, but mostly science fiction, and mostly to Galaxy Magazine. Stories of mine like "Name Your Symptom" and "The Place Where Chicago Was" have often been anthologized. I will shortly have my first collection of SF published as *Harmon's Galaxy*. I could not sell enough short stories to make a living, and then it was very difficult to sell novels. On the advice of famed fantasy personality, Forrest J. Ackerman, I moved to the Los Angeles area and found it easy to sell quickie mystery and adventure novels, mis-named "sex novels" because there was virtually no sex in them —the publishers were afraid of prosecution. I wrote many on my own, collaborated with a number of other writers, and for a group of beginning writers I plotted and oversaw the production of their books for 20% to 50% of the money, running a virtual factory. I thought these minor efforts would all soon be forgotten, but these books seem to have become collector's items and go for $30, $65, $100 a copy at specialized conventions like the Paperback Show in L.A. Some of my titles were *The Man who Made Maniacs* and *Vixen Hollow*.

My hobby of old time radio produced a book, *The Great Radio Heroes*, Doubleday and Ace, which became a "modest best-seller." A number of other books followed: *The Great Radio Comedians, Radio Mystery and Adventure, Radio and TV Premiums* and others. I have had, off and on, various programs playing old shows and commenting on them, and on several occasions I have written and produced new professional radio drama. For Ralston-Purina, I created a short series of new Tom Mix radio adventures for their Fiftieth Anniversary of sponsoring the show, once again starring an original radio Tom Mix, Curley Bradley, and featuring myself as his sidekick, Pecos. I also helped design premiums for Ralston, and wrote and edited two Mix comic books (only one of which they actually published). More recently, with the approval of the great radio mystery writer, Carlton E. Morse, my friend of thirty years, I produced a new edition of one of the classic *I Love a Mystery* radio serials, "The Fear that Creeps like a Cat," offered in a three-cassette album during a time period that has run out.

Today, I am far from retired. I am editing a series of books for BearManor Publications involving new short stories about famous radio characters, *It's That Time Again*, working on one book about science fiction on radio, and another on Westerns on the air. I continue to make radio and TV appearances, and love to come to conventions, like Left Coast Crime.

TONY ALBARELLA is the co-author of *The Twilight Zone Scripts of Earl Hamner* and the editor of *As Timeless as Infinity: The Complete Twilight Zone Scripts of Rod Serling*. His magazine articles have appeared in publications that include *Filmfax, Outré* and *Radiogram* and he is a Board Member of the Rod Serling Memorial Foundation. Tony lives in New Jersey with his wife, Cindy, and his two daughters, Alyssa and Veronica.

DR. CHARLES A. BECKETT grew up in St. Louis, MO., during the 1930s and 40s— in the era of the golden age of radio. He did homework while listening to his favorite after school serials. Sunday evenings were always reserved for listening to the Jack Benny and Fred Allen programs. During the Korean conflict, Sergeant Beckett continued to stay true to his love of old time radio in its waning days, by short wave radio. He finished his military career about the same time old time radio was beginning to fade away. After military service, Beckett concentrated on continuing his education, and helping his wife raise their three children. Then, in the 1980s, he rediscovered old time radio in a little tourist shop that had a small collection of programs on cassettes. He has been an avid listener and collector ever since—and has writen several articles and short stories about his favorite programs and performers for old time radio publications.

FRANK BRESEE. The 1940's was one of the happiest times of my life. It was in 1942 that I began playing Little Beaver on *The Adventures of Red Ryder* radio show. Tommy Cook and I spent many hours in the part, and I will never forget those days at the Don-Lee Mutual studios on Melrose Avenue.

Red Ryder was a program that was heard from 7:30-8:00 p.m. on Mondays, Wednesdays and Fridays. (For a time it was also heard on Tuesdays, Thursdays and Saturdays on the NBC Blue Network.)

After school (both Tommy and I attended John Burroughs Junior High School), I'd take a bus to the studio, arriving around 3:30. The cast would sit around a table and read the script for the first time. After marking our scripts and making any changes, we would do a second reading "on mike" with sound effects and music.

Paul Franklin, the writer/director of the *Red Ryder* program, would make the final cuts (or additions) to bring the program to the proper time. Then we went to dinner, usually next door to the studio at the Melrose Grotto. After dinner we would again meet in the studio, and within twenty minutes, or so, we would be on-the-air.

Several times I thought of submitting a story line for a show, but Paul Franklin did such an incredible job, that I never offered an idea.

When my friend Jim Harmon asked me to prepare a story for this book, I jumped at the chance. But without his help and ideas, I never would have been able to pull it off. Thanks, Jim.

T. WAYNE CLAY is a relatively young writer, actor and filmmaker. He especially loves horror movies and Westerns. He appeared as the Frankenstein Monster in a music video a few years ago, and recently played the Master Vampire, Dracula, in a Donald Glut film concerning Countess Dracula. A few years ago Tony Clay was acclaimed by hard-to-please radio fans for his portrayal of Don Long in Jim Harmon's production of Carlton E. Morse's *I Love a Mystery: The Fear that Creeps like a Cat*, an audio novel in a cassette album. Clay has also produced, directed, and starred in a Western film, *Six Gun Women*, soon to be released.

CHRISTOPHER CONLON is the editor of *The Twilight Zone Scripts of Jerry Sohl* and *Filet of Sohl,* both from Bear Manor Media. He has written about classic television for *Filmfax* magazine and old-time radio for the Sperdvac *Radiogram.* The author of two books of poetry and one collection of short stories, Conlon first fell in love with audio drama as a teenager in the 1970s, listening to the *CBS Radio Mystery Theater* on KNX and ordering cassette tapes of *Dimension X* and *Lights Out* from advertisements in the back of *Galaxy* magazine. Conlon's website can be accessed at www.christopherconlon.com. He lives in Silver Spring, Maryland.

JOSEPH CROMARTY has been (and still is) in love with radio for most of his life. He was weaned on Kate Smith and Helen Trent, Major Bowes and *The $64 Question.* (My, that was a long time ago.) His fiction has appeared in *Rod Serling's Twilight Zone Magazine,* (that, too, was a long time ago) and *Prime Time Magazine.* He is currently working on a detective novel that takes place in 1940.

JUSTIN FELIX also published a story in the first volume of *It's That Time Again! The New Stories of Old Time Radio.* He has written an essay about science fiction concept rock albums in the Winter 2000 issue of the academic journal *Extrapolation* and many movie reviews for various Internet periodicals. He lives in Bowling Green, Ohio, and is working on a doctorate in rhetoric and composition. His interests include old time radio, science fiction and horror, film, composition, and education.

JACK FRENCH is the author of *Private Eyelashes - Radio's Lady Detectives,* published by Bear Manor Media in 2004. He currently edits *Radio Recall* and is the former editor of *Nara News.* He has over 2,000 shows in his personal collection and specializes in articles about radio's juvenile westerns, aviators, and RCMP heroes, in addition to feminine sleuths. Jack has lectured on OTR topics at the Smithsonian and National Press Club. He received the Allen Rockford Award in 1993 for his contributions to vintage radio research. Jack is a former Navy officer and a retired FBI Agent. A member of SAG and AFTRA, he has appeared in several movies and television shows, in addition to his stage roles. Jack is a past president of the Metro Washington OTR Club and lives with his wife in Fairfax, VA.

MEL GILDEN is the author of many children's books including multi-part stories for children which appear frequently in the *Los Angeles Times*. Books for grown-ups included *Surfing Samurai Robots*, which received excellent reviews in the *Washington Post* and other publications, and which has spawned two sequels. He has also written Star Trek novels, books about Beverly Hills, 90210, and other media phenomena. He has written cartoons for TV, and has developed new shows. Gilden spent five years as co-host of the science-fiction interview show, *Hour-25*, on KPFK radio in Los Angeles, and was assistant story editor for the DIC television production of The Real Ghostbusters. His interest in dramatic radio goes back many years. Sometimes he thinks he was born in the wrong era. He lives in Los Angeles, California, where the debris meets the sea, and still hopes to be an astronaut when he grows up.

MARTIN GRAMS, JR. is the author and co-author of numerous books about Old-Time Radio including *The Have Gun – Will Travel Companion*, *The History of the Cavalcade of America*, *The Alfred Hitchcock Presents Companion*, *Inner Sanctum Mysteries: Behind the Creaking Door*, *The I Love A Mystery Companion*, *Information Please*, *Invitation to Learning*, *The Sound of Detection: Ellery Queen's Adventures in Radio*, *Suspense: Twenty Years of Thrills and Chills* and others. Martin is the recipient of the 1999 Ray Stanich Award for excellence in documenting Old-Time Radio.

BARBARA GRATZ has a husband, a writer, one grown daughter, an economist, and two cats. She is currently employed as a lab technician and microbiologist at Los Angeles Pierce College in Woodland Hills, California. All her previous publications have involved bacteria and disinfection by ozone and have appeared in technical and trade journals.

MICHAEL KURLAND is the author of over 30 novels and a melange of short stories, articles, and other stuff. He gave up his career in the theater and took up writing when the horse died. His stories are set in epochs and locations from Ancient Rome to the far future; anyplace the reader won't spot anachronisms too easily. His works have appeared in many languages, sometimes three or four on the same page, and are believed to be fragments of one great opus, a study of the *untermensch*. More can be learned at his website: michaelkurland.com

RICHARD A. LUPOFF never heard "The Witch's Tale" in its original incarnation, but his favorite Aunt Marion grew up on the creepy show and loved to recreate the voices of Old Nancy and Satan when Richard was a child. By 1960 he was a corporate executive longing to dump that career and become a writer. Enter Jim Harmon as temporary house-guest and volunteer tutor. It took another five years before Richard's first book was published and five more before he switched over full-time, but he's been at it ever since to the tune of fifty-odd books plus assorted screenplays, magazine features and other projects. He was also a founding member of the New Retro Radio Players, a troupe that had at least as much fun re-creating golden age radio as their audiences did watching and listening to the magic.

WILLIAM F. NOLAN (author of *Logan's Run*) is twice winner of the Edgar Allan Poe Special Award. Most recently, he accepted the International Guilds Living Legend Award for 2002. He has 75 books and over 300 anthology appearances to his credit.

DONNIE PITCHFORD, a native of East Texas, is married to the former Laura Pearson. Both are Christians and educators. The National Lum and Abner Society was founded in 1984. Donnie serves as its President, contributing audiovisual support, art, articles and character voices, working with Vice-President Sam Brown and Executive Secretary Tim Hollis. Since 1985, Donnie has taught broadcast journalism (CHS-TV) at Carthage High School (Texas) where Mr. P's students produced an eight-hour OTR marathon (on cable TV) entitled *The Golden Age of Radio!* For more NLAS information, check out http://home.inu.net/stemple/index.html. To learn more about CHS-TV, look for their link at http://www.carthage.esc7.net/.

BEN OHMART is a writer and publisher. His current and coming projects include biographies of Paul Frees, Don Ameche, Daws Butler, Walter Tetley, The Great Gildersleeve, The Bickersons and others.

BRYAN POWELL is a freelance journalist and musician based in Lawrenceville, Ga., near Atlanta. He holds a Master's degree in Mass Communication, print journalism concentration, from Georgia State University. He has written for more than a thousand articles for various magazines and newspapers, primarily covering blues and jazz music. Bryan is married, with two daughters, and is the happy owner of several thousand hours of old-time radio programming.

JON D. SWARTZ has been a fan and collector of OTR programs, premiums, and other radio-related memorabilia for many years. A retired psychologist, he received his Ph.D. from The University of Texas in 1969 and taught at several colleges and universities before retirement in 1999. For ten years before retirement he was Chief of Psychological Services at Central Counties MH-MR in Temple, Texas. He has written widely on both psychology and popular culture, including the *Handbook of Old-Time Radio: A Comprehensive Guide to Golden Age Radio Listening and Collecting* (Scarecrow Press, 1993). The following materials were used in the writing of his story about the adventures of *Jimmie Allen in World War II: The Sky Parade* (1936) by Wallace West, *Jimmie Allen in the Air Mail Robbery* (1936) by Wilfred G. Moore and Robert M. Burtt, the Jimmie Allen radio programs from the 1930s, and the several OTR books by the editor of this volume, Jim Harmon, who also suggested that the story about Jimmie Allen be set in World War II.

LAURA WAGNER is a freelance writer, and a steady contributor to *Classic Images* and *Films of the Golden Age* for almost a decade. She has been *Classic Images'* resident book reviewer since 2001.

BearManorMedia

It's That Time Again! The New Stories of
Old-Time Radio   ISBN: 0-9714570-2-6   **$15.00**

The FIRST collection of old-time radio fiction ever published! New short stories based on the shows we love: Our Miss Brooks, Quiet Please, Yours Truly Johnny Dollar, The Bickersons, and more. 20 stories in all, including real rarities like The Clyde Beatty Show and Capt. Midnight!

"The enthusiasm of the writers and their respect for the period is infectious."
— Ellery Queen's Mystery Magazine

"A terrific bunch of writers, all with the ability to make these shows sound as fresh as they were in their heyday."
— Classic Images

Have You Seen The Wind?
Selected Stories and Poems by William F. Nolan
ISBN: 0-9714570-5-0   **$14.95**

This is the first collection of Nolan's horror fiction and verse to share a single volume: Six chilling tales of murder and madness, guns and obsession; "Behind the Curtain," a brand new story written just for this collection; Delve into Nolan's darkest worlds of murder and revenge from beyond the grave; A celebration of Nolan's widely-praised poems on topics ranging from Bradbury to Vienna, from Hammett to Hemingway.

FILET OF SOHL
The Classic Scripts and Stories of Jerry Sohl
Edited by Christopher Conlon   ISBN: 0-9714570-3-4   **$16.95**

Included in this volume: Ten classic short tales, including two adapted for the legendary *Outer Limits*; Two never-seen scripts for *The Twilight Zone*; An intriguing story treatment for *Alfred Hitchcock Presents*; A powerful foreword by William F. Nolan; Essay-appreciations from George Clayton Johnson, Richard Matheson, and Marc Scott Zicree; *And Much More!*

The Pulp Western:
A Popular History of the Western Fiction Magazine of America
by John A. Dinan
ISBN—1-59393-002-X   **$14.95**

Private Eyes In the Comics
by John A. Dinan

ISBN—1-59393-002-X   **$14.95**

BearManor Media • PO Box 750 • Boalsburg, PA 16827 • www.bearmanormedia.com
Add $2.00 per book for postage.

Printed in the United States
18411LVS00004B/1-66